I Thought I Saw You Today

by

Patricia Seager

Dedicated to my family

who continually encouraged me and

to Ian Seager who picked up the baton

'after they stepped out of the room

Special thanks to my dear friend Avril Causier

whose continued support is invaluable

Other titles by this author

Same Beginnings	Published 2015	
Waiting for the Light Taylor Mystery	Published 2016	A DCI James
No Peaceful End Taylor Mystery	Published 2016	A DCI James
Stolen Years Taylor Mystery	Published 2018	A DCI James
Into the Shadows Taylor Mystery	Published 2019	A DCI James
Lost in the Picture Taylor Mystery	Coming Soon	A DCI James

Contents

PROLOGUE

Her heart was racing, it was beating so hard she was sure that those around her would hear the thud of its every beat and she felt as if it was about to burst out of her chest. She felt sick and dizzy and her mouth had suddenly become so dry that her tongue was sticking to the roof of her mouth. With shaking hands she picked up her glass of wine and took a gulp trying to wet her palate and calm her nerves. She looked around her and saw a waiter whose attention she tried to attract in order to get the bill but he didn't look her way. She strained in her seat twisting her body and head around in order to get him to notice her but he was too busy taking an order and as soon as he finished he hurried back into the restaurant.

She couldn't see any other serving staff so grabbing her handbag and the till receipt which had printed on it what she owed, she stood up hurriedly, knocking over her chair which clattered to the ground. The noise drew the attention of the other customers who turned to look at her and her face burned. As her whole body shook she thought they would probably think she was drunk as she bent to pick up the chair which she lifted and pushed back under the table.

She turned and made her way to the restaurant interior to pay her bill but the commotion she had caused had brought the waiter hurrying out to see what was happening, 'Boró na pliróso,' she asked in Greek if she may pay the bill, handing him the slip of paper. She didn't wait instead she followed the waiter inside. The restaurant felt cold and dark after the bright hot sunshine outside and she pushed her sunglasses on to the top of her head..

All she wanted to do was flee the restaurant and get to the safety of her home and he seemed to take an age to find a slip that matched hers in order to confirm what she owed. 'For God's sake,' she thought, 'I only had a bloody glass of wine!' What was taking him so long? Couldn't he feel her sense of urgency? She could feel her impatience growing and she snapped at him as she said that it was only one glass of wine she wanted to pay for and he looked up at her surprised at her manner.

Although she was a private person having few friends on the island all the locals knew of her referring to her as 'O Syngrafeas' meaning 'the author'. They were fiercely proud of their famous resident and she was well liked for her mild pleasant manner.

Now looking at the hurt look on the waiter's face she immediately apologised, making the excuse that she had an appointment. He smiled at her but her words didn't make him move any faster as being typically Greek he only had one speed and that was laid back slow.

She wasn't thinking clearly and realised she should just give him more than the amount of the bill but as she pulled some notes out of her purse he produced the slip and she paid, thanking him with a politeness she didn't feel although she added a generous tip to make up for her impatience. She rushed to the doorway where she hesitated as the light blinded her and she took a moment to readjust to the brightness. Putting her sunglasses back on she peered out and when she saw the coast was clear she hurried out into the sunshine and made her way quickly to her car. She pressed the remote to unlock it but her hands were shaking as she fumbled with the door handle. Eventually she was sitting in the driver's seat but she couldn't get the key into the ignition as her hands shook. She stopped, took two deep breaths and tried again and this time she was successful.

She drove down the harbour road only looking ahead afraid to catch anyone's eye and was frustrated as she reached the entrance to the ferry as there were several cars waiting to board and the queue was causing a delay. She cursed as this was so unusual on this small island where the traffic was normally light and she felt as if forces were against her and she would be discovered.

Eventually she was driving out of town, turning the corner at the end of the road she started to climb the hill which would take her home. She had been into town to do a bit of shopping and as she loaded her purchases into her car parked on the harbour she had glanced over at the restaurant across the road with the tables set outside looking so inviting and she felt tempted. She had looked towards the sea and could see some distance away a ferry making its way towards the island. This made up her mind as she loved to watch boats arriving and watching people disembark. They didn't get hordes of visitors on Skopelos but people watching was one of her favourite things to do and she would take a seat at a restaurant on the harbour road and watch the boats come in and the few individuals who would arrive.

It was a beautiful day in late May and the sun was becoming very hot so she chose a table with a parasol, ordered herself a cold glass of Rose and settled herself to wait for the ferry to come in. She sipped her drink as she watched a small sailing boat moor up and watched a man whose skin was turned dark brown by extensive exposure to the sun tie the boat to the dockside. He jumped back in the boat and settled himself on a chair on the deck of the boat and then she saw a woman emerge from below deck carrying two mugs, one of which she handed to the man. She then took a seat beside him and the two looked towards the arriving ferry. She envied their shared experience.

Her mind spun as she drove, she thought it must be her imagination as it wasn't possible or was it? She couldn't think straight. She had been driving for about ten minutes and had reached the top of the island where the road levelled out and her villa came into view. As she approached she pressed the remote for the electric gate across her drive in enough time for it to be open when she arrived. She parked her car in her drive and heard the gate closing again. She jumped out of her car, opened the boot took out her shopping and then hurried into her home making sure she relocked the door which wasn't usually a priority of this small, friendly island..

The coolness of her hallway was welcoming and in stark contrast to the building heat outside. She made her way to the kitchen and put her shopping away with a calmness that she didn't feel and once it was all where it belonged she opened the fridge and took out a bottle of Rose. She poured herself a large glass, picked up her laptop and made her way outside to the large patio area where she sat at the table under a canopy.

The view from her home was spectacular which is why she had bought this villa all those years ago although it was impossible not to enjoy wonderful views from wherever you were on the island of Skopelos. She had a clear view of the harbour and during the warmer months enjoyed watching the boats come in and out from a distance but today she stared out unseeing.

She was confused as she couldn't believe what she thought she had seen and as she tried to process her thoughts a movement from the harbour jolted her back and she saw that the ferry was leaving for its return journey to Skiathos loaded with the cars she had seen waiting to board.

Although she felt much calmer now her stomach did a little flip as her mind returned to what she thought she had seen. She switched on her laptop and watched it load up, picking up her glass she noticed that her hand was shaking, she took a large drink of wine and putting the glass down she turned her attention to her laptop and started to type,

'I thought I saw you today'.

CHAPTER ONE

EMINE

She awoke to the darkness that surrounded her and she felt the pain that wracked her body immediately. There wasn't one part of her that didn't hurt and as she tried to sit up she winced. Pain shot through her head as she wondered where she was. She laid back down and could tell she was on a hard floor, she was very cold and the air smelt stale and then slowly memories started filtering back to her. He had taken her totally off guard, grabbing her from behind and at first she had been shocked but had soon started to fight her attacker like a wild cat. She kicked back and screamed, struggling to get free from the arms that held her. She could smell the stale odour of his body which became stronger as he put a hand over her mouth to muffle her cries and she sank her teeth into his flesh and he shouted out as he moved his hand away.

He span her around and she came face to face with her assailant who was a man she guessed was in his early forties with sun dried skin and a dark beard. He wore a headdress common to Turkish men of red and white cloth and a beige kaftan type gown worn by many traditional Turks. He slapped her hard and she felt her head spin as she literally saw stars. She staggered back and he grabbed at her but even though she managed to kick out the raising of her leg made her lose balance and she fell to the ground. She felt the kick in her ribs and the breath left her body as she gasped for air and pain seared through her body. He continued to beat and kick her until she almost lost consciousness.

She felt him dragging her across the cobblestones of the street she had been walking on and through a haze she saw him opening the tailgate of a truck. He dragged her to her feet and she cried out in pain as he had hurt her badly but he ignored her complaints and pushed her into the back of the truck where she lay engulfed in agony. She heard the engine start and then endured a painful ride to their destination.

They left the cobbled street and she lay on her back unable to move watching as buildings flew by as they drove onto a smoother road and then she could see nothing but the dark sky and the twinkling stars as they drove on. She could hear the sea gently lapping at the nearby shore but eventually the noise grew quieter and quieter until she couldn't hear it anymore. She heard the odd dog bark but nothing else and every now again she would see houses but then nothing for what seemed like hours. She could tell they were climbing a hill as they turned several times and she tried to sit up but the pain that shot through her limbs forced her to remain still. She fell in and out of consciousness and when she finally came around she could tell they were on some kind of track. As each bump in the road magnified the agony she felt. She tried to get up again but fell back as it was too painful however she knew she had to get away.

She tried to make a plan but must have passed out again as the next thing she knew was the feeling of being dragged again and as she tried to find her footing she stumbled along being supported by the rough hands of the man who had caused her pain. She could see several run-down buildings around her and heard a male voice call out. The man supporting her answered the other voice and then dropped her by the door of one of the buildings. She tried to crawl away as she saw him opening the door to the building that looked like an animal store and he laughed out loud. He dragged her back by her hair and she screamed out as he threw her into the room. Before the door closed she could see the straw strewn earth floor which she fell to crying out in pain.

She now looked around her hoping for her eyes to adjust but it was pitch black in the room and she could hear no sound. She shuffled back wincing in agony and each movement until she found a wall that she managed to pull herself up enough to lean against. It was so cold in the room and the effort it had taken to get her to this sitting position had taken it out of her and she passed out again.

She came around and once again tried to get up but it was impossible but all that she could think of was that she was in grave danger and must escape. She somehow managed to summon up the strength to move and laboriously felt her way around the wall stopping every few minutes to catch her breath as the pain was so bad. The walls were cold stone but as she felt around eventually she felt wood and knew she was at the door. She tried to stand but it was useless and she realised if she did manage to escape she wouldn't be able to go far but perhaps she could hide somewhere until she felt more able to run.

She tried to pull herself up but even though her mind was strong her body wasn't and she couldn't manage it. She reached up with her hand to try to find a handle or someway out of the room but it was useless and she fell back on the ground.

She hadn't been in Bodrum long but had thought it was perfectly safe to walk alone as she had many times before. She knew that there were places in Turkey where she shouldn't venture alone but Bodrum wasn't one of those places. She had been walking home from work and had turned down a cobbled alleyway which had small shops on one side but it was late and they were all closed. She hadn't been aware of any danger and was lost in her own thoughts when he had grabbed her. She felt cross with herself for not being more aware of her surroundings and realised that someone was behind her. She couldn't imagine what he wanted with her but she was scared.

She must have fallen asleep as she had no idea what time it was when she awoke again but realised that what had woken her was the door being unlocked and opened.

CHAPTER TWO

OLIVIA

Olivia Weber and Maggie Richards disembarked from the ferry that had brought them from Portsmouth to Bilbao in Spain. They had excitedly boarded the same ferry over twenty four hours earlier and after exploring the ship had found comfortable seats where they could spend their journey.

They had taken it in turns to make several trips to the bar whilst the other saved their seats before settling down for the night. They were surrounded by other travellers and there was a real buzz to the atmosphere but as the early hours arrived quietness fell over the room as most people slept.

Olivia and Maggie continued to chat in whispers until they too fell into a fitful sleep. The seats didn't make the most comfortable of beds and both kept waking and each time they would check their backpacks were safe.

They had graduated from university a week earlier where they had worked and partied with equal enthusiasm. They met in the first week of study at Norwich, Olivia from Leeds and Maggie from Penarth near Cardiff they had recognised something in each other and had hit it off immediately. Both girls were guarded and didn't make friends easily although both appeared friendly they kept a lot back. After their first year they moved into shared accommodation and spent the next two years living together. They shared their ups and downs and forged a strong friendship.

Both had dated during the three years at University and both had had what they considered serious relationships in their final years however both had split from their respective partners around the same time two months before graduating.

Maggie had been heartbroken when her relationship with Guy a local lad whose brother studied with her had broken down. He had become distant but Maggie chose to ignore the signs even though Olivia had quizzed her about it but she was surprised when she shut her down and realised that the subject wasn't open for discussion. She had noticed that he wasn't around as often and when he was he seemed more interested in speaking to their small group of friends. One night he didn't turn up as arranged and Maggie couldn't get hold of him. This went on for days until she was dumped by proxy when Guy left it to his brother to tell her that he didn't want to see her anymore.

Olivia had come home to find her friend in floods of tears and had spent the night trying to placate her. She herself had split from her boyfriend Nick a week earlier when he had told her that when they graduated he would be moving back home to Leicester. It was obvious that he didn't want her to join him and that suited her as she had been fighting the feeling for some time that she didn't really like him.

She had no intention of settling down yet and wanted to travel imagining visiting distant shores. Her friends described her as a bit of a dreamer although she preferred to think of herself as a free spirit but Nick called her irresponsible and accused her of suffering from commitment phobia. He liked to jibe at her fantasies and dreams and she sometimes found his mockery cruel.

Olivia and Maggie had sat up all night talking through what Guy had done and by the morning Maggie felt better and the girls had had decided to go backpacking for a year around Europe before looking for employment. Of course it had been Olivia's suggestion but Maggie had readily agreed saying that she wanted to put the whole upset about Guy behind her although she harboured a secret wish that Tom would step in when he heard of her plans, declaring his undying love and stop her leaving.

The girls excitedly made their plans, mapping their way across Europe and intended spending at least a month travelling across Spain to Barcelona in order to catch a ferry to Genoa in Italy which was their next destination. They had a good idea of their route but it was flexible and nothing was set in stone as they agreed they would play it by ear.

It was the early nineties and as they stood at the dock in Bilbao, both sported the bootleg denim jeans, baggy loose fitting tops, denim jackets and trainers popular in the era and carried large rucksacks on their backs crammed full with their belongings. They planned their route from hostel to hostel and both girls were excited at the adventure that lay before them.

Although they had had little sleep they were not tired as their excitement grew as they looked around them. They walked to the small harbour and were delighted with the prettiness of it. It was July and the weather was very hot as they sat on a wall on the harbour to cool down watching the small boats bob about in the calm sea. Both sat quietly taking in their surroundings, calm and relaxed in the atmosphere they enjoyed.

They wandered the cobbled streets that ran between small interesting shops and they gazed in the windows at jewellery and pottery knowing they wouldn't buy anything. They didn't have a lot of money and knew they had to make what they had go a long way. They intended to pick up work as they travelled in order to boost their coffers but the thought of the new experiences that were to come only added to their excitement.

They had a small paper map which showed them where the hostel was where they intended to stay and they strolled in the hot sunshine to the building where they would sleep. It was a rundown large house with peeling paint on the walls. They were put in a dormitory with four other young women and decided on the first night that they must find somewhere else to live as it was only temporary accommodation.

They spent two nights in Bilbao where they familiarised themselves with the town and a few bars there but decided when they couldn't get in better accommodation to move on in the next few days. One of the girls in the dormitory was leaving the next day to go fruit picking and they decided to join her. It was hard work in the hot sunshine but they were given tents to sleep in and they had one to themselves which they preferred to sharing with others and they stayed there for two weeks before moving on towards Barcelona which would be their final destination in Spain.

They worked their way across the country working in bars and restaurants and at one point were even threading beads for a small jewellery maker called Alejandro who Maggie was having a fling with. She thought herself in love again but it fizzled out within three weeks. Olivia felt for her as she knew that Maggie fell in love easily and heavily only to have her heart broken.

On the other hand Olivia who for no obvious reason didn't totally trust the opposite sex found it harder to connect. Although she had been fond of a couple of young men she had never really been in love. Had she known that this was all about to change would she have blindly run towards it or run in the opposite direction?

CHAPTER THREE

RACHEL

When Rachel Ross was born her father, Roger immediately fell in love with her even before she was put in his arms. He thought his heart would burst when he laid his eyes on the pink, squirming bundle and couldn't believe that he had been part of creating something so beautiful.

Her mother, Catherine took longer to bond with the child she had given birth to. The doctors thought she was suffering from post-natal depression however the truth was that she had no maternal feelings. She was a self-centred woman who had never wanted children and had never really had any intention of settling down with one man and marrying. One man was never enough for her as she craved attention and although the initial adoration of the men she met fed her craving it couldn't be sustained and she soon grew bored.

Roger and she had met when he attended an art show in London where he lived and he had been enchanted by the beautiful, free spirited young woman who seemed to laugh constantly. He enjoyed the carefree way she made him feel and he had fallen completely under her spell.

She had seemed a little aloof and not as keen on him as he was on her but this didn't deter him. He knew she was seeing other men and although she seemed constantly distracted when they were together he was happy for any time she would give him.

He was a patient man and bided his time, fighting hard to get her to fall in love with him by the way he treated her. He adored her and showered her with the small gifts his meagre salary would allow. He had spent his first few years after graduating working in a research laboratory which didn't pay well but he enjoyed the work.

She dabbled in painting but her main interest was literature and she had found a job lecturing at the local college. She would quote famous historical authors and always seemed to have something to say on every subject. Her personality could be described as a bit 'airy fairy' but she could do no wrong in Roger's eyes.

On her part Catherine amused herself with Roger as she considered him a bit of a lap dog. She couldn't deny he was very handsome but the real draw for her was that his good looks together with his muscular build and air of seriousness reminded her of one of the heroes from a Bronte or Jane Austin novel. The only thing he lacked was the sternness of these men as he would do anything she asked.

Despite the lack of respect she cared deeply for him and without realising came to rely on him more and more. He would come when she called dropping whatever he had been doing and would fix whatever she needed fixing. He lived some distance from her but it was never a chore for him to attend to her every need.

He lived in a bedsit in a large Victorian house whilst she lived in a small flat which was slightly grander than his as she earned more money, something she was very aware of. Another thing she didn't admire about him was his apparent lack of ambition.

This all came to the surface when he eventually suggested that they move in together. She told him that although she had feelings for him she didn't really want to restrict herself to one man. She saw the hurt on his face and uncharacteristically softened her remark by adding that if she did want to settle down it would be with him.

She saw this gave him hope and thought this was a good thing as he would stay around to do her bidding but shot herself in the foot when she couldn't stop herself saying,

'The thing is Roger you will never earn enough money working in that little lab of yours. I plan to travel and see the world and your wage will hardly subsidise that.'

He had been crestfallen as he loved his work but loved her more and knew there was a solution. He presented this to her a month later when he announced, 'I have been offered a position to lecture in biology at the University of Birmingham. The money is very good so if you will come with me we could have a good life and travel as much as you want.

She stared at him in shock and he was scared of what she was going to say so spoke again before she could, 'The money I'll earn will keep us both as it's cheaper living there than here in London but if you want you could easily get a job there I know.'

She still didn't speak so he continued, 'Please think about it Catherine.'

'I don't need to think about it,' she said, 'why on earth would you think I'd want to move out of London?'

'So we could be together,' he answered, 'I applied for the job because you said you needed me to earn more money.'

'My God Roger,' she laughed, 'don't you have a mind of your own? If I say jump you always bloody jump.'

The conversation turned into a huge row with Roger slamming out of her flat with her words ringing in his ears, 'It's over Roger. Just go to Birmingham but I will never come with you.'

He went and she was surprised how much she missed him. How could this have happened?' she asked herself as she yearned for the attention he lavished on her and when four months later she visited him in his new flat in Birmingham it was her turn to fight for him.

He had said he had not wanted to see her but she had turned up anyway and found herself begging him to take her back. She said she would move immediately and look for a job there if he gave her a chance.

He thought about it for the evening they were together and then as he took her to the train station he stood by the barrier and said, 'I'd love you to come to live here with me,' and he saw her smile but added, 'there's one condition to us getting back together...'

'Anything,' Catherine gushed.

'Marry me,' Roger said simply.

She stared at him blankly, 'that's your condition?' and he answered 'Yes, that's my condition.'

When she got home, she phoned him and said she would marry him and enjoyed how happy he sounded. He adored her it was obvious and it made her feel good..

They married in a small ceremony and she soon found a job lecturing at the same university in literature. She made connections in the art world and started to build up a group of arty friends which Roger wasn't part of but he was just happy to have her as his wife.

She hadn't told him she didn't want children as the subject hadn't come up but when he broached starting a family two years after they had married she put him off saying that she wanted them to visit more countries and it would be hard with a baby. They had had several holidays since marrying and although he enjoyed the travel it was not his dream in life.

She had become pregnant by mistake and had been deeply disappointed but her spirits had lifted a little when she had seen how overjoyed Roger was. Although he loved her very much the initial pandering to her every whim had waned a little. She saw it return whilst she was pregnant and this was a great consolation to her and as she looked at him now cradling their child and cooing to her, 'Hello Jelly Bean, you are my girl,' he looked up and the love that shone from his eyes made her smile.

CHAPTER FOUR

EMINE

The door swung open and she could see it was dark outside but the man who entered the room carried a lantern and she could see by the dim light that it was her attacker. He dragged her to her feet and the agony she experienced made her dizzy but she still tried to fight him. He slammed her against the wall and pain shot through her body. He grabbed her again an dragged her through the door. She managed somehow to stagger with him out of the room.

As before she could see that there were several other buildings surrounding them and some of them had light coming from them. It was hard to make out where she was but it seemed like a small settlement. She heard goats bleating but apart from that she could hear nothing.

She tried to take it all in as she looked for an escape route but it was hard to make out her surroundings clearly in the dark. The man was rough with her as he dragged her as she tried to keep her footing across the ground to one of the larger buildings which she could see light coming from.

He had the lantern in one hand and had to let her go but it was only for a moment as he pushed the door to the building open. She was greeted by the murmur of men's voices and then he grabbed her again and pushed her inside ahead of him. The room was lit by many lanterns and she could see several men sitting around talking. They went silent as she and her captor entered and she was pushed towards an old looking man who smiled menacingly showing that he had several teeth missing.

He was dressed in the same way as her captor but was fat with a straggly beard and he looked dirty. He drank from a dirty glass and looked around at all the men in the room smiling.

He then turned his attention back to her and stared for some time, took another swig from his glass and she saw liquid dribble down his chin which he didn't wipe away. After what seemed an age he told her captor to bring her nearer. She was pushed forward and then painfully brought to a halt She stood there for a good fifteen minutes whilst the old man drank and ate some meat with his hands and she could see the grease on his face. All the time he didn't take his eyes off her and every now and again he would smile at her but it wasn't a pleasant look.

Eventually the old man stood up and walked towards her slowly, his eyes piercing into her. He stood in front of her staring into her face for a few minutes and she held his gaze and then he told the man holding her to let her go. She staggered a bit but manage to keep her footing and then the old man slowly circled her until he came back to stand in front of her staring first at her face then at her breasts where his gaze lingered, 'Nice,' he said..

She shuddered as his eyes moved down her body and then back to her breasts where his gaze remained and she tried to shrink away but her capturer had moved back behind her blocking any movement with his body. She shuddered again as she touched his body and the man in front of her laughed.

Looking over her head at her captor he spoke in a thick accent, 'You have done well my son.' and then turning his attention back to her, 'We will get good money for you.'

'I have nobody to pay a ransom for me if that's what you mean,' she said and he laughed again.

'Your people will pay,' he said and looked back into her face as if he was trying to see inside her mind. She once again stared back at him. 'You have spirit, you suit the name Emine with your show of fearlessness.' Then he laughed, 'If your people won't pay to get you back I know many men who will pay for this,' he put his hands out and caressed her breasts. She tried to move away but the man behind her blocked her way and put his arms around her to prevent her moving as the old man continued to touch her. She felt nauseous as she felt the two men touching her, one mauling her whilst the other held her his body pressing into her. The old man then moved away from her, much to her relief, and sat down again, looking at her, he held up something in his hand and she realised it was her passport. Of course they would have her bag and she always carried her passport with her as the lock on her rented room was not very secure.

He waved the document at her and said, 'We will wait to see what your people do and if they refuse to meet our demands,' he laughed again, 'perhaps I will have you for myself'.

'I will kill myself first,' she screamed at him and he got up quickly moving towards her. 'No,' he said, 'but I might kill you after'. All the men in the room laughed and fear filled her mind but she wouldn't let him see how scared she was so her back straightened and she spat in his face. She saw his leering smile replaced by rage as he grabbed her face with one hand and moved his face close to hers.

She could smell his rancid breath as he squeezed her face painfully and saying through gritted teach, 'You will never do that again.' She continued to stare into his face and he added, 'It would be a shame to damage this lovely body.'

Then she saw his anger replaced by a leering look, 'Perhaps I'll sample the meat anyway.' He continued to hold her face but started to roughly fondle one of her breasts with his other hand hurting her as he squeezed and pinched her. She tried not to cry out at the pain but a small groan came from her and he smiled, 'you like that?' he goaded her deliberately mistaking her groan of pain as one of pleasure. He turned to the men in the room, 'She likes it rough,' and then turning back to her, 'we will have a lot of fun, you and me.'

She shuddered again and he laughed saying to the room, 'Look how she trembles at my touch. Perhaps I should take her now.' He turned to the men in the room, 'Should I take her now?' The men cheered and started to clap and her fear grew.

He put up a hand to silence the men and turned back to her. She tried to pull away scared of what was about to happen and he let her go, 'You are eager to start, I can tell,' he leaned forward and licked her face hard from top to bottom.

Her skin crawled and he laughed again as he turned and started to walk back to his seat, 'I have no people to pay for me,' she protested to his back not sure this was the right thing to say and knowing in her heart of hearts this wouldn't placate him.

'We will see but if you are right then so be it, I will have you until I tire of you and then we will sell you to the highest bidder,' he laughed at the hatred in her eyes and said, 'The look in your eyes tells me you will be a hell cat, I hope so, I will enjoy taming you.' All the men in the room laughed and her face burned.

She wanted to scream but it would do no good, she thought of begging but that would be a waste of time too. 'Be patient,' he sneered, 'we'll know soon if your people want you back and if they don't we'll be together.'

He waved his hand, 'Take her away,' he said adding something she missed and she was roughly escorted once again back to the building she was being held in. she knew better than to try to run away at the moment as she was injured and wasn't strong enough and she knew that she had to recover first but as soon as she could she'd try to escape.

CHAPTER FIVE

She spent days in the room lying on the hard floor and as the days passed the pain subsided until she tried to walk and she would wince with every step. She felt sure the man who had taken her must have broken some of her bones.

She had to go to the toilet in the room and felt totally filthy. Various men came into the room to bring her water some of which she would use to clean herself as best as she could but there was never enough to do a decent job. They would bring her bread which tasted surprisingly good as it was freshly baked and sometimes she'd be given some kind of stew with rice. Some of them hardly looked at her and others leered. Sometimes the door would open and men would just stand and stare at her.

A week after she had arrived at the camp a man with a rifle entered her room and grabbed at her arm dragging her outside. It was dark as he pushed her towards the house she had entered a week earlier where the old man had threatened her. She was pushed inside once again but this time there was only the disgusting old man and four other much younger men.

'Look at our prize,' the old man said as she came to a standstill in the room and the other men murmured.

He stared at her as he did before, 'So far we have no word from your people so soon you will be mine.' He let out a loud laugh and got up to walk towards her, 'Or maybe I'll let one of my sons have you,' he waved towards the men in the room.

'Look my sons how ripe she is,' he again reached forward but this time didn't touch her, 'Aren't these just perfect.' She moved away and he laughed, 'Look how the thought of my touch makes her jump. She is begging to be taken but she must wait.'

She relaxed a little at his words as she realised he wasn't going to force himself on her today.

'Would one of you like her,' he asked his sons.

'I'm the first son, I should have her,' a man stood up and walked towards her leering at her and she shrank away..

'I think she wants you too, my son,' the old man said, 'look how she shakes with desire.' As he spoke his son reached out and grabbed her right breast, squeezing it hard.

'Yusuf,' his father shouted, 'do not touch her.' He slapped him at the back of the head hard and his son looked annoyed and embarrassed.

The man turned back to her, 'I must apologise for my son's eagerness,' he laughed, I am thinking that I will have you first and then perhaps Yusuf can have you. My second born Mustafa can have you when Yusuf is done with you and then you can get reacquainted with Mirac who you already know. She hadn't looked at the men in the room but as he stood up she saw the man who had grabbed her on the streets of Bodrum and beaten her before bringing her here.'

He turned to Mirac and spoke angrily, 'Unless you have already tasted our prize.'

'No father,' Mirac protested, 'I promise I haven't.'

The old man seemed placated and turning back to her, 'That will just leave my youngest, Omer to enjoy you.' He turned and smiled at the young man who looked rather shy. 'We don't know if Omer has ever enjoyed a woman's flesh but he will enjoy yours.''

They all laughed and prodded and jibed at the young man who protested and told them that of course he had had a woman. She felt a great anger burning in her, 'You will have to force me as you all make my skin crawl. You can do what you want but you won't break me. I will never belong to any of you.'

'We make your skin crawl,' the old man spat the words out 'you need to see yourself. You are dirty and you smell bad. You would have to be cleaned before any of us would touch you.' He turned to the guard who had brought her into the room, 'take her away and wash her.'

As the man dragged her from the room the old man said, 'Emine,' she turned at the name, 'I will enjoy forcing you.' She heard the laughter in the room as she was dragged out.

The guard took her over to a trough on one side of the area and taking a bucket he filled it and threw the water over her. The water was icy cold and she jumped as it hit her but she then started to enjoy the feel of the water cascading down her clothed body. He threw several more buckets of water over her before taking her back to her prison before pushing her inside. The room was cold and the wet clothes sticking to her body made her start to shake.

Within minutes the door opened again and she saw the young man called Omer, the youngest son of the fat old man standing there, 'It will be cold for you in there when you are wet, come outside.'

She was grateful and stumbled outside as he took her arm steering her to a post which he proceeded to tie her arms to, 'The night air will warm and you will dry here.' He then left her and she eventually fell asleep.

She was woken Omer when it was light and she felt very stiff. He untied her and reached out and she shrank away, 'You have nothing to fear from me Emine,' he said so she allowed him to help her up and lead her back to her cell.

It became a regular event for her to be dragged to the house where the old man would threaten her with what he would do to her but although he didn't touch her again she expected him to every time she was taken there. She dreaded the night when he decided to go further but for the time being he was happy to amuse himself trying to break her mentally.

They continued to feed her regularly and 'wash' her every few days. She didn't like Yusuf coming for her as although all the others were rough with her, he would always make sure his hand brushed one of her breasts as he pushed her around.

Omer was the only one who showed her any kindness and he was the one who would release her out into the sunshine sometimes securing her to the post. She would watch as an old man made bread every day baking it in a stone oven where she could see the coals glowing red.

She noticed that there were no women in the camp but once a week she would be locked away and she would hear the men shouting and laughing mingled with the voices of women. She was scared that she would go mad as she lost herself in thoughts and dreams as the days passed by.

One night she was taken by Mirac, her original captor, over to the house where the old man who she had learned was called Berat told her they had heard nothing from her people, 'They don't want you Emine,' he said and then laughed, 'but you are wanted here. It won't be long now before we will lie together.'

She had grown used to his taunts and they almost had no effect on her anymore but something about the way he said it tonight sent panic racing through her.

CHAPTER SIX

OLIVIA

It was their last night in Spain and as they finished their drinks in the noisy bar in Barcelona before leaving for the hostel they were staying in that night Olivia's eye was caught by a young man standing near the bar who was staring at her. He stood at over six feet tall, was slim but muscular and as she took in his handsome face and floppy dark hair he smiled at her. The smile filled his face and totally disarmed her and she found herself smiling back. Maggie saw her and looked over her shoulder at the young man staring at her friend.

'He likes you,' she said, 'he looks nice, shame we're leaving tomorrow.'

Olivia didn't answer but thought that it was indeed a shame as there was something engaging about the young man and she had felt an instant connection as he smiled at her. She was being daft she realised, she didn't know him and that thing about seeing someone across a crowded room was ridiculous. She brought herself back to reality, finished her drink and suggested that they leave. The man had turned back to the bar for a moment and didn't see the girls leave but Olivia would have been surprised to see the disappointment on his face when he turned back and she had gone.

The next day as the two girls waited for the ferry to take them to Genoa they were both aware of a sudden movement and then the young man from the bar was standing in front of them. 'Where did you go so suddenly last night?' he addressed himself to Olivia but then turned slightly smiling at Maggie.

'Our departure wasn't sudden,' Olivia said smiling, 'it was planned.'

He stared at her with a smile on his face, 'Are you catching the ferry to Genoa?'

'We are,' Maggie answered, 'are you?' he nodded and Olivia smiled again.

'Jack,' a voice called and the young man turned and waved to two other young men making their way over to where the girls were standing.

'Who are these two lovely ladies?' one of the young men who was about five feet ten with a nice face framed by a mop of ginger curly hair asked.

The young man from the night before turned to the girls saying, 'I'm Jack Lynforth, this ginger nut is Robbie Nixon and the devilishly handsome one is Jason Barker,' he turned to his other friend who was indeed classically good looking. He was smaller than the other two men and had blond spikey hair. He smiled at the two girls but then his eyes were looking elsewhere taking in all the people around him. Olivia thought he was very handsome but rather bland as he had no character in his face unlike Jack and Robbie. She took an instant dislike to him without knowing why except that for a feeling which grew as she watched him eyeing all the girls who walked past them.

Olivia introduced herself and Maggie to the young men and they chatted whilst they queued for the ferry and boarded together. They fell into easy conversation and enjoyed each other's company as they travelled to Genoa and Olivia was pleased when she heard they were heading for the same hostel as them.

She found out the boys who were all medical students were also backpacking around Europe and that Jack who came from Norwich had studied medicine at Leeds which made her laugh as she lived in Leeds and had studied in Norwich. He was three years older than Olivia and had already spent the years since graduating working his residency which he had just completed in Casualty at a large hospital in Bristol but wanted to specialise in Paediatrics. He had been offered a positon at a hospital in Edinburgh and had decided to take some time off before taking up the position.

Although they all got on well Olivia and Jack were drawn together and found themselves alone on several occasions in deep conversation. They exchanged stories of the two cities they were both familiar with sharing experiences of places visited that they both knew.

Maggie seemed to be getting on well with Robbie and whilst the four of them laughed together Jason excused himself to go to speak to a stunning blond girl standing nearby.

'He has a short attention span,' Jack joked as his friend moved away but Olivia didn't smile as there was something about Jason that made her feel uneasy.

When they disembarked in Genoa it seemed natural for them all to travel together to the hostel where they stayed for four weeks. At first they did their own thing, Maggie and Olivia getting jobs in a bar within two days of arriving. They spent some time with the boys but they seemed to have more money than the girls and could afford to do more.

One night when they were working the three boys came to the bar Olivia and Maggie were working in sitting on the bar stools they chatted to the girls when they had a moment and it became a pattern in so far as Jack and Robbie would show up whenever they were working sometimes accompanied by Jason.

Olivia enjoyed their company but her feelings towards Jack were growing and it scared her especially as she didn't believe he felt the same way. She was also concerned about the way Jason flirted with Maggie as she didn't want to see her friend hurt again but when she broached the subject with her friend she brushed her off.

There were many nights Jason didn't arrive with the boys and they didn't hide the fact he was off with some girl he had met. Some nights when he did accompany his friends he would leave with a girl he met in the bar but then there were other times when he would chat to Maggie and she would laugh up at him and Olivia dreaded what might happen.

One night when he had spent the whole night flirting with Maggie and then just before closing time had disappeared with a dark haired girl he had only spoken to for moments Olivia decided to broach the subject again with Maggie.

When they were walking back to the hostel she hung back from the boys and Maggie joined her, 'Maggie do you like Jason?' she asked.

'Of course I do, I like all the boys,' she answered.

'I thought you were getting on particularly well with Robbie,' Olivia said.

'I do get on with Robbie, we have a laugh,' Maggie said.

'But you like Jason more?' Olivia said holding her breath.

'I don't know what you mean,' Maggie answered not looking at her friend.

'You know exactly what I mean,' Olivia felt frustrated and a little annoyed that her friend was making her say it out loud when she was sure she knew what she was getting at. 'You know that Jason will shag anything that breathes. He doesn't care about anyone's feelings.'

'Ooh do you fancy him yourself,' Maggie asked and Olivia turned her head towards her to see a playful smile on her friends face. It wasn't a pleasant smile and Olivia was shocked. 'C'mon Liv why are you so concerned about Jason and me if you don't want him yourself?

'You're being ridiculous,' Olivia said, 'I just don't want to see you get hurt.'

''Doesn't sound like that to me,' Maggie said, 'don't you have enough with Jack. Don't be greedy.'

'Maggie I don't know what's got into you,' Olivia said, 'You're my friend and I have seen you hurt before. Jason will hurt you, he's a serial shagger. I really am worried for you.'

'I'm a big girl Liv,' Maggie laughed, 'besides how do you know that Jason wouldn't be different with me?'

Olivia stopped herself sighing out loud and decided not to get in this discussion with her friend as she didn't want to fall out with her. They had never had an argument and she didn't want to start now, 'Be careful,' was all she said.

CHAPTER SEVEN

Olivia didn't broach the subject of Jason with Maggie again as after the last time there was an awkwardness between them for a couple of days. They had been so close since the met and now Olivia felt as if Maggie was shutting her out.

When things went back to normal Olivia relaxed as she realised that there was nothing she could say that would stop Maggie hooking up with Jason if that's what she wanted and all she could do was be there to pick up the pieces after the fall out.

They didn't work every night and would go out themselves to bars but towards the end of their stay in Genoa the boys started tagging along when they ventured out. Jason rarely joined them which suited Olivia as she always felt awkward when he was with them.

One night when all five of them were together they had had a lot to drink and as they made their way back to the hostel Jason and Maggie were walking ahead together chatting and then Olivia saw Jason pull Maggie down an alley. Maggie laughed and didn't protest. Robbie walked by the alley but Olivia stopped and looked down to see her friend in a very close clinch with Jason. Her back pressed against a wall as he pushed into her kissing her hard. She looked for a sign that Maggie was in distress but her friend was kissing him back and had a hand on the back of his head pulling him into her.

Olivia felt a hand take hers as she was propelled away by Jack, 'They're fine, leave them to it.'

She stopped and stood her ground, 'I don't like Jason,' she said to Jack, 'he is a predator and Maggie is vulnerable. He'll hurt her.'

Jack laughed, 'You're being a bit dramatic aren't you?' he said, 'they're both adults.'

'I know that,' she said feeling as if he was belittling her, 'but you don't know Maggie like I do. She falls hard for blokes and then is heart broken when they let her down.'

'You're not responsible for her,' Jack said, 'she's old enough to make her own mistakes.'

'So you know it's a mistake for her to go with Jason?' she asked.

'They're just having a bit of fun,' Jack said, 'you should try it. Lighten up.'

She felt as if he had slapped her in the face and she thought she had misunderstood him. She had liked him but he was obviously the same as Jason. 'I thought you were different,' she said.

'Different?' he echoed, 'what does that mean? Different to what?'

'Different to blokes like Jason,' she answered.

'And what is Jason like?' Jack demanded.

'He's shagging his way round Europe,' she almost spat the words, 'he doesn't care who it is or who he hurts. I didn't think you were like that.'

'Have you seen me shagging my way round Europe?' he asked.

'No but,' she said 'you're condoning it.'

'If he wants to shag his way around Europe and the girls are willing then he's not doing anything wrong,' Jack said and saw Olivia was about to speak but stopped her by saying, 'it doesn't mean it's what I want to do.'

She stared at him realising what he was saying made sense but it didn't sit right with her especially as it involved her friend. He looked back at her, 'Look Olivia each to their own. I don't think he promises the girls anything. They all know it's a bit of fun.'

'It's not what I'd call fun,' Olivia said.

'You don't shag then?' Jack said smiling.

She spluttered as she didn't know how to respond then said, 'I certainly wouldn't make a hobby of it.'

He laughed and she started to laugh too at her remark and the tension was broken and he moved towards her and before she knew what had hit her he took her in his arms and kissed her. She found herself kissing him back lost in the moment and then coming to her senses she pushed him away, 'I'm not shagging you if that's what you're thinking,' she said walking away.

He laughed, 'Spoil sport', and following her he took her hand and they walked back to the hostel in contentment without speaking.

After that night Jack didn't try to kiss her again and she decided he had been drunk and forgotten She was okay with that although she couldn't deny the strength of the feeling when he had kissed her. She was scared of how much it had moved her as she liked to be in control of her feelings and therefore she was happy to continue with their friendship.

What she wasn't happy about though was the way Jason was treating Maggie. He would disappear with other girls but then turn up on occasion and snap his fingers and Maggie would be there for him hanging on to his every word. They would then disappear together and although Olivia knew it wasn't her business she really wanted to ask her friend what she was doing but decided to keep her feelings confined to the diary she wrote in every night recording the adventures she was experiencing.

Once she had decided not to interfere in Maggie's love life she started to relax and the girls grew close again. She hadn't realised that there had been a strain between them until she let it go but she tried not to feel bad about it as she wanted them to have a good trip. Although she still didn't like Jason and avoided him when she could, she didn't let it spoil her time in Italy.

They spent the next two months travelling together, hiring scooters and jumping on trains exploring Italy. During this time Jack and Olivia grew close but although they didn't kiss again he often took her hand and Maggie and Robbie seemed to have developed a good friendship constantly horsing around with each other when she wasn't off somewhere with Jason.

Olivia's feelings for Jack were growing and sometimes would catch her off guard as she would catch her breath when he brushed by her or she unexpectedly caught sight of him. Although he was especially nice to her he never expressed similar feelings so she decided to just enjoy the time they spent together.

Maggie and she had planned to move on to Greece next intending to spend several months island hopping. As the final day in Italy approached Olivia felt as if she was walking on egg shells as she worried that Maggie wouldn't want to part from Jason but didn't dare discuss the subject. She felt sad at the thought of leaving Jack behind as the boys didn't have any set plans.

Olivia was filled with the strongest feeling of foreboding when that all changed two days before the girls intended leaving Italy.

CHAPTER EIGHT

RACHEL

After Rachel was born Catherine ensured there were no more mistakes as one child was more than she ever wanted. She looked after her daughter, never complained and even developed some affection for her but it wasn't until Rachel could hold a conversation that they really bonded. She began to enjoy her company and like the love she had for Roger had been slow burning so it was for Rachel.

She could see how Roger doted on the child but she didn't feel jealous about that as he still gave her plenty of attention and it kept him occupied allowing her to follow her own pursuits.

Growing up an only child Rachel had been the focus of her father's attention although her mother was there when she wanted her. She was unaware of the coldness her mother had shown towards her in the early years as once she was talking properly her mother always seemed to be there for her.

She was aware however that her mother wasn't as warm as her father but was used to the differences between them. She would cuddle down with her father on an evening watching television whilst her mother worked away in her studio but she also enjoyed sitting in her mother's light airy studio watching her painting which she did more these days and she would ask her many questions most of which would be answered philosophically. Often she didn't understand her mother's answers but that just led to more conversation.

Both parents had encouraged her in everything she did. From an early age she had a thirst for knowledge and it wasn't clear whether she was born this way or it was because her parents spent so much time with her in conversation never boring of the questions their daughter had for them.

Both her parents, Roger and Catherine were academics but worked in very different fields. Her Father had lectured in biology for many years before moving into the field of cancer research. Her mother was involved in literature and the arts and lectured part-time in creative writing and had her own studio at home where she spent hours painting wonderful pictures many of which she had found buyers for.

Rachel knew that they had both been born down south and that they had moved to Birmingham before her birth moving again further north when she was a year old. She never tired of asking them questions about their lives before she was there. She loved the story of how her mother had followed her father to Birmingham where he had asked her to marry him. In her mind they had been so in love they hadn't been able to live without each other.

Roger had come to enjoy travelling abroad as much as Catherine for holidays as Rachel grew as he saw everything through her eyes. Rachel's thirst for knowledge grew as they travelled the world. She was fascinated by different cultures and the languages that were spoken. As she grew it became apparent that she had a good ear and the ability to learn different tongues and over the years she became fluent in many European languages.

When they were away she enjoyed seeing the tourist attractions and learning about the traditions of the countries they were in but preferred it when they went off the beaten track. Those were the times when he felt she learnt more about the culture of the people and as her knowledge of languages grew she was able to talk to locals and spend time learning the raw history of places they were visiting.

She had many books at home about travelling and foreign countries many of which had been bought for her by her parents whilst on their travels.

They would spend at least four of the six weeks summer holiday abroad when they would spend time exploring but they would also take other more relaxed holidays twice a year on the two bank holiday weeks. To her it was a way of life and although she realised her friends didn't go on holiday as much as she did, she didn't actually appreciate how fortunate she had been until she was much older.

Like her mother she enjoyed writing and started a journal about the countries they had visited. She decided to take what she felt were the the best parts of the journal and create a book. Her mother who encouraged her was happy to guide her with her writings and helped her publish her first book when she was only sixteen.

Although she had a close relationship with her mother and they shared the love of literature the relationship she had with her father was more loving and therefore stronger. Although they spent a lot of time as a family the time spent with each individually was very different.

Her father appeared to others as a serious man whereas her mother came across as a social butterfly full of fun but Rachel knew better. Her mother was arty and bohemian in her appearance, wearing long flowing dresses and caftans, her brown hair long and curly cascading down her back. She smoked brightly coloured cocktail cigarettes and drank wine from hand painted glasses. She had friends around often who all belonged to the arty set and although Rachel enjoyed their company to a point she generally found them quite shallow.

Her father on the other hand was a loving, deep thinking person and would openly talk to Rachel about feelings and discuss his thoughts on the reasons people behaved the way they did encouraging her to think about her actions.

He was full of joy and the two of them laughed together and shared jokes and all the time she spent with him she never realised she was learning as he made everything so much fun.

She was the apple of his eye and his chest would visibly swell when she walked in a room. He made her feel very special and she always felt safe when he was around and saw him as her champion. Although this may not have prepared her for the hard knocks of life the love of her doting father was a precious thing.

It was her father who taught her to ride her first bike picking her up again and again as she fell, kissing her grazed knees better. When she had finally mastered it her mother had joined them and clapped in glee at her daughter's achievements before returning to her studio. After this Rachel and her father would go riding on their bikes in the evenings and at weekends as there was a cycle path nearby.

It was her father who plucked her from the ocean when she was drowning.

CHAPTER NINE

They had been travelling around Italy for two weeks now and the weather was glorious. Rachel who was only five was fascinated by the culture and was constantly being told to stop staring at people by her parents.

Although she had been having swimming lessons from a very young age her father was always at hand and on this particular day he was teaching her to swim in the sea. They had been in and out all morning as she loved the feeling of floating on the water but there came a time when he thought she had had enough and told her that she needed to come out. She protested but he managed to coax her out with the promise of ice cream.

He carried her until she could stand in the water and placed her down holding her hand all the time as they walked through the waves and then up the beach to where her mother was laid on a sunbed reading.

He asked Catherine to watch their daughter but she didn't put her book down until he insisted and then he left Rachel on the beach with her mother whilst he went to get them all one of the amazing ice creams the Italians are so famous for and that Rachel loved.

Her mother lay back down on her sun bed on the sand under a parasol and told Rachel to wrap a towel around herself. She then picked up the book she had been reading which was a novel by her favourite author and continued, to read lost in the story. The only time she read dramas and novels was on holiday and she enjoyed the escapism whilst warmed by the sun.

Rachel grew bored waiting for her father to return and started to speak to her mother asking her about where they were going the next day but her mother didn't seem to hear. Rachel was used to this when her mother was reading and started to look around, She could see families chatting and eating, children playing on the sand and people swimming in the sea.

She stared out to sea and smiled deciding rather than bother her mother whilst they waited for her father she would go back to the sea and try to swim by herself.

She thought how proud her father would be when he returned to see her swimming by herself. Her mother didn't notice as her daughter rose, discarded her towel and skipped over the warm sand down to the sea. Rachel stood for a short while watching others in the water, enjoying the feeling of the gentle waves lapping at her feet.

She looked down and watched the water caressing her toes and the sand working its way between them. She looked up, turned back to look at her mother who was still engrossed in her book and then started to walk slowly into the sea.

Her steps at first were taken gingerly but as the water rose up her legs she became bolder. The water was lovely and warm and as she was so small, soon it was at her waist. She hesitated for a moment as when she had been in the sea with her father he had carried her in and then when the water was at his waist he would lower her into the water and supported her weight on his arms until she was floating in the water. All the time his arms would be hovering below her as he instructed her in how to move her arms and legs ready to lift her out of the water if necessary. Then they would spend time playing in the waves laughing as he lifted her in and out of the water.

Now as she stood alone she was unsure how to start swimming but then she remembered how she had seen her father launch himself into the waves arms stretched out and raising her small arms she plunged forward. She was alarmed immediately as she didn't float like she did when her father was with her. She thrashed around trying to remember what her father had told her to do with her arms and legs but nothing worked and she started to swallow the salty water. The sand that she disturbed with her thrashing made the water murky and she couldn't see much apart from tiny bubbles that seemed to fill the water around her.

Her little chest felt like it was exploding as water started to fill her lungs and she was very scared as she could hear ringing in her ears. She didn't know how to get her head back above water. She couldn't think straight as the fear filled her little body. At such a young age and in her sheer panic it didn't dawn on her to just put her feet back on the ocean floor.

It seemed an age to her that she was drowning but in fact it was less than a minute before she felt strong arms lifting her out of the sea.

'Jelly Bean,' she heard her father's voice saying his pet name for her as he carried her back to the sand whilst she choked in his arms. He placed her down and knelt beside her, tapping her back as she coughed and spluttered. A small crowd had gathered around them and she looked around her with eyes as big as saucers.. When she was breathing normally she looked at him with her scared eyes and he bundled her up in his arms, 'you mustn't go swimming alone Jelly Bean. You must always wait for me.'

She nodded as he scooped her up and carried her back to where her mother was standing looking shocked holding three ice cream cornets in her hands the creamy liquid running down her arms.

Her father set her down and wrapped the towel she had discarded earlier around her rubbing and patting her gently. When she was settled he took an ice cream from her mother who had not spoken and presented it to Rachel telling her to eat it and she was then aware of whispered words between her parents.

She heard her father say, 'We could have lost her.' To her young ears it sounded like her father was scolding her mother but she knew this couldn't be as she had never heard them argue. She hoped he wasn't cross with her mother because it was she who had gone off on her own but her concern soon waned as she enjoyed her ice cream.

She was too young to notice the coolness between her parents for the rest of the day.

CHAPTER TEN

EMINE

The days passed and the routine was the same, she would sleep on the hard floor of the dark, musty stone outbuilding and be taken out in the morning, secured to the post and left there for the rest of the day. Her hair was matted and her skin dry from the sun on her unprotected skin through the day. Although they threw water over her every few days she never really felt clean.

Most days she was fed with scraps of bread, rice and stew but sometimes they forgot to feed her although they always provided her with water.

She would be taken outside and tied to the post most days by various men who were generally rough with her except Omer and his brother Mustafa. Omer continued to be kind to her, lingering to talk. He would tell her about what the weather was going to be like and ask her how she was. She had nothing to say as her days were all the same but when she asked him when they would let her go he would clam up and move away which worried her and once when she asked him to help her escape she had seen a dark look cross his face and he hadn't spoken to her for a few days after.

Mustafa would speak to her and always tied her loosely sometimes only by one hand and she realised that if she was ever be free it would be when he secured her to the post and so she spent her time making plans for her escape.

The men would sit around together in the shade through the day talking and laughing but as the day grew hotter they would retreat indoors where they would generally stay for the rest of the day opening the doors at night when she could hear them talking.

She watched carefully trying to become familiar with the movement in the camp. Most days some of the men would drive off in the trucks which were parked nearby. She had no idea where they went but they would be away most of the day returning late in the evening announcing their presence with lots of hooting of horns and shouting.

There were some young boys who were little more than children who would wash clothes most days in the large water trough and then hang them over a makeshift washing line strung up between two outbuildings. Most days she would watch in shock as they were taught to use rifles by the older men and saw them learning to use knives and fight.

The old baker would make bread every day and then later he would cook over an open fire in two huge pots and the young boys would help him. She would watch as they carried individual bowls to the men who gathered to eat together and would wait expectantly hoping they wouldn't forget her.

Every week there would be one night when they would start drinking hard, shouting and laughing raucously and she would feel relieved when she was locked in her cell. As the nights got lighter she would be allowed to stay out longer before being returned to her cell. One evening she saw the men start to drink but nobody came to lock her up and it made her nervous. She had heard the trucks returning hooting their horns and the men shouting and suddenly Yusuf came hurrying out of the main building and ran towards her.

He untied her but it took him longer than usual as he was trying to rush and his fingers fumbled with the rope. He eventually released the rope and dragged her to her feet pushing her towards her cell shouting at her to hurry and she wondered what was wrong.

She heard the men walking into camp and turned to see that there were several women with them, some of whom ran to various other men in the camp who grabbed at them roughly. She realised that they had not been meant to see her and as she stared at them as Yusuf pushed her hard towards her cell she caught the eyes of a young woman.

The woman stopped and stared at her with sad but kind eyes and Emine didn't shift her gaze from the woman until she was pushed to the floor in her cell and Yusuf slammed the door shut. She could hear the noises outside of drunken shouting and laughter and the sound of women's voices. She thought of the woman she had seen who had looked at her with gentle eyes and wondered if she would help her.

Two weeks later once again the men forgot to lock her away as she had become such a usual sight in the camp and the women arrived. This time nobody came running out to lock her away and she watched as the men shouted with excitement as they walked into the camp and some took hold of the women gently kissing and caressing them whilst others grabbed at them roughly.

There was so much activity in camp and she sat quietly as she didn't want to be treated in the same way when she was aware of someone standing near her. She turned expecting to see a man leering at her but she was surprised to see the woman whose eye she'd caught previously.

'Will you help me? Emine asked.

'I cannot,' the woman replied, 'they would kill me.'

'Please,' Emine begged but the woman turned away and because she didn't want her to leave she called after her, What's your name?'

The young woman turned back to look at her but hesitated before saying, 'I am called Esin.'

Before they could talk anymore Berat's voice bellowed close by, 'Why is that girl still out here?' to nobody in particular. He grabbed Esin by the arm and shook her roughly, 'What did she say to you?'

'Nothing father,' she said and he slapped her asking he once again what Emine had said.

'She just asked me my name,' she said.

He shouted for Yusuf and Mirac to come to him. Mirac appeared first and his father pushed Esin towards him, 'Look after your woman.' Emine realised Esin must be his wife as he had called Berat father and she watched as Micar grabbed Esin and pull her towards one of the buildings where they disappeared inside.

Yusuf arrived at his father's side and he hit him hard across the face, 'Why is this girl still out here? Why can't you do anything right? Take her to her room.'

As Yusuf bent to untie Emine his father kicked him and he saw the man wince and then his face set in anger as he stared into her face. She felt very scared as he hauled her to her feet and pushed her towards her cell.

As he threw her into the dark room he said angrily to her, 'I will make you pay for this.'

She shuddered as the door slammed shut as she was sure he meant what he said.

CHAPTER ELEVEN

The days after their alcohol fuelled nights when the women visited the camp would be quiet as the men slept most of the day and she was rarely brought from her cell until early evening. They would all be nursing hangovers and their unwarranted anger towards her would be more exaggerated so on those occasions she would always comply with them and not fight them in order not to antagonise any of them.

Life went on as before and she was rarely taken into the main house anymore for Berat to torture her with his taunts. Yusuf would look at her with anger every time he saw her and on the occasions he fetched or put her in her cell he would be very rough with her. On one occasion he said, 'Your time will come,' and she could only imagine what he meant.

One day he opened the door and hauled her to her feet and continuing to hold on to her arm he dragged her into the bright sunshine which blinded her. She couldn't see for a few seconds as he proceeded to drag her to the main building where the door was standing open. He pushed her inside with such force that she almost ran across the floor coming to a stop a few feet from Berat.

He was sitting down, leaning back in his seat and he looked up at her with a serious face. Fear struck her as she waited for what him to speak. He looked at her for a few moments but there was none of his usual leering, 'Nobody will pay to get you back,' he said, 'you are of such little value.'

She was scared what this might mean for her and stood stock still as the old man continued, 'What are we to do with you?' She didn't answer as she could tell it was a rhetorical question. 'I will decide soon,' he said with none of his usual threats, 'but first we have business.'

She couldn't imagine what kind of business he would have with her except for the obscene threats he had made but when he told Yusuf to take her away she was confused. He took her over to the post where he tied her making the knots so tight the rope cut painfully into her wrists, 'Soon,' he said, 'you will pay.'

Berat came to the door of the main building and shouted that it was time for business and she saw most of the men walk towards him and sit down on the ground around him. The old baker didn't even look up but remained making his bread and the young boys were shooed towards him by another man.

Berat greeted the men loudly as they took their seats and then lowered his voice as he started to speak in hushed tones and however hard she strained she couldn't hear what he was saying but it wasn't long before she realised the 'business' Berat had mentioned didn't involve her.

When the old man stopped speaking, she saw Mirac, her original captor, take over and then the men fell into deep conversation for some time. Eventually they all got up and disappeared into various buildings from which they all brought guns which they started to clean. She felt very nervous and wondered what was going on. When Omer brought her some water she asked him what was happening but he wouldn't say and didn't linger to talk to her.

Mustafa later brought her a bowl of food and as he loosened her ties to release one of her hands so she could eat he commented that her bonds were too tight. He loosened both and rubbed her wrists gently. She asked him what the men were doing and he looked at her with suspicion in his eyes and then she saw them soften as he tied one of her hands again to the post.

'We plan an attack and tomorrow we go on a raid,' he said.

'What kind of raid and attack?' she asked him.

'We fight against the regime,' he said, 'they will not expect this.'

She pressed him about what he meant but as he started to speak Berat shouted him over to where the other men were sitting. His father seemed to be angry with him and she thought he had probably said too much to her.

The next day Omer took her out of her room early taking her to her usual spot. She saw all the men gather and the boys serve them with food. They were particularly quiet and after about thirty minutes Berat appeared from the main building and spoke to them. They all rose, picked up their guns and made their way to the trucks. Two men remained behind and she watched Berat follow the men to the trucks. She heard the engines start up and then the trucks started to leave and when all was quiet again she saw Berat return. He looked at her without speaking and returned to his home.

From what Mustafa had said she understood that the men had gone on some kind of planning mission and she assumed that they would leave another day for their attack. She studied the camp closer than she had ever done before as she knew that this would be her chance to escape.

The men who had remained behind didn't stay outside for long and she found herself alone. The old baker would go inside in the afternoon and today was no different and the young boys disappeared inside when it became too hot.

This would be her best time to get away and although it was the hottest part of the day it would be her only chance and she would take it. She looked around and her eyes fell on the pile of rough stones outside the building they kept her imprisoned in and an idea formed.

The men returned late the horns sounding and they all seemed excited as they entered camp. Some of them went in to talk to Berat and she observed everything closely. When she was returned to her cell she deliberately stumbled and fell onto the pile of rocks. She grasped on to one of the stones and slipped it inside her top as the guard roughly pulled her up and pushed her inside her cell.

Once inside she retrieved the stone and felt it in the dark. She was pleased with her prize which she would use to cut the rope. Most of the guards just secured one of her hands now except Yusuf and she prayed that it wouldn't be him that would come for her in the morning.

Her heart sank the next day when the door opened and she saw Yusuf standing there. She had put the stone inside her top earlier and was scared that it would fall out as he was so rough with her. He pulled her outside and as they approached the post Berat came out and shouted to him. He looked at her and then pushed her towards Mustafa who was standing close by. Yusuf walked towards his father as Mustafa tied one of her hands to the post loosely as was his usual practice.

She felt optimistic as she said, 'Are you going on your attack today?'

He looked around to see if anyone was listening and when he saw the coast was clear he turned back to her, 'Yes,' he said, 'today the regime will feel the pain.'

She could barely contain her excitement as she watched the men eat and then leave camp as they had the day before. She was impatient for midday to arrive and was relieved when she saw the baker disappear into his home and one of the guards who remained behind herded the young boys inside. She was alone in the camp but realised she must wait a short while so she was sure that the coast was clear.

She wriggled her hand and the tie came loose, she didn't need the stone after all. Soon she was free but she kept her hand up as if she was still tied in case anyone came out. She stayed like that for about ten minutes before she carefully rose to her feet. Her heart was pounding so hard she was sure that the men would hear it.

She crept across the ground towards the trail where the trucks had driven down earlier and as she passed the last building she started to run as if the devil himself was on her tail.

CHAPTER TWELVE

OLIVIA

The friends arrived in Bari two days before the girls were due to take the ferry to Corfu in Greece.

They checked into their hostel and then explored the maze of narrow streets of the capital of the Puglia region of southern Italy which stands between two harbours. They spent the evening in a bar on one of the harbours and Olivia noticed that Maggie and Jason seemed to be getting on particularly well. What should have made her happy made her heart sink.

The next day she wanted to visit Basilica di San Nicola an eleventh century pilgrimage site which holds some of St Nicholas' remains. It was on her wish list of things to do in Italy and Maggie had said she too would really like to see it but when Olivia asked her what time she wanted to set off, her friend acted as if she didn't know what she was talking about. the idea of there being St Nicholas' remains there was fascinating.' Her friend said nothing so Olivia said, 'look I don't mind waiting whilst you get ready. We'll still have most of the day.'

'I'm sure I didn't say it was fascinating,' Maggie said, 'it all sounds rather macabre to me.' Olivia started to protest again not believing what she was hearing when Maggie cut her off, 'I really don't remember Olivia,' she said adding, 'besides Jason and I have plans for today.'

Olivia understood immediately and she was very angry at her friend and she couldn't keep that anger out of her voice, 'So not only are you dumping me for a shag you're lying to my face about it.'

Maggie turned on her, 'It's not just a shag, he loves me.' Olivia snorted and Maggie continued, 'I don't know why you're so against Jason and me getting together. You know how I feel about him but you have to spoil it all the time. I think you're just jealous because Jack doesn't feel the same way about you.'

Olivia felt as if she had been slapped in the face, 'You can't believe I'm jealous,' but Maggie just stared at her and Olivia tried to use a more gentle voice, 'Look Maggie I know you care for Jason but doesn't it bother you about all the other girls he goes off with?'

'I don't know what you mean,' Maggie said.

'You're kidding, right?' Olivia said, 'it's most nights and you know it. That's not the actions of a man who loves you. You deserve better than that. It appears that he only comes to you when there's nobody else around.'

She could see she had hit a nerve and Maggie looked furious, 'You are jealous, I was right! Why else would you say such hurtful things. You moon around Jack and he doesn't even notice you but that's okay I suppose because that's you. You can't stand that I've found someone who loves me and you'll say and do anything to spoil it.'

Olivia stood looking at her friend stunned without speaking and Maggie turned, picked up her bag and left the room.

Jack found her sitting on the harbour an hour later where she was lost in thought staring out to sea. She told him what had happened leaving out the part about her feelings for him.

'Jason's just like that, he's just a lad I suppose,' Jack said, 'not that I like the way he behaves but to be fair to him he doesn't promise anyone anything.'

'Then why does Maggie seem to think he loves her?' Olivia asked, 'could he have told her that?'

Jack sat staring out to sea for a few moments, 'Maybe I'm giving him too much credit. I think he might say whatever he needed to in order to get what he wanted from a girl.'

'That's disgusting,' Olivia said, 'he has no scruples.'

'Oh Liv,' he smiled at her and her heart constricted, it was the first time he had called her 'Liv', 'I love that you are so fair minded but it's a little naïve. Lots of men and women for that matter don't have scruples especially when it comes to sex. Jason is hardly a one off.'

'That doesn't make it right,' Olivia protested.

'Of course it doesn't make it right,' Jack said, 'but not everyone plays fair Liv. Unfortunately Maggie's making it very easy for Jason to take advantage.'

'So it's her fault?' Olivia felt annoyed.

'Whoa,' he said, 'I'm just saying. Look I'm sure Jason's very charming and has won her over but c'mon Liv all the warning signs are there. All those other girls she sees him with…'

Olivia sighed, 'I know, I said as much to her but she said I was just jealous.'

Jack laughed, 'Jealous? What have you got to be jealous of? She really has got it bad.'

They sat in silence for a few minutes and then Jack said, 'C'mon Liv don't let it spoil your time here. It's your last day in Italy so let's go to see the Basilica di San Nicola

The day got better for Olivia as they spent a lovely day together. At one point Jack took her hand to help her climb down from a wall and didn't let go for several minutes. Her heart sang but then remembering what Jack had said about her being naïve she wondered if she wasn't being a bit pathetic.

As they passed the harbour on the way back to the hostel they heard a voice calling Jack and as they both turned Olivia saw Jason and Maggie sitting with Robbie at a table outside a bar. They went over to join them and Jason said, 'Where have you two been?' with a wink which put Olivia's back up but before she could answer Jack told them what they'd been doing.

She could see Jason wasn't interested and noticed that Maggie wouldn't look at her. When Jack had finished speaking Jason said, 'We've all been talking and Robbie and I think it would be a good idea for us to go with the girls to Greece.'

Olivia looked at Maggie's beaming face which was now turned to her. Olivia stared at her incredulously and Maggie looked back at her with a smug expression on her face.

When they were alone at bedtime Olivia asked her friend if they could forget their argument and Maggie replied, 'Yes we can but now you must see that I'm right, he loves me.'

Olivia didn't want another argument so said, 'I'm just worried for you.'

'There's nothing to worry about,' Maggie said but Olivia didn't believe that for a moment.

CHAPTER THIRTEEN

The next morning Maggie acted as if nothing had happened between them but Olivia couldn't shake off the bad feeling she had. It had surprised her how Maggie had turned on her and although she realised that her friend wasn't happy with what she had said she couldn't forget the accusation she had thrown at her. She hated the way Maggie had shouted at her and couldn't understand how their friendship had soured in this way. She knew she had to get over it as they had months to spend together but it made her wary. She had thought she knew Maggie and although she had always known that she liked her own way she had always found her fun to be with and thought she was a loyal friend.

One thing she realised she had learned from what had happened was that things said in anger although perhaps not true were hard to forget and she decided then that she would try not to say things in anger as they couldn't be taken back.

As they walked to the harbour Robbie, Jack and Olivia walked together with Jason and Maggie lagging behind as they walked with their arms around each other stopping to kiss on several occasions.

They boarded the ferry at seven fifteen and found some seats on deck, Jason and Maggie sitting slightly apart from the other three. They were departing at eight o'clock and knew the journey would take almost eleven hours so had wanted somewhere they could be comfortable. They had bought some sandwiches on the way to the ferry which Olivia had carried and she now handed them out. She sat between Robbie and Jack and they chatted happily as the boat sailed out of the harbour and they watched Bari grow further and further away.

It was a lovely day and Robbie went to buy them all water leaving Jack and Olivia sitting in comfortable silence. Olivia looked over the Maggie and Jason who were kissing and cuddling. She could hear Maggie giggling every now and then and it made her cross. She gave herself a talking to. She hated that Maggie was making such a fool of herself but at the end of the day it was her friend's choice and it really shouldn't bother her so much. She decided to let it go and be ready to be there to pick the pieces up when it all went wrong which she was sure it would.

It was a long journey to Corfu and the friends, chatted, walked around the boat and as Olivia snoozed she felt Jack's arm go around her so he could cradle her whilst she slept. Maggie hardly spoke to Olivia for the whole journey as she spent all her time with Jason. It was almost eight o'clock in the evening when the friends stood on Corfu harbour studying a map in order to work out where their hostel was. It only took them ten minutes to walk to their accommodation and Maggie dumped her bag and left immediately telling Olivia that she'd see her later.

Olivia went to find the boys and went to a bar nearby where they relaxed and enjoyed the evening. The boys who had no plans listened as Olivia told them that she and Maggie had planned to spend some time in Corfu exploring the island and then intended taking the ferry to the mainland where they would make their way across Greece to Volos where they would take a ferry to Skiathos and from there visit Skopelos and Alonissos where the marine park had been formed to preserve the seals and marine life.

From there they had planned to travel to Athens where they would spend some time and then island hop the Cyclades Islands visiting Naxos, Pars, Piraeus, Santorini and Syros although they were open to visiting any of the other islands.

She spoke with such enthusiasm that the boys got caught up with her excitement and before long they said they'd tag along if that was okay. She said she was fine with that and assured them that they would love Greece. She then told them they intended ending up in Patras in March for the final event of the Patras Carnival. When they asked her about the Carnival she explained that it was the largest event in Greece which starts mid-January and lasts until forty eight days before Easter.

'Bloody hell,' Robbie laughed, 'that's what I call a carnival.'

Olivia laughed with him, 'It's not just one long event. It's made up of various things like, balls, parades and kid's treasure hunts but it finishes with a big parade of floats and the ritual burning of the carnival king's float on the harbour.'

They all agreed that it sounded like fun and looked at the map Olivia had as she pointed to the route they'd take.

It was late when Olivia went to bed that night. There were no other backpackers in the room apart from her and Maggie but she never heard her friend come in as she was exhausted and fell into a deep sleep.

When she woke the next morning Maggie was in her bed but took an age to get up and Olivia wondered exactly what time she came in but she wasn't her mother and she could do as she pleased. She told her that she was going down to meet Jack and Robbie for breakfast and Maggie said she'd join them.

Olivia met up with the boys and was surprised to see Jason was with them. He listened as they told him about their plans of travelling Greece and he showed little interest until Maggie joined them and Olivia thought she may have been wrong about him as he seemed pleased to see her draping his arm over her shoulder as she sat next to him.

They spent most of their time together exploring Corfu visiting various coves and bays, swimming in the sea and sightseeing the local attractions including several monasteries. There were times when the boys went off together and Olivia would find herself with a distracted Maggie. She knew she was thinking about Jason all the time but tried to get her involved in activities which she would join in with however with little enthusiasm.

After almost two weeks they decided to move on and agreed to start their journey to Volos the following Monday which was three days away and as they sat together in the evening at a bar excitedly talking about their plans Olivia noticed that Jason didn't seem interested. He was staring across the bar and as Olivia followed his gaze she saw a pretty blond girl smiling back at him. She froze as she realised what this could mean and tried to draw him into the conversation but after a few minutes he excused himself from the table.

She watched as he made his way over to the blond girl who beamed up at him and she turned to see Maggie watching too, her face set.

'Maggie,' she said reaching over to her friend who shrugged her off and gave her a look that appeared to Olivia of pure hatred. It made her almost reel back and all she could do was repeat, 'Maggie.'

Jack and Robbie had also witnessed what Jason had done and both looked very awkward and the evening remained strained with Maggie not speaking at all. The girls didn't see Jason in the following days and Olivia hardly dare broach the subject with her friend who followed her around like a zombie. When she asked if she was okay Maggie would say yes but she knew it wasn't true.

Jack and Robbie would join them for a drink in the evening but spent the days apart from them as they didn't want to get into where Jason was. Robbie would try to cajole Maggie when they met but she wouldn't be brought out of her mood.

The night before they were to leave for their journey to Volos Olivia asked Jack, 'Are you still coming with us tomorrow?'

He looked surprised, 'Yes of course we are. I'm sorry about Jason but it's between Maggie and him. I think moving on is the best thing we can do.' Olivia didn't see the point in discussing it with him as there was nothing they could do to improve the situation.

The following morning they got their things together and once again Olivia asked Maggie if she was okay. Her friend smiled, 'Yes I'm fine. We're leaving Corfu and Jason and I will sort things out. It'll all be good again.'

Olivia was stunned that her friend thought things would be okay with Jason but decided to leave it. She would stick to her resolve of not getting involved anymore. When the girls went to the bar near the hostel for breakfast to meet the boys Olivia saw that only Jack and Robbie were there and she immediately felt concerned.

'Where's Jason?' Maggie asked and the boys said he was on his way.

Maggie looked brighter as she sat down to join them and ordered some food and coffee. They chatted and Olivia was happy to see her friend back with them even if she didn't like the reason. She saw him before Maggie who had her back to him did. Jason was walking towards them with his arm around the blond girl he had joined in the bar three nights before. She didn't know what to do but wanted to warn Maggie however before she could Jack who was sat next to her saw them approaching and the look on his face made Maggie turn around.

Olivia saw her back stiffen as Jason joined them sitting down and pulling the blond girl down next to him. 'Hey guys,' he said with not a flicker of embarrassment, 'this is Stacey.' He didn't even look at the girl as he said it and they all mumbled a hello. 'Stacey and I are going to spend a bit more time in Corfu but I'll catch up with you later.'

Olivia glanced at Maggie who looked totally stunned and silence descended on the table but Jason didn't seem to notice as he asked Stacey if she wanted anything and then ordered coffee for both of them. They spent an awkward fifteen minutes before Jason got up from the table pulling Stacey up with him, 'see you guys in a few days,' he said.

CHAPTER FOURTEEN

RACHEL

One Summer when Rachel was nine years old they made their first trip to Greece together and this is when for her the love affair with everything Greek started. They were going island hopping and chose the Cyclades island group to spend four weeks in.

They flew into Mykonos and as they drove towards their costal accommodation Rachel was mesmerised by the little white houses with blue windows and doors. She stared out of the window in wonder at the windmills and numerous small churches that she saw on their way.

They had hired a small cottage on the coast where they would spend five days whilst they explored the island and the smaller islands nearby. They stopped for supplies and Rachel begged them to buy her a book about the island which she saw on a book stand. When they pulled up outside the small white cottage they were staying in Rachel climbed out of the car, book tightly in hand and smiled at the sight before her. The cottage was as others she had seen on the way, white washed with a blue painted door and windows to match. She thought it was wonderful and as she turned to look at the sea she could see islands in the distance and she immediately fell in love.

They spent days driving and walking around the island and hopping on a couple of ferries which took them to less commercial islands nearby. Rachel spent the whole time in awe of the beauty that surrounded her and thought it was just the perfect place.

She read about how the people of the island were once very poor surviving on fishing and breeding stock and land that wasn't suited for livestock. She learnt that tourism had turned the economy of the island around but she imagined how it was to have lived here before the hoards of tourists arrived. Although they visited commercial towns where holiday makers outnumbered locals including Chora where she saw the windmills and fed pelicans she always preferred stopping in the villages and hamlets scattered over the island where she could witness the real life of the locals.

Her imagination was well fed when she read that according to mythology Mykonos was where Heracles killed the giants and that the rocks around the island were supposed to be their corpses. She would stare at the craggy rocks trying to see any resemblance to the giants they were supposed to be.

They ate in small tavernas, swam in the warm sea and explored but as night drew in they would sit outside the cottage watching the lights twinkling in the harbour. On the second evening as they left a local taverna her mother said she wanted to visit the local town but her father said that Rachel wouldn't like it.

That night she had woken to raised voices but the next day she believed she had dreamt it. However the next night her mother said she was going into town and her father protested but it made no difference as they watched her mother drive away and Rachel could tell from her father's face he wasn't pleased. Her mother didn't return before she was asleep but was there in the morning and she didn't notice the frosty atmosphere.

On the last evening in Mykonos her mother once again said that she was going into town and this time her father said nothing instead he put an arm around Rachel's shoulders and to her this meant that all was fine.

From Mykonos they moved on to Naxos but Rachel found it too large and busy being more interested in seeing the cave where according to Greek Mythology Zeus was raised.

After that they went on to Paros, Sifnos and Sikinos and she enjoyed exploring loving the atmosphere that Greece offered but her imagination was set alight when the island of Santorini came into view. She was standing on deck with her father as the ferry approached the island and Rachel held her breath as she saw the beauty before her.

It rose steeply out of the sea and all she could see was the abundance of white washed houses. It was the prettiest thing she had ever seen. Her mother appeared wine glass in hand and

Rachel exclaimed, 'Oh Mum look, you nearly missed it. Isn't it the most beautiful thing you've ever seen?'

Her mother smiled at her and said it was and how much fun they would have exploring. She noticed that she didn't look at her father but dismissed it as she turned her head back to the view before her.

When she read that the island was the site of one of the largest volcanic eruptions in history she was a little worried until her father assured her that it was quite safe.

They spent days exploring the steep winding cobbled streets and pathways that meandered between the lovely houses with pretty flowers growing on them. Rachel adored the island but found that she was spending more and more time with her father whilst her mother went off alone. Her father would explain that she was shopping but she rarely came back with any purchases and Rachel doubted the shops were open at night.

She enjoyed the time she spent alone with her father but was worried that her mother was missing out on the fun they were having. They spent a week there and many mornings her mother slept in and her father would take her off on adventures. It was the end of the adventure and Rachel supposed that her mother had grown tired as they had been very active.

When there were only three days left of their holiday she asked her father if her mother was ill as this had worried her but he reassured her that she was fine and she was pleased when her mother spent all the rest of their time on the island together with them and for Rachel all was well with the world.

When they arrived home all she could talk about was Greece and pestered her parents about returning there and they promised that one day they would go back. She wrote in her journal about the islands she had fallen in love with and life went on as usual.

She didn't notice that her parents spent less and less time together as it had been a gradual thing and that her mother's friends spent more time at their house. Her father didn't really mix with them and spent his time either in his study or with Rachel which she was happy about.

CHAPTER FIFTEEN

The family continued to holiday together and visited Australia, New Zealand and the United States as well as other European destinations. Catherine still disappeared when they were on holiday and over the years Rachel no longer questioned her absences as it became the norm. At home she was used to her mother not spending much time with her father and herself and she would seek her out in her studio.

Although Catherine from time to time baked with Rachel and sometimes cooked for the family it was Roger who made most of the meals. Catherine would usually join them then sitting at the large kitchen table and they would all chatter until the meal was finished. It was one of Rachel's favourite times.

Her mother's friends still called at the house and she had many impromptu parties where much alcohol was drunk. Rachel thought little of it as she rarely saw her mother without a large glass of wine in her hand.

Her father usually dropped her off at school and her mother collected her at the end of the day however when she was twelve years old they allowed her to catch the bus which passed the end of their road and dropped her outside her school. It made her feel very grown up and it gave her time to catch up with friends who also caught the bus.

She took extra classes in languages after school three days a week and on the other two she went straight home. She rarely let her mother know she was home as she didn't want to disturb her painting or writing and as her mother had no concept of time she didn't worry. Instead Rachel would spend an hour or so completing her homework before her father returned from work. Sometimes he worked late and then she would either watch television or wander into her mother's studio.

One day leading up to a school holiday she arrived home with no homework to do as she hadn't been given much to do and what she did have she had been able to complete in a rare free period. She grabbed an apple from the kitchen and wandered through to her mother's studio where she could hear her mother's voice drifting out. As she entered the studio she was shielded by the painted screen that was set up just inside the room.

Rachel didn't know why her mother had placed the screen there but it had always been in this place for as long as she could remember so thought nothing of it. She took a few steps into the room from behind the screen and then stopped in her tracks her breath leaving her body.

Her mother stood behind her easel wearing one of her loose fitting kaftans whilst on a chaise in front of her lay a naked man with everything on display. Rachel stood rooted to the spot staring. She had heard stories from other girls who talked about how men had a penis but what they said sounded ridiculous to her. She had never seen a naked man before and looking at this man now she knew everything she had heard was true. She couldn't take his eyes off his penis and was horrified and fascinated at the same time.

She heard her mother laugh, 'Rachel, darling have you never seen a penis before? Please spare Mark his blushes and stop staring.'

She felt her face burn red as she realised that her mother and the man named Mark who didn't alter his pose were both looking at her.

'Darling, this is Mark, come and look at my work,' Catherine said.

Rachel started to walk slowly towards her mother suddenly feeling very uncomfortable until she could hide herself behind the canvas. It wasn't finished but she could see a good likeness of the man on the chaise taking form on the canvas.

Her mother spoke to her, 'The naked body is the most natural thing in the world darling, don't you think Mark has a marvellous body?'

She hesitated before answering, 'I don't know,' she stuttered a bit feeling rather foolish as she continued, 'I've never seen one before.'

She heard Mark laugh from behind the canvas as her mother smiled and said, 'Don't expect all men to look like Mark when they take their clothes off. Everyone is different.' She looked around the canvass speaking to Mark she added, 'It's only right to set her expectations.' They laughed and Rachel who didn't really understand the comment felt they were laughing at her. She made a move to leave but her mother insisted she stay a while.

She went to sit on a seat behind the canvas so she couldn't see Mark but her mother told her to move it so she could see Mark and observe her work at the same time. Rachel did as she was told but didn't look at Mark again.

After about half an hour Catherine told Rachel she could leave if she wished and she didn't need telling twice. She rose and walked towards the door but as she reached the screen she slipped behind it as she couldn't resist one last look at the man lying on the chaise without being observed.

As she peeped out she saw her mother was walking over to where Mark was lying and stopped in front of him shielding his body from Rachel's prying eyes. She started to turn to leave when she saw her mother pull her kaftan off over her head revealing her total nakedness.

Rachel was confused and didn't understand why her mother needed to take her clothes off to paint but something inside her made her run from the room. The temptation to slam the door was immense but for a reason she didn't understand she closed it quietly and stood for some time with her back resting on it.

She didn't know why her face was burning and her head was spinning but every fibre of her body told her that what she had seen wasn't right and she decided then not to ever mention it to anyone.

CHAPTER SIXTEEN

EMINE

Emine continued running until her lungs felt as if they would burst when she stopped and looked around. The land was dry and flat and there was no cover for her to hide herself. She looked back and saw nobody was chasing her but knew that she couldn't relax as they may soon notice she was missing. If today played out like yesterday it would be hours before anybody came outside but she couldn't take this for granted.

She saw some way ahead a wooded area and set off again towards it as she could take cover here. There was nobody around and all was quiet as she ran, her panic pushing her on. She had to stop twice to catch her breath before she reached the wooded area and fell to the ground where she leant against a tree. There were few leaves on the trees as the area was very dry but she felt some element of safety however she knew that she couldn't be complacent.

She started to walk through the woods following the direction of the rough road as she was sure that she would eventually reach a main road. From time to time she stopped to listen but was only met by silence each time. She had no plan as she didn't know where she was but thought if she continued to follow the road she would eventually find someone who could help her.

She didn't know where she would end up or what she would do when she got there but her only goal was to find some kind of civilisation that wasn't hostile.

The branches of some of the trees scratched and cut her but she hardly noticed as her only thought was of escape. They offered some protection from the hot sun however the temptation to stop and rest was great but she pushed on desperate to get as far away from the camp as possible.

She could see the wood was thinning out and wondered what would be waiting at the end of the wood. As it came to an end she saw an open field ahead of her which had long grass dried out by the sun. It was empty but she listened carefully. She could see that the road she had been following came to an end and formed a t junction with another road at the farthest edge of the field. Beyond that there was another wood.

She would make her way to this wood but wasn't sure whether to go through it or follow the new road and if she did which way would she go?

After looking around again she set off running. The dry grass cut her legs as she ran but she didn't care she just needed to get to cover again. She was half way across the field when she heard the sound of an engine and fell to her belly in the field hoping the long grass would hide her.

Listening she could tell the vehicle was on the road that ran along the edge of the field and for a moment she was tempted to show herself in the hope that she would be rescued but it was too risky. She decided to wait and put more space between her and the camp before seeking help.

She raised her head slightly to see which way the vehicle was going and saw an old truck on the road. As it passed by she sat up further and saw it was full of watermelons. She laid down again to think and decided there were so many that the driver must be taking them somewhere to sell. She made the decision that she would travel in the same direction.

She waited for the sound of the vehicle to disappear completely before rising but as soon as she did she saw a man with a herd of goats coming towards her from the far side of the field. She fell to the ground again her heart beating fast.

She knew that she wasn't so far from the camp that those living around here wouldn't know it was there. She assumed that anyone around here would either be affiliated with Berat and his men or be scared by them so would offer her no help.

She lay still hoping he hadn't seen her and then started to crawl on her belly towards the road and wood. She could hear the goats coming nearer to her their bleats breaking the silence.

She was very scared of being discovered. She flattened herself to the ground as they passed close by her and she held her breath. They passed by and the herder was some way behind and it seemed an age before he eventually passed her without seeing her.

She let out a sigh of relief but waited for some time before lifting her head above the grass and saw that the goat herd were some way in the distance but she decided not to take any risks and crawled the rest of the way to the edge of the field on her belly.

When she reached the road she poked her head out of the grass and looked both ways from her lying position. She could see the road was clear so she sat up and looked back to see the goat herd was a long way off now. She rose to a crouching position and ran hunched across the road into the second wood.

There was nobody around but she felt sheer panic coursing through her body and felt a great relief when she entered the cover of the second wood. She slumped to the floor until she got her breathing under control. She suddenly started to panic and tears filled her eyes but she scolded herself and took some deep breaths.

Once she was calm she gathered her thoughts. She had been walking for over an hour she was sure and worried that her time was running out. She would only be two or three miles from the camp and she knew now that by following the road she had seen the vehicle on she wouldn't be putting much distance between herself and the camp as the road probably ran parallel with it.

She had no choice and set off through the wood but rather than staying close to the road she went further into the wood so she was moving at a diagonal way hoping that she was putting further distance between herself and the Berat family.

She had been walking for over another hour when she saw another road cutting through the wood. She crossed it and continued on hoping she was heading somewhere safe. She thought she heard something and stopped to listen but it was quiet and she moved on but then she heard it again. She stopped and this time she heard voices. She kept close to the trees as she moved carefully forward.

The voices kept stopping and starting and she could tell the voices were women. She suddenly felt some hope and moved a little faster. She saw the trees thinning out and could see the shape of buildings. She approached them cautiously hiding behind the trees as she moved. She saw two women come into view and saw they were washing some clothes and chatting as they worked.

She hesitated and decided to watch for a while before approaching them. They finished their washing and picking up the clothes they started to walk towards the buildings. She couldn't decide what to do when she saw another woman approach them, say some words and then carry some washing of her own to the trough to wash.

Her heart was suddenly in her throat, her mouth dry, it was Esin.

CHAPTER SEVENTEEN

She hesitated, trying to decide what to do but this woman had looked at her with kindness and she made her decision. She slowly emerged from the woods and moved cautiously towards the young woman who had her back to her. She stepped on a twig which cracked under her foot and Esin turned around fast.

When she saw her she jumped up, panic on her face, 'What are you doing here?'

'I escaped, I need help.' she said.

'You can't be here,' Esin said fear in her voice.

'Please Esin,' she said, 'please help me.'

'They will kill me,' the young woman said, 'they will kill us both if they find you here.'

'Could I have some water please,' Emine said, 'I don't want to put you in danger so if you could just point me towards a town I'll go.'

'Why are you at the Yilmaz camp?' Esin asked.

'They snatched me off the street,' Emine said, 'I have to get away.'

'Come,' Esin said beckoning her to follow. She walked carefully behind the young woman who carefully looked around her as they walked. There was nobody else around and Esin led her into a small building nearby. It was cool inside and as her eyes adjusted to the darkness inside she could see a chair, table and bed in the room. There were various ornaments and utensils around the room and a small pile of clothes.

'Sit down,' Esin said, 'rest.' She brought her a cup of water which Emine drank thirstily and as soon as she finished it Esin replenished it.

'How long have you been at the Yilmaz camp?' Esin asked

'I don't really know but it must have been months,' she answered, 'Berat said they were trying to get money for me but he said that didn't work.'

'They need money for the cause,' Esin said, 'they will sell you to get money.' Emine started to panic as it sounded like Esin was defending their cause but then she smiled at her. 'You can rest here until it's dark and then you can move on. It will be safer by night.'

'Thank you,' Emine said, 'what is the cause that they need money for.'

'They fight against the regime,' Esin answered, 'but I don't really know what they do.'

A thought struck Emine, 'Is it just women here?'

'Yes apart from two men who guard us,' Esin answered and when she saw fear in the other woman's eyes she added, 'they are on the road outside the camp. They walk around now and again but they don't come into our homes.'

'Why are you kept here?' Emine asked.

'We belong to the men in the Yilmaz camp,' Esin answered simply'

'I don't understand,' Emine said but Esin just smiled gently at her and so Emine continue, 'Berat said if he didn't get money for me that he would have me for himself or give me to one of his sons.'

'I think it's unlikely' Esin said, he needs money and I think he would rather sell you. If any of the men went with you word would get around and he wouldn't get much for you.'

Emine hesitated, 'I'm not sure what you mean, I'm not a virgin.'

Esin smiled, 'It doesn't matter. It would lessen your value if one of the Yilmaz men went with you. They are powerful around here and feared by all. No man would want to buy you if they thought you had laid with a Yilmaz because it would be like you still belonged to them.'

'Well thank God I got away,' Emine said, 'how can you live not being free Esin?'

'This is my life,' she answered, 'it was decided a long time ago,'

Emine looked at her in pity and she saw anger flash in the other woman's eyes, 'Don't look at me as if you pity me. This is my life. I always knew what was ahead of me.'

'I'm sorry,' Emine said, 'I didn't mean to offend you it's just that my freedom means a lot to me.'

'You are fortunate that you have that luxury,' the other woman said, 'now rest.'

Emine laid down on the matress on the floor which was so comfortable after the hard floor she had been sleeping on and fell into a fitful sleep.

Esin awoke her and told her night was drawing in. She gave her a bowl of food which Emine ate hungrily. When she had finished the woman handed her a bottle with water in it for her journey and told her which direction she needed to travel.

'Come with me,' Emine said.

'That is impossible,' Esin answered, 'they would hunt me down wherever I went until they found me and then they would kill me. My place is here.'

She excused herself and said she would be back shortly and after about fifteen minutes she returned. She told her that it would be safe to leave in about an hour and they sat talking quietly.

When Emine got up to leave Esin asked her to stay a bit longer and Emine suddenly felt fearful. It must have shown on her face as Esin said, 'it's not quite dark yet.'

They sat a little longer but Emine couldn't shake off a sense of foreboding and decided she was going to leave. She got up and Esin followed her to the door of her home, where Emine thanked her for her help and started to walk through the door.

She heard the noise of engines close by and the sound of tyres on the road. She turned to look at Esin wondering if she had given her away but she had turned away and was walking back into her house, 'Come back, hide in here.'

Emine didn't know what to do but walked back into Esin's home.

'Wait here,' Esin said, 'I will go to see what's happening. You'll be safe here.'

She closed the door behind her and Emine listened carefully. She couldn't stop the panic she felt and made the decision to leave as she felt anything but safe here. She grabbed the bottle of water and opened the door. She peered outside and seeing there was nobody about she moved outside.. She had only gone a few steps when she heard voices.

She didn't know which way to go and turned to her left and ran around the building there. She stopped and listened, the voices had gone and so she ran forward straight into the arms of Mirac, the man who had first brought her to the camp.

He was with other men and as she managed to struggle out of Mirac's clutch they surrounded her, she was trapped. She could see Esin standing nearby watching and she looked at her pleadingly. Mirac followed her eyes and laughed, 'Don't look to Esin for help, she brought us here.'

'No,' the cry escaped Emine's lips and then all the men laughed at her despair. Mirac beckoned Esin who walked towards him but wouldn't look at Emine. He grabbed her and turning with his arm around her waist he said what Emine had suspected, 'Esin is my wife.'

CHAPTER EIGHTEEN

OLIVIA

Maggie hardly spoke on the ferry trip from Corfu to the mainland but Olivia kept trying to draw her into conversation. She sat with her all the way whilst the boys kept their distance, 'You know Maggie,' Olivia said, 'sometimes things are just not meant to work out.'

'But he said he loved me,' Maggie objected, 'why would he say that?'

Olivia decided not to be derogatory about Jason, 'Perhaps he did feel like that at the time but maybe he's one of those people who fall in love easily,' she said lamely.

'I just don't know what I did wrong,' Maggie said and Olivia had to bite her tongue before she said that she had made it too easy for him and accepted his bad behaviour at every turn. Why wouldn't a bloke love her for that? Instead she said, 'You didn't do anything wrong Maggs. It was all him,' although she didn't believe that all the fault laid with Jason.

'You never liked him,' Maggie accused.

'Here we go,' Olivia thought but said, 'It's got nothing to do with how I feel about him it's about how he's made you feel. I just hate to see you hurt like this.'

'No you hate him!' Maggie was getting agitated, 'I bet you're happy that he's not with us.'

'That' not true,' Olivia protested, 'I only care about you.'

Maggie turned her head away from her friend and they fell into a silence which lasted for the rest of the journey and Olivia was pleased that it only took two hours.

They docked in Igoumenitsa on the mainland where they intended to spend a week or so exploring the large town and surrounding area. Maggie was very quiet for the first few days but slowly she started to join in especially as Robbie constantly teased her and as they had got on so well from the start it seemed to do the trick and she started to laugh again.

The girls managed to pick up some temporary work for a few days as they didn't think anything would be available as they travelled across Greece. They were not running out of money but agreed that any top up was welcome. The boys who didn't seem to have any worries about money enjoyed their time in Igoumenitsa. The girls managed to do some sightseeing with the boys and on one of their free days travelled to the Pamvotida Lake which had been recommended to them.

It was a lovely walk from Mavili square passing the castle walls and down to the cycle path which took them by the lake, their only company apart from the odd walker were ducks and seagulls. They saw a fisherman on their way and they stopped to watch the patient man sitting still waiting for a bite and Jack took Olivia's hand in his, she looked up at him but he continued to stare at the fisherman. Although he had taken her hand before it was usually only momentarily and she pleasantly surprised as they continued their walk hand in hand trailing Robbie and Maggie who were fooling about most of the way.

They came across a boat which offered trips to the island in the centre of Pamvotida lake and the friends piled on, Jack helping Olivia and sitting very close to her on the boat. The trip was only about fifteen minutes but as they slipped away from the sight of the city they got a perfect view of the Aslan Pasha Mosque and the calm serenity of the lake affected them all as they smiled at each other. Olivia felt very happy, she loved peace and quiet and as she snuggled up to Jack she couldn't imagine a better day.

Once on the island they bypassed the tavernas and made their way up the cobbled streets to the Saint Panteleimon monastery. They passed the museum where the Ali Pasha had hidden from his enemies before they found and beheaded him. Olivia was taken off guard when Jack pulled her down a small quiet alley next to the museum and kissed her. He looked down at her stunned face and smiled kissing her again and this time she responded. As they wandered around the building looking at the ruler's personal belongings Olivia took little in as she thought about what had just happened.

They spent another two weeks in the city before taking a bus to their next port of call which was Ioannina. All the time the relationship between Jack and Olivia grew and by the time they left for Ioannina Robbie and Maggie could see they were becoming a couple. Maggie hated that her friend was happy when she had lost her love and refused to talk about Jack with Olivia as she couldn't bear the way her eyes shone when she spoke of him so she would cut her off changing the subject. Olivia noticed what she was doing and knew why and even felt a little guilty about what she and Jack had which spoiled it for her.

They spent some time around the area where there's another beautiful lake called Panvotida and explored the monuments in the Ottoman mosque of Veli Pasha and enjoyed the atmosphere of the historic town. They were supposed to move on to Larissa next but as the bus journey took nearly three hours Olivia had suggested that they stopped off at the National Park which was a vast woodland half between Ioannina and Larissa. She told the others that there were some camp sites there and they all agreed it sounded like a good idea.

Maggie hadn't mentioned Jason much apart from asking Jack how he would know where they were and Jack had assured her that he had a mobile phone. Mobile phones were a recent addition to everyday life and unlike today not everyone owned one and the boys who had one each only used them when necessary as call charges were expensive. Maggie did periodically ask Jack if he'd heard anything from Jason and only once did he say that he had been in touch. He said that he was getting bored with Corfu and they all saw Maggie's face light up.

When they reached the camp site Robbie suggested that Jack and Olivia share a tent and both the girls protested but for very different reasons. Olivia felt embarrassed as although they had kissed many times now it had gone no further between them but

Maggie just didn't want them to be together. Robbie grabbed at Maggie and swung her around, 'I promise there won't be any funny business,' he said laughing and it was decided as she would have shown herself up by protesting any more.

Olivia felt a little awkward when she and Jack retired to their tent but that didn't last long as he smiled at her and took her in his arms. That night they cemented their relationship and Olivia knew beyond a shadow of a doubt that she loved this man deeply.

They had been at the campsite for four days, taking long walks and spending evenings drinking, singing and having fun. They were returning from a long walk when they saw a figure walking towards them. None of them took much notice at first until they heard the familiar voice call out, 'Bloody hell, you guys took some finding,' it was Jason.

Maggie couldn't hide her pleasure but Jason took little notice of her and that night the three boys shared a tent whilst Maggie moved into the tent that Olivia had been sharing with Jack and talked non-stop about Jason until Olivia fell asleep.

When they got up the next day the boys said they thought they should move on to Larissa and Olivia agreed happily and they all packed up and caught the bus to the capital city of the Thessaly region. They could see the mountains rising around the city as they approached and Olivia commented on how spectacular it looked.

They spent ten days in the city visiting all the tourist attractions commemorating the Byzantine period. They travelled up the hill to visit the ruins of the ancient theatre and took in the views.

Olivia watched as Maggie and Jason gravitated towards each other again starting from the first night and by the time they left Larissa they were once again all over each other with Maggie following him around like a puppy dog.

From here they moved on to Volos where they would get their ferry to Skiathos. Olivia was happy to see the sea again as she was so drawn to it. She was struggling with Maggie again who spent every moment she could with Jason and had said to Olivia one day that he had come to his senses and realised how much he loved her but Olivia very much doubted that.

Volos has a mythical background which captivated Olivia's imagination and as she and Jack explored together he was caught up in her enthusiasm. Olivia had read about Volos which is an area of Magnesia and he listened with great interest as she told her tales about it being the birth place of the Centaurs, the half horse, half man creature, that Achilles had spent time here as the pupil of Chiron, the wisest of Centaurs and that the Argonauts had set off on their expedition from the port here.

They thought that it had to be one of the most beautiful cities either of them had visited as they looked in wonder at the grandeur of the architecture. There was an amazing seafront with lots of small restaurants which made it a most romantic place to walk and Jack and Olivia took advantage of this many times.

The day arrived for them to board the ferry to Skiathos and Jason was nowhere to be seen. Jack and Robbie said they had no idea where he was but decided not to mention that he hadn't come back to the hostel the night before. They had thought he was with Maggie but when they saw her that morning they realised that that wasn't the case. Maggie was visibly anxious even saying to Olivia that if he didn't come this time she was staying too. Ten minutes before the ferry was to leave he strolled on to the boat without a care in the world. Maggie hurried to his side and Olivia felt a rush of despair which was nothing compared to how she would feel about what was to come.

CHAPTER NINETEEN

There were no backpacking hostels in Skiathos so the friends stayed in a cheap hotel, the two couples having their own rooms and Robbie on his own which he said he didn't mind as it was only for sleeping. The beaches on the island were delightful but Olivia found the area too commercialised. They spent just over a week in the area before moving across to the island of Skopelos.

They made their way along the harbour road and saw a large restaurant with tables outside where they sat down and ordered drinks. They asked about a cheap hotel but were told there were only two which were expensive but the owner said he had an apartment that he let out to holiday makers.

It turned out to be a small house which was split into two apartments which were very basic but none of them seemed to notice. The town was built on a hill and behind the main road there was a narrow cobbled street which ran parallel with it with various alleyways and stone steps leading off it which climbed steeply up the hill. It was at the top of one of these narrow stone stairways that their new temporary home sat and offered an amazing view across the harbour.

As there were only two apartments Olivia had to go back to sharing with Maggie whilst the boys shared theirs and Olivia missed the quiet time that she and Jack shared alone before going to sleep.

They explored the island in the first few days enjoying the spectacular views it offered and Olivia asked Jack, 'Do you love it as much as I do?' and she felt contented when he had said he did. They swam in the warm seas, travelled by ferry across to Allonisos where they spent two days before returning to Skopelos.

Olivia said she'd like to stay there for a while and the friends agreed as for what the island lacked in nightlife it made up for in beauty. She knew that she and Maggie would have to get some work as their funds were running a bit low now and although there weren't many restaurants on the main harbour road they had noticed that the restaurant owned by their new landlord advertised for English speaking staff. Olivia felt as if was all meant to be.

One early evening when Olivia was working at the restaurant she was standing outside looking after customers but as it was quiet she watched the ferry approaching the island and imagined who may be arriving. Her thoughts were broken when she saw Jack and Robbie sit down at a table and she smiled broadly as she went over to take their order. As she went over to serve them she saw Maggie and Jason on the other side of the road. Something made her stop and stare at them as she realised that something was wrong and thought they were arguing but then realised it looked more like Maggie was pleading with Jason and she thought, 'Oh no, he was leaving her again.'

The boys ordered two beers but she noticed they weren't their usual selves and when Jack said he needed to speak to her fear struck her heart and as she walked back to get their beers an involuntary shudder passed through her body. When she returned she could see that Jason and Maggie were still across the street and she saw Jason start to walk away but Maggie grabbed his arm and it was then that Olivia noticed he had his back pack on. She looked at the boys and could see their backpacks were on the ground next to their table. She made the final few footsteps with stiff movements as her limbs suddenly felt very heavy and when she reached them she said directly to Jack, 'You're leaving.'

'Please Liv,' Jack said, 'can we talk?' She wanted to say 'no' as she was afraid of hearing the words but told one of the other waiters that she was taking a break. Jack followed her further down the street where they too crossed and as they sat on the sea wall she asked why they were leaving.

'Jason is keen to move on,' Jack said and before Olivia could say that his friend had been on his own before he added, 'Robbie wants to go too, I don't feel like I've got a choice.'

'Of course you have,' she said, 'you could stay with me.'

'You have no idea how much I want to, you've been the best part of this adventure,' he said, 'but we want to see as much as we can.'

'I don't understand,' she said, 'I saw you three hours ago and you didn't say anything, why all the rush?'

'Jason and Robbie just decided they want to move on to the Cyclades and then on to Turkey,' he answered.

'But we intend to move on to the Cyclades,' she said, 'can't you wait a few days?'

'Please Liv,' he said, 'don't make this more difficult, the whole Jason and Maggie thing has already become such a drama,' and suddenly she thought of how Maggie had looked pleading with Jason and she realised she didn't want to be like that.

'I'll miss you,' she said and turned away as a tear ran down her cheek. He pulled her to him and whispered, 'Not as much as I'll miss you.'

She didn't believe him because if he felt the same as her he wouldn't leave her, 'Here, take this,' he said and she turned her head back to see him offering her his mobile phone. She looked at him quizzically, 'We can keep in touch,' he said, 'I'll let you know my new number as soon as I get another on the mainland.'

Tears filled her eyes and he wiped them away and kissing her forehead he said, 'We'll see each other again Liv, this isn't the end for us.'

She had to go back to work and she watched the boys walk towards the ferry which was preparing to leave for Skiathos she could feel physical pain in her chest. She could see Maggie trailing on behind Jason still pleading with him and was tempted to do the same as she saw Jack turn back to look and wave at her several times but knew that it would only make her feel more wretched.

When she got back to her room that night the emptiness inside her was physically painful and she wanted to scream. Maggie wasn't there and she was grateful as she couldn't handle her grief at the moment but that didn't last long as the door opened and Maggie walked in but neither girl spoke. She turned the lights on in the darkened room and Olivia could see that Maggie looked pale, her eyes red from crying.

Olivia didn't know what to say as she thought asking if her friend was okay didn't seem adequate but it was Maggie who spoke first, 'I suppose you blame me for your precious Jack leaving but let's be honest if he cared about you he'd have stayed.'

It felt like Maggie had stabbed her in the heart, 'I don't know what you mean?' she said trying not to visibly smart at Maggie's hurtful words. Maggie stared at her without speaking and Olivia added, 'Jack said Jason and Robbie wanted to get on with their travels.'

Maggie laughed but it sounded hollow, 'He didn't tell you, did he?' she said but before Oliver could enquire what Jack hadn't told her, Maggie said, 'I'm pregnant.'

CHAPTER TWENTY

RACHEL

The incident with Rachel's mother and the man called Mark was never mentioned. Catherine had not known that her daughter had witnessed the intimacy and had she known she would have been alarmed not because she was too worried about Roger finding out but rather she wanted the pretence of their perfect family to continue for her daughter's sake.

She was always wrapped up in herself however Catherine had noticed a slight awkwardness after Rachel had visited her studio when she had seen Mark lying naked on her chaise lounge but she thought it was because it was the first time she had seen a naked man and dismissed the feeling.

She had long thought that Roger suspected her of being unfaithful, which she had been several times, although she could not be totally sure. He was a gentle, naïve man completely wrapped up in his work and their daughter and perhaps he didn't realise what was going on.

They were generally intimate once a week these days and it had become like a thing of routine rather of desire. She never refused him but it was all a bit of a chore which was usually over quickly with little affection shown on either side. For her, her dalliances were just sex, a fix she needed like the wine she drank every day.

She didn't know how her husband would actually react if he was faced with her infidelity but she had no intention of telling him and she would never leave him. She enjoyed her life too much and she wanted Rachel to have a stable home life. She cared for Roger in her own way but there was no passion and when she looked back she didn't think there ever had been on her part.

Although she made a living through her painting and teaching it was his money that afforded them the wonderful holidays they took every year. They meant so much to Catherine and sometimes when they were away she did feel a mild desire for him. She would show this by behaving seductively and she could tell that he enjoyed these moments.

Sometimes she would catch him looking at her the old feelings showing in his eyes and she would feel a small stab of guilt that she didn't return these feelings but it would soon pass.

He had accepted that when they were away she needed time alone and didn't try to stop her going out in the evening. He never commented on how drunk she was sometimes when she returned or the smell of men's cologne on her body.

Sometimes she envied the relationship Roger and Rachel shared, they always had their heads together, chatting and laughing. They often spoke in foreign languages as Roger had a limited knowledge of many and Rachel would practice with him They never excluded her and would welcome her into their conversations but she never felt totally part of the closeness they shared.

She enjoyed the time she spent alone with her daughter and although she was disappointed that she showed no real interest in art she was delighted by the interest she took in reading. They would discuss literature and she was encouraged by the talent Rachel displayed in her writings. It was something they shared that Roger wasn't part of, something where she could guide her daughter, something that made her feel of some use to her daughter's development.

She introduced her to many different authors who were often advanced for her learning level but she encouraged her to stretch herself and Rachel was always only too happy to learn new things.

Rachel would write in her journal her observations about places they visited, people they met and was happy to share this information with her mother. She encouraged her daughter to take the information and make it into book form rather than jotted notes. She helped her meet this goal showing her how to connect the points and embellish them so they didn't appear as if they were just a list of experiences.

She would sit with her whilst she read parts to Roger but she could see that whilst he was proud of his daughter's efforts he had no real understanding of the work that had gone in to producing the work she presented.

She bought Rachel books about other countries which she devoured always wanting to know more about the people and the history of the places she read about. She knew that Rachel enjoyed travelling as much as she did and was happy that they could offer her these experiences. She felt a slight sadness that when they reached their destinations Rachel seemed to make her memories with Roger rather than her but it was a connection she didn't seem able to make.

Each year Rachel had begged her parents to take her back to Greece. It wasn't that she didn't enjoy learning about the other countries they visited but she could never forget the affinity she felt with Greece.

It would be four years since their first visit before they would return.

CHAPTER TWENTY ONE

It was a year after Rachel had witnessed the very naked Mark in her mother's studio that the family landed in Athens to spend four weeks of the summer holiday exploring the island.

Rachel found Athens too busy for her liking and although she was never bored as they spent their time seeing the tourist attractions such as the Acropolis and the Parthenon it wasn't her favourite place. Her mother was keen to visit the museums and art galleries and Rachel and her father tagged along. Whilst they could appreciate the works they saw they couldn't spend the length of time that Catherine stood staring at the art and would usually end up outside waiting for her.

Their penultimate day in Athens was spent in the National Museum of Contemporary Art which is Athens' answer to the Tate Modern and it didn't take Roger and Rachel long to make their way through the building. They found a café nearby where they could see the exit and settled down with soft drinks whilst they waited for Catherine to reappear.

They waited for almost an hour looking around them people watching and taking in the sights. They could see the colourful canopies of a small street market nearby and eventually Roger suggested that they wander over to have a look at the stalls. He kept an eye on the exit of the Museum and after they had finished there they once again took a seat at the café across the road. It was another two hours before Catherine emerged from the Museum and they made their way back to the hotel they were staying in.

On their last day they went to the Museum of Cycladic Art where artefacts of ancient Greek and Cypriot art are housed. Roger and Catherine arranged that they would meet back at the hotel if Rachel got through quickly but Roger found himself on his own as Rachel was fascinated by the distinctly shaped slender marble figurines and statues dating back to the Bronze Age.

She got lost in the history of the ancient Greek art collection including vases and weapons grouped by themes such as Gods and Heroes which had always enthralled her.

They made their way across Greece heading towards Skiathos via the island of Skyros where they spent four days in a white painted villa exploring the many beaches, jagged coastline and sea caves. Rachel especially liked the seaside villages and was fascinated by the Byzantine castle which stood on the crag above Skyros town.

She nagged her parents to visit the castle and when they took her at last Rachel was struck by the marble lion that is built into the wall over the main entrance. She particularly enjoyed the vista as the viewpoint overlooked the whole area taking in the town and the sea. The ruin wasn't well preserved but Rachel loved discovering the history of how the fortress which protected the island from the pirates that frequently marauded its shores. She thought it was like a fairy tale and wove stories in her imagination as she walked around.

They eventually reached Skiathos and spent two days exploring before taking the ferry to Skopelos where they would be spending a full week. As they approached Skopelos Town Roger took Rachel up on deck and she stood in awe looking at the scene before her.

There was a full bank of houses rising before her built on a hill closely together, one behind the other. Similar to all over Greece most were painted white but here each and every one had a terracotta roof. Only a few had the traditional blue doors and windows that Rachel loved so much and yet the sight was spectacular. For her it was like falling in love with Greece all over again.

Disembarking from the ferry they found themselves on the harbour which had the main street running next to it. Across the road were a few tavernas, a bakery and a car hire shop where they paid for a vehicle to take them around the island. Being a small island it didn't take them long to find their villa which had the most spectacular view overlooking the town and sea.

Rachel sat on the veranda of the villa the first night and told her parents that she had never seen anything so beautiful. Although they could have covered the island in a day they took their time so they could fully explore each place they visited. It was a relaxing beautiful island and it totally encompassed Rachel's soul. There were few villages as such and the only other town was Glossa where there was also a port smaller than Skopelos Town.

The day they took the ferry to Alonissos she stood on deck with her father and was amazed when they spotted a pod of dolphins following the boat. They pointed in wonder as they watched the creatures jumping out of the water and frolicking in the wake the boat left behind it as it cut it's passage through the sea.

She had never felt so completely at home in any place they had visited and was already completely transfixed by the island. The icing on the cake which was unnecessary for Rachel was when they visited the church of Agios Ioannis Kastri which sat perched on top of a rock that lies in the sea immediately next to the island. As she looked up at the church straight out of a fairy tale and the steps carved into the stone of the rock that went on for ever before her she thought what a magical place it was.

Like those before her and many who would follow years later when the film Mamma Mia would make the church famous she started to climb counting the steps as she went her parents following and by the time she reached the top had counted one hundred and ten steps.

She stood looking over the sea and surrounding islands and could see a gleaming haze rising from the ocean and waves gently crashing against the rocks. As she turned back to enter the church which housed beautiful icons she felt a sudden sadness that she had to leave the island at all.

When they left to go home she felt incredibly sad and couldn't wait for the time when she could return to the island. She went straight up on the deck of the ferry so she could watch the island disappearing from sight and for once her mother joined her. She told her that she like Rachel had also fallen in love with the island. Those words made her feel confident that they would soon return little knowing that she would indeed return within two years, her whole world turned upside down by the most devastating event so far in her short life.

CHAPTER TWENTY TWO

EMINE

Mirac tied her hands and leaving some rope he led her out of the small women's settlement and as they passed Esin, Emine managed to catch her eye and looked directly at her but the woman who she thought was helping her dropped her head. As she was dragged towards the trucks Emine looked back and saw Esin staring after her and she realised that she was crying.

She was taken to the waiting trucks and Mirac threw her in the back of one telling her not to move. She expected a beating but it didn't come and two guards jumped in to keep watch over her whilst Mirac got in the cab of the truck. They set off with two other trucks following and made their way back to the Yilmaz camp. She stayed where she was lying on the back of the truck being jolted around as they drove on the uneven tracks.

She contemplated her possible fate and could hardly bear to let her mind go to the horrendous things Berat might do to her for running away. For a moment anger sparked in her as she thought, 'how dare he? I'm a free person' but she knew that thoughts wouldn't save her.

It only took fifteen minutes and she couldn't believe she had travelled such a short distance after her efforts. She was dragged out of the truck and taken into the camp where all the men gathered to watch her arrival and she started to cry silently as she was very scared.

She saw Berat standing there flanked by Yusuf and Omer and as they stopped before the leader of the camp she saw Mustafa standing behind his father looking furtive.

'Mustafa,' Berat shouted as if he didn't know that his son was skulking behind him and the man stepped out, 'Tell me how this woman escaped from our camp?'

'I don't know father,' Mustafa said and she could see that he was scared.

'I am told that you never secure her well,' Berat said, 'did you plan for her escape?'

His son protested but Berat cut him off, 'Whose fault is it that she escaped my son?' Mustafa squirmed before his father like a small boy but didn't speak and Berat said, 'I believe that you didn't plan her escape but it's your fault and you must pay for your mistake.'

He turned to Omer and spoke his name and Emine saw him hand his father a baton of wood. All the men apart from Berat and Mustafa moved back to make a space and Berat hit his son with the baton. She heard the sound of it hit his body, the cry that escaped Mustafa and turned away as Berat continued to beat his son.

Mirac told her to turn her head and watch and when she didn't he asked her if she wanted him to make her watch the beating so she complied and saw that Mustafa was now on the ground with his father standing over him raining blows down on him. Eventually the beating stopped and she could see the sweat pouring down Berat's face after the effort he had used to punish his son. He turned to her, 'This is your doing,' he said.

He handed the baton back to Omer and turned to her and she started to shake as she thought if he would do this to his son what would he do to her? He stepped towards her putting his face close to hers, she could see the droplets of sweat running down his skin, she smelt his sour body odour and she froze, 'Emine,' he said, 'the fearless one, you live by your name.' Then he drew back, 'you don't look so fearless now.' He looked around but continued to speak to her, 'You cannot get away, you belong to me. That is until I say different.'

He turned back to her and came close again, she could feel the heat of his breath on her face, 'Do you promise not to escape again,' he asked.

She looked at him and wanted to shout 'no' but she realised she wasn't that brave, 'Yes, I promise.'

He slapped her with the back of his hand, 'Liar,' he shouted. Then turning to the men standing around watching, 'do you hear how she lies. Her lips say she won't try to escape but her eyes say different.'

'What should I do with her?' he asked the men and there were a rumbling of voices from the men and he laughed. Turning back to her, What should I do with you?' he asked her.

'I promise I won't run away again,' she pleaded, 'please don't hurt me.'

He smiled, 'Oh you will be hurt,' he said, 'look at my son Mustafa. He is weak. He has had his punishment but his crime was that he didn't tie you up properly he didn't have my men running all over the countryside looking for him.'

She was very scared and she saw a twinkle in his eyes and realised that he was enjoying torturing her, 'How should I hurt you? That's my dilemma.'

He studied her for a while and then said to Mirac, 'Untie her.' When she was free she stood before him shaking wondering what he was about to do. 'I am the law here and you defy me,' he said, 'and it is still there in your eyes. You are so proud,' he said, 'what must I do to break you?'

'Why,' her voice was a whisper, 'do you have to break me?'

'You dare to question me?' Berat roared, 'You will do my will.' He turned from her and looked around his men and then back to her. Should I remove your clothes so you stand naked before all these men with only your pride to protect you?'

'No,' she cried, 'please no,' she begged she couldn't bear it.

He started to laugh, 'Are you scared that the sight of your naked form will drive the men wild?' He turned back to the watching men. 'Look at this skinny, filthy creature with her dirty clothes and matted hair,' Berat said turning back to her and for a moment she felt ashamed 'no man here would want you.'.

He turned to Yusuf, 'Wash her.'

Yusuf grabbed one of her arms which he twisted painfully as he dragged her to the trough but she fought him all the way to no avail. Instead of filling the bucket with water to throw over her as usual he lifted her off her feet and threw her in the trough and as she hit the stone sides of it she went under the water and she let out a cry of pain allowing water to enter her lungs. She came up for air choking and spluttering but Yusuf forced her down again and she was sure he was going to drown her. She had never felt such terror as the realisation hit her that this might be her end.

He pulled her up by her hair and she gasped for air, her head spinning as he saw Mirac had joined his brother and they started to run their hands over her kneading her as if they were washing a bundle of clothes with nobody inside. She choked and coughed as Yusuf took the opportunity to grope her breasts several times and when each time she pushed his hand away he would duck her again and she fought for breath.

Yusuf pushed her under the water again and again and at one point she felt his hand groping between her legs and she fought hard to push him away. She succeeded in getting him to remove his hand but it resulted in him once again pushing her under the water. Eventually she was pulled out of the trough bent over coughing the water out of her lungs.

Mirac and Yusuf dragged her back to their father soaking wet with her clothes clinging to her, 'Better,' Berat said, 'Now someone will have you. Who shall I give you to?' Adem,' he called and she saw the old baker come forward. She was crying and begging him, 'Please don't do this.'

The old baker leered at her body so hard she felt as if she was naked, he smiled a gummy toothless smile and a dribble ran down his chin.'

Emine screamed in horror but was no more horrified about the old baker raping her than any other man in the camp.

She started to fight as best she could but Mirac caught her arms and held her so she couldn't move. Berat waved Adem, the old baker away and Yusuf said, 'Can I have her father, I'll teach her a lesson.'

Berat turned to his eldest son, 'I'm sure you would but nobody is having her. Her people don't want her so we will fatten her up and sell her to the highest bidder.' He turned to the watching men, 'If any man touches her they will be beaten to within an inch of their life and be forever banished from the camp.' She almost felt relieved but that feeling didn't last long as he continued, 'We will get a good price for her but not yet, first she must learn her lesson.' He turned to his youngest son, 'Omer,' he said his name.

As with Mustafa Omer held out the baton to his father but he waved it away and told him that he must punish her. She wasn't so fearful as Omer had always been kind to her and as he approached her she pleaded with him with her eyes. She saw no kindness in the eyes that looked back at her and felt none as he slammed the baton into her body.

CHAPTER TWENTY THREE

He hit her again and again in the body and once in the face knocking her head back, pain shooting through her skull and she heard Berat telling Omer not to damage her face.

He moved away for a moment and she thought that was the end of her punishment as she shook her head trying to clear it and it was hard to ignore the pain in her body. He stopped and turned back to her, walked towards her, no pity in his eyes as he started to hit her body viciously again until she fell to the ground. It didn't stop as he continued to beat her, the pain was intense and she thought it would never end. She cried at the intensity of the agony she was feeling and the barrage she was suffering.

She was almost unconscious when she heard Berat shout for Omer to stop and she felt herself being lifted off the ground and carried. Every inch of her body was in pain and it wasn't long before she felt herself put down gently onto something soft and she realised she was on a mattress. She felt hands removing her clothes and she wanted to fight but she couldn't move.

She must have drifted off as she was suddenly aware of someone gently bathing her body with a wet cloth. She tried to open her swollen eyes and managed a crack and she could see that the person tending her wounds was her attacker Omer and she tried to move but was unable to as the pain was so bad. He wasn't hurting her now but suddenly she remembered having her clothes removed and but then she realised that she wasn't naked but that she was still wearing her underwear she was grateful.

'Your punishment has finished,' he said in a voice that had some of the old kindness back in it, 'my father is the law here and you must do as he says if you don't want this to happen again. I will look after you until you are recovered.'

'You did this,' she said accusingly. She had thought he was kind but she no longer trusted him and his words didn't make her feel better.

'No,' he said, 'you did this. Anyone who defies my father is punished.'

'I thought you liked me,' she said feebly knowing how pathetic she sounded.

'That has nothing to do with it,' Omer said, 'we all have to obey the rules.'

She was in so much pain it hurt to talk so she fell into silence and she winced every now and again as he bathed her sores. When he had finished he placed a blanket over her and left the room, locking it behind him.

She slept for over twenty four hours although she was sure some of the time that someone was in the room but she thought it was probably one of her dreams. One of her dreams where she escaped this nightmare, swimming in the sea and sipping ice cold drinks in the shade of pretty parasols. She would lose herself in sleep but every time she awoke she was back in the nightmare.

She was in a room which had only a chair and a mattress in it, there was a small window which had bars on it but unlike the cell she had been kept in before there was light in this room and it wasn't cold and dank. Omer continued to tend to her and she laid on the mattress unable to move for almost a week before he insisted she try to get up.

He supported her as she hobbled around the room and then he sat her back down on the mattress. He had brought food for her and she had noticed she was being given food three times a day and had an endless supply of water. He brought her buckets for her to use as a loo which he emptied and large bowls of water for her to wash in. He would leave them with her and leave the room allowing her privacy and one day he even brought her a plain cotton kaftan which is what the men wore and left it on the chair for her.

She removed her underwear and after washing herself washed it in the bucket and hung it on the back of the chair. She dried herself with the thin bit of cloth Omer provided for her and donned the Kaftan. She felt a bit better but was still suffering a lot of pain from the beating he had handed out.

Omer returned, took away the buckets and came back with a fresh bread and a large bowl of stew. He sat cross legged on the floor opposite her, tore off some bread and dipped it in the stew and then nodded at her, 'Eat,' he said and they sat eating as if they were friends.

'This is good,' she said and he nodded.

'You need to put weight on,' he said, she was aware of how thin she had become and knew what he said was right but why was he so keen for her to gain the pounds.

'What is going to happen to me Omer?' she asked hoping to hear something different from what Berat had said.

He looked at her and she saw tenderness in his eyes, 'Once you are recovered and have put some weight on my father will find a buyer for you.'

'No,' she cried but he put up his hand, 'There's nothing you can do, accept it, my father will sell you to the highest bidder. We need the money for the cause for the sake of the people.'

'Please help me Omer,' she begged, 'please help me get away.'

He stood up abruptly, picking up the bowl of food, 'No more,' he almost shouted, all his softness gone, 'do not talk of escaping and do not ask me to help you,' and with that he almost stormed out of the room slamming the door shut. She felt total despair and could see no way of getting away.

Later that day it was one of the guards who entered the room with food which he placed on the chair and then left and Omer didn't return to the room again for another five days. On more than one occasion Yusuf brought her food and water and he would stand and watch her eat and wash as best she could with his eyes on her. She asked him where Omer was and he just snapped at her to eat.

When Omer returned he was distant with her for the first few days and then he softened his treatment of her. She was kept in the room for four weeks, as with no medications her recovery was slow, before Omer considered her strong enough to go out. She hadn't mentioned escaping again as he was her only ally and she saw how it angered him.

He walked her around outside supporting her as she staggered a little allowing her to stop to rest before returning her to her room. Every step hurt and she thought he had probably broken some bones but she was healing and although she welcomed it she was scared what would happen when she was well again.

She started being able to walk without support and one day Omer directed her to walk past the main building and down a small rough path. She hadn't been down here before and she wondered where they were going. There was yet another ramshackle building which looked as if it had a tree growing through it.

He led her inside and she saw that it was a shower room. It looked old with grimy, cracked tiles and there were unglazed windows around the top of the walls through which bushes grew. Although normally the shower cubicle would have made her balk she was so desperate for some kind of normality it actually looked inviting to her. He handed her a large piece of soap that had previous users hairs stuck in it but she couldn't afford to be proud.

He placed a clean kaftan and a rough overused towel on a chair in the room and left, 'I will be outside the door,' he said, 'I will give you fifteen minutes,' and she was grateful.

She undressed and stepped into the shower turning on the tap. She knew the water would be cold but it made her jump as it hit her. The soap didn't lather much but she did what she could and even managed to wash her hair which was filthy and matted. She combed it with her fingers ending up with strands of it entwined around them.

She dried herself with the towel which was like using sandpaper on her skin but when she had finished she dressed in the clean kaftan and realised it was the first time in a long time that she actually felt clean. Omer would take her to the shower every other day and one day he presented her with a comb. It was made of wood and as she accepted it she smiled broadly at him and thanked him so much he blushed.

On occasions when Omer was out of the camp other guards would take her to the shower and like Omer they would wait outside, she actually looked forward to these times but one day Yusuf entered her room and told her it was time for a shower.

As they walked to the building where the shower was housed he held on to her arm so hard he hurt her. He pushed her into the shower room and took up his position against the wall where he could watch her shower.

'I'm usually allowed this time alone,' she said unsure of how he would react.

He laughed, 'Well today you will not be alone.'

CHAPTER TWENTY FOUR

OLIVIA

It had been almost three weeks since Maggie had told Olivia that she was pregnant and the boys had left the island. Olivia missed Jack so much it hurt and her misery wasn't eased as Maggie had hardly spoken since. Both girls were in their own individual worlds of pain although Olivia did try to talk to Maggie she got little response.

She had broached the subject of leaving the island as although she loved it they had planned to go south to explore the Cyclades islands. She thought that her friend would probably want to go home in a few months when her pregnancy made it uncomfortable to travel. That's if she kept the baby as Olivia didn't know what she was thinking as Maggie wouldn't discuss it.

She was heartbroken that Jason had so callously left her and for the first ten days or so she seemed convinced that he would return but as the days passed she became less sure and sadder.

It was Maggie's day off from the restaurant where they were working and Olivia had an hour before she started her shift. Maggie was lying on the couch staring into space and Olivia sat on a chair opposite her, 'Maggie we need to talk.' Maggie stared at her saying nothing so Olivia pleaded, 'Maggie please.'

She saw her friend slowly sit up and felt hopeful. 'What do you want to talk about?' Maggie asked and Olivia felt a stab of impatience.

Their friendship had been strained for some time now but Olivia didn't want another argument so said, 'Have you thought about what you want to do about the baby?'

'I don't really think about it at all,' Maggie answered, 'I just want Jason to come back.'

'I know Maggs,' Olivia said gently, 'but I don't think he is coming back ' She saw a flash of anger in Maggie's eyes and added as patiently as she could, 'Look what do I know? He might come to his senses and come back to you but just in case he doesn't, we need to make plans.'

'Why?' Maggie asked.

'Because you have a baby on the way and that isn't going to wait,' Olivia said. Maggie just stared at her again and so Olivia continued, 'Do you want to stay here a bit longer or do you want to continue with our plans of visiting the Cyclades islands or perhaps you want to go home?'

'I don't care Olivia,' Maggie said, 'don't you understand I don't care about anything but Jason.'

'You have a baby to think about,' Olivia reminded her.

'This,' she said grabbing her stomach, 'it's because of this that Jason left. I hate it. Jason didn't want it and nor do I.'

'Maggie,' Olivia said 'don't say that. Jason left you and the baby. He doesn't deserve either of you.'

'Oh here we go,' Maggie said in a voice full of sarcasm, 'You hated him and tried to spoil it from the start.'

'No,' Olivia snapped, 'I could see what he was like which is more than you could. You were blinded Maggs. He was sleeping his way around Europe and you didn't seem to notice.'

'You don't understand,' Maggie said, 'those other girls didn't matter. He loved me. At least he did until this,' she punched her stomach this time.

'You're right,' Olivia said, 'I don't understand how you can care for someone like Jason but I do understand that you are hurt.' Maggie looked at her sneeringly and so she added, 'I lost Jack too you know. That hurts too.'

Maggie snorted, 'Jack? It wasn't the same. You two didn't have the feelings that we had.'

Olivia felt as if her friend had slapped her and tears pricked her eyes. She decided that there was no point in talking anymore and standing up she told Maggie she was going to work. As she made her way down the steps to the cobbled lane below she thought about what to do. She would have to make a decision and then just tell Maggie what they were going to do. She couldn't decide about what her friend would do about the baby but she could make a decision about their future plans together. She loved this island but she thought it was best if they moved on and continued their journey as it may take their minds off their misery.

It was early September and the weather was glorious and Olivia thought what a hot one it was going to be. It hadn't been her dream to work continuously in the same restaurant as it had been more of a means to an end rather than a fixture. The owner liked her a lot as she was a hard worker but he would grumble to her about Maggie as he said she wasn't friendly with the customers.

Although the island wasn't commercialised it was still popular with many discerning travellers and there was little competition to the restaurant she worked in so she was kept busy for the day which took her mind off her problems with her friend.

She had a break and chose to go across the road and sit on the harbour wall watching the sailing boats that were mooring up. She loved the sea and it calmed her and as she relaxed her mind drifted to thoughts of Jack and what could have been. She had never felt like this for anyone before and perhaps one day they would meet up again, she could only hope. He had texted her letting her know where they were travelling and once he had tried to phone her but she couldn't hear what he was saying but they were in touch and that made her hopeful. She hadn't told Maggie that Jack was still in touch as she knew that she would pester her about Jason and Jack never mentioned him.

'Oh well,' she thought, in the meantime she had to deal with Maggie. She felt the gloom descending on her again and sighing stood up and made her way back to the restaurant where she started to work again.

She was working until seven that evening and it was proving to be a long day as it was so hot. It was almost six o'clock when she heard a commotion coming from down the road. She heard a scream and raised voices and wondered what on earth was going on as there was rarely any drama on this sleepy island. Everyone sitting outside the restaurant started to stand to try to see what was happening and the owner and waiters came out to look.

A young woman was running quickly towards them and as she got closer Olivia saw the fear on her face. She ran up to Olivia, 'Come quick. Your friend. She's hurt.'

Olivia didn't give it a seconds thought as she took off after the panicked young woman who led her back to cobbled lane where the steps were that Olivia had walked down earlier. She could see a small crowd of people standing at the bottom of the steps and they parted when she approached to reveal something lying on the ground.

Olivia sucked in her breath as she realised it was Maggie who wasn't moving and was lying at an awkward angle, 'Oh my God,' she cried.

Someone standing by Olivia said, 'She fell down all the steps.'

Olivia stared up to the top of the long steep steps and then looked at Maggie. She started to move towards her friend when she felt a hand on her arm. She turned to see the woman who had brought her here. She looked concerned and said to Olivia, 'She didn't fall.'

CHAPTER TWENTY FIVE

As Olivia knelt next to Maggie she was relieved to see she was breathing, 'What have you done?' she whispered. She reached for her friend's hand and then drew back as she noticed her arm was bent in the wrong direction as was one of her legs. There was a movement behind her and she saw a middle aged man with a bag standing looking down at Maggie. She realised he was a doctor and moved away so he could examine her friend and it wasn't long before he stood up and asked if he could use someone's telephone.

He spoke to Olivia and the woman who had run to get her said, 'He says she has to go the hospital in Skiathos.' The doctor smiled gently and nodded at her saying in broken English, 'I ring hospital,' and then disappeared into a house on the cobbled street and reappeared moments later announcing that the ambulance would travel over on the next ferry. It was almost two hours before the ambulance arrived and the doctor tended to Maggie as best he could on the cobbled street.

He helped the ambulance men protect Maggie's neck and then gently move her limbs, tying her legs together and her broken arm to her body and then they transferred her to a stretcher. She didn't stir during all this and Olivia prayed that she would wake up. She travelled in the ambulance with Maggie and the doctor on the ferry back to the mainland where she was transferred to the hospital. Olivia told the doctor that her friend was pregnant and the doctor looked alarmed.

She was examined and Olivia waited with the doctor for two hours before a surgeon appeared. The island doctor put a hand on her arm which suggested she stay where she was whilst he got up and walked towards the surgeon. They appeared to be in deep conversation and the island doctor kept glancing at Olivia.

She watched as the surgeon went back through the swing doors and the island doctor returned to sit beside her. He explained that she had a bad break to her left arm, had broken her leg in two places and had badly bruised her spine. He added that she had damaged a kidney which would have to be removed and that she would need at least three operations on her limbs.

Olivia couldn't take it all in but something in his face made her hold her breath, what more could he say? He then said that she was lucky to be alive and then after hesitating a moment he added that she had lost her baby.

Olivia cried silently for the loss of the life of the baby who hadn't been wanted and for a moment wondered if that is why Maggie had thrown herself down the steps or was it because of Jason. The doctor sat quietly beside her for a few minutes and then said, 'You can do nothing here. We return to Skopelos. I will tell you when your friend wakes up.'

She travelled back to the island in silence and even the sight of the dolphins following the ferry didn't lift her spirits. What had Maggie been thinking of? She felt guilty as she had thought her friend selfish and not realised how very depressed she was.

She felt completely lost unsure of what to do and just worked and slept for the following days. Five days after Maggie's accident she tried to ring Jack as she needed to hear a friendly voice but couldn't get a connection.

It was ten days before Maggie regained consciousness although she understood from the doctor that she was heavily sedated and that was why she hadn't come around sooner. When she saw her friend in the hospital bed she was shocked to see that she was black and blue and linked up to various machines but didn't know why she was surprised. She had her left arm in plaster and there was a cage over her legs raising the bed covers. They sat quietly Olivia holding her friend's hand all the time and this was the pattern of the visits over the next three weeks. They hardly spoke but when they did it was small talk but on one of the visits Maggie told Olivia that she was to be released from hospital in two days The doctor came to speak to them and told them that she would be immobile for another five to six weeks and would need care. After that time the plasters would be removed but that even then her recovery time would be several weeks more.

Maggie explained that they lived on Skopelos but Olivia realised that their apartment wouldn't be suitable for Maggie with her injuries and so told the doctor that they could move to Skiathos as she was sure she could find work. The doctor told her that wasn't necessary as he could have Maggie transported to the island and that he would attend her and Olivia didn't protest for now. She told Maggie she had to go as she needed to make plans but would come back the following day.

She caught the ferry back to the island and went straight to the restaurant where she worked to tell them she had to leave explaining her reasons. The owner was visibly upset and asked her to reconsider but Olivia told him that she wouldn't be able to get Maggie up all the steps to their apartment and she couldn't afford anything nearer the more accessible harbour. She had never intended staying anyway but at this moment it seemed a safe place to be as she knew nobody on Skiathos. She told the owner that she would be back to do her shift that evening and turned to walk away but he called her back.

'I have an idea,' he said, 'I have a small house I rent to holiday makers just outside town. There's someone in at the moment but they leave in four days and then it's empty until next year. You can use it.'

'I'm sure I won't be able to afford it,' she said but the owner replied that she could pay what she paid now for the apartment. Olivia realised that she would have to work all of Maggie's shifts as well as her own to cover the costs but what choice did she have. She accepted his offer as she didn't know what else to do.

She persuaded the hospital to keep Maggie four days more and on the morning of her return to the island the owner of the restaurant took Olivia to the house. It was on a rough road off the end of the main road through town and was about a ten minute walk. It had two small bedrooms, a bathroom and an open plan kitchen and sitting room. The furniture was old and dated but it was more than adequate and Olivia was delighted as the owner went around opening the shutters on the windows allowing the sun to stream in. He then opened the shutters on double doors which he proceeded to open onto an outside area and as Olivia followed him outside her spirits lifted and she felt happier than she had for some weeks.

She was standing on a fair sized veranda with a small table and four chairs and barbeque but the thing that won over Olivia's heart was the unobstructed view across the sea. Maggie arrived by ambulance in the afternoon and the ambulance men carried her in to the house. Olivia pointed them to one of the bedrooms but Maggie protested, 'I have had enough of being in bed,' adding, 'couldn't you have got somewhere which wasn't such a rough ride. I felt every bump.'

Olivia bit her tongue and directed the ambulance men to the veranda and Maggie said, 'I can walk with help, put me down.' Olivia put her rudeness down to the pain she was in as she watched her struggle supported by one of the men whilst the other went outside to inspect the area. He moved the furniture around outside and suggested moving one of the armchairs out there which he and Olivia carried out.

They settled Maggie in the armchair supporting her fully plastered leg on one of the garden chairs and gave Olivia her friend's medication, brought a pair of crutches from the ambulance and then they were gone.

Olivia made some coffee and took it out to her friend who took it saying, 'I know I sound ungrateful but I'm in a lot of pain and so frustrated.'

'I'm sure you are Maggs,' Olivia said, 'it's just good to have you here.'

Maggie looked around her and then out to sea saying, 'It'll do.'

Olivia left everything Maggie would need on a chair next to her before leaving that evening for work and was worried that she would be okay. As she walked down the road her phone rang. It made her jump as she didn't get many calls. When she answered her heart did a flip as she heard Jack's voice as clear as if he was next to her. As she walked on he started to break up so she moved back to where she had been and he was clear again. He told her he was in Paxos and he had to tell her something. He started to break up again but when he came clear again she told him what had happened to Maggie and then he was gone. She tried to ring him back but there was no connection.

She worked over the next two days and looked after Maggie as best as she could and she felt rewarded as her friend's spirits began to rise. She wasn't working that night and was sitting with Maggie on the veranda and decided to be blunt, 'Did you want to die Maggie?' Maggie turned to look at her but didn't answer so Olivia repeated her question, 'Did you want to die when you threw yourself down the steps?'

'No Liv I didn't want to die,' Maggie replied, 'I wanted the baby to die.'

Olivia was stunned and angry but before she could speak there was a loud knocking at the door. She rose feeling numb at the words she had just heard but she was jolted out of her mood when she opened the door to see Jack standing there.

'Jack,' she said smiling, 'what are you doing here?'

'Not quite what I hoped you'd say,' he said and then laughed at her protestations, 'I had to come. When I said I had something to tell you on the phone you didn't ask what it was.'

She stared at him and then shook her head, 'What do you have to tell me?' she asked smiling.

'I love you,' he said simply.

CHAPTER TWENTY SIX

RACHEL

The rest of the year passed and Rachel started to learn Greek which she found harder than the other languages she was learning. She couldn't imagine that she would ever be able to read or write it as the letters looked alien to her but the language itself she started to pick up. She read everything on Greece that she could get hold of and soon had read all there was to know about Skopelos as it was such a small island.

Things at home were much the same although she was sure that she heard her parents arguing on more than one occasion and her mother started occasionally staying away overnight. She asked her mother about this and she said that it was related to some work she was doing and wouldn't be drawn on the subject further.

It played on her mind and she tackled her father on one of the nights Catherine was away. She rather sneakily asked the question as if it was the first time she had enquired about the subject, 'Where is Mum tonight?'

'She's gone to see an old school friend,' her father answered but when Rachel asked which friend he answered he had forgotten. She was confused as that is not what her mother had told her.

'Why does she have to stay out overnight?' Rachel pressed the point.

'Her friend lives a bit of a distance away' Roger answered, 'and they will be having a drink so she won't be able to drive home.'

This was exactly the reason that Catherine had given Roger when he had asked her why she needed to stay overnight at her friends and the words didn't sound any more convincing to his ears when he repeated them to his daughter than they had when his wife had said them to him.

He had long suspected that Catherine might be cheating on him as she had several male friends who would call around regularly through the day when he was at work. He sometimes wondered if he was just been paranoid because she never lied about the callers as far as he knew.

He chose to ignore his suspicions as if he was honest he was afraid of the answer and he didn't want to rock the boat. When he reached for her in the night she would turn to him but there was no response from her in their lovemaking. For a long time it broke his heart as he had loved his wife so deeply for so long but he knew she didn't feel the same.

He had always known that she didn't feel as strongly for him but he had hoped that the love would grow and for their first few years together he thought that was the case as she seemed happy but then she slowly changed. She preferred to spend time with her arty crowd and she had started drinking a lot. Sometimes she would be quite drunk by the time she came to bed and in the early years that would be when she would initiate love making. He didn't refuse but he didn't enjoy the crude words she would use as she fell on to the bed asking him what he wanted to do to her.

In these moments she was not the woman he had fallen in love with and eventually he would pretend he was asleep when he knew she was drunk. There were occasions where she would roughly wake him up but he would tell her he was tired and then she would mock his virility and abuse him verbally.

The following day she would behave as if none of this had happened however this together with her other behaviours was slowly killing off the love he had for her. The only saving grace for him was Rachel whom he could never imagine living without and because of this he chose to ignore his wife's behaviour.

He was struggling now though as she was staying away overnight at least once a week but he still didn't dare push the subject. If she admitted she was cheating what would happen if she spoke the words out loud? Would they be able to carry on living together? It was not a possibility for him to leave his daughter.

During the October school holiday they visited Murcia in Spain and did a little exploring but mainly just relaxed and enjoyed the sunshine. They all seemed to be getting on well as they did when they were away but Catherine disappeared on three occasions in the evening as she had had before.

Christmas was always a jolly time in their home and that year was no different. Rachel got lots of presents as usual but the thing she loved the most was not one of her own presents but the large turquoise coloured bohemian earrings that her father gave her mother. She didn't know but her father had commissioned their making and she thought they were beautiful. Both of her parents were surprised and amused that she would be so taken by something that she couldn't wear herself.

Early the next year her father announced that they would be spending their long summer vacation in the Caribbean. She knew her father had always longed to go there especially Haiti and her excitement grew as they spent many evenings looking at photos of the area and pawing over the plans for a route to take.

Rachel noticed that in the two months leading up to the holiday her mother seemed to spend more time with her and her father and they all discussed their plans for their holiday. She didn't stay out overnight at all during this time and Rachel mentioned it to her mother who said that the work she had been doing had finished. She was quite confused as this was different to what her father had said but perhaps the work her mother had been doing was for an old school friend she thought.

The holiday approached and the excitement in the household grew especially for Rachel little knowing that heartache lay ahead.

CHAPTER TWENTY SEVEN

The year after Rachel and her parents visited Greece for the second time they set off to the Caribbean to visit the many islands in this region. Rachel had read about their destination and was excited but she was a little disappointed as she had lost her heart to Skopelos and knew she had left part of it there. She thought about it often and one day she would live there, she was convinced of it.

She was caught up in her father's enthusiasm as he had always wanted to visit the Caribbean and he was so excited about visiting Haiti he was like a child. She knew that they would be taking various flights between the islands rather than taking ferries and this was her least favourite part of holidays.

They were first flying to Antigua which took eight hours and from there they would explore the island and islands around and then fly on to Peurto Rico. They were spending longer there as they would also visit the British Virgin Islands from there but would eventually end up in Haiti which would be another flight.

They arrived in Antigua all quite tired, it had been a long day and they drove straight to their hotel. They didn't often stay in hotels, preferring to stay in rentals which gave them their own space and the freedom to come and go as they pleased. Rachel was thirteen now and old enough to have her own room in hotels as long as they connected to her parents. She enjoyed this as she liked her own company and whilst she wasn't antisocial she enjoyed quiet space to herself. It allowed her the room for her imagination to run wild and it was the time she got her best thoughts down in writing.

Rachel had her breath taken away by the stunning bays and beaches on the island and could see why her father had wanted to visit the area. He was totally smitten and whilst he spent hours soaking in in the views Rachel in turn soaked in the history. For the first time in a long time Catherine spent most of her evenings with them painting the scenery.

Rachel read that Christopher Columbus who was the first European to visit the island named it Antigua. The island had originally become populated by people of various surrounding islands the first and most influential to the birth of inhabitation on the island were the Arawak people who paddled their canoes to the island where they introduced agricultural cultivating many crops especially the 'black pineapple'. When she read about this the first thing Rachel wanted to do was try one and her father was enthusiastic to fulfil this wish.

Roger and Rachel did more exploring than Catherine as she preferred to paint the fabulous scenery. Rachel poured over her books whenever she could and learned that the island had been raided by the Venezuela Carib people who were superior to the Arawak in the seafaring and weapon prowess and that after the fighting the remaining original inhabitants were either cannibalised or enslaved both fates totally horrified her.

She knew about slavery but not in detail and was now devastated to read about free people being captured and made to work for nothing. On the island the slaves died by the thousands and historians put this down to the stress of slavery and the malnutrition they suffered. The people were used to diet of fresh fruit and vegetables fortified with protein by the vast abundance of sealife however the slavers fed them on a starchy, low protein diet which caused malnutrition which in turn caused them to easily succumb to disease.

Sugar became the most successful crop on the island but it was a gruelling and dangerous crop to work requiring long days which were back breaking under the sun that beat down on the slaves. The only relief from the sun was if they were put to work in the plantation mills where they were at risk of losing limbs in the metal rollers used to crush the cane or they worked in the sugar boiling houses where the temperatures were unbearable and slaves risked being burned in the boiling mixture..

Rachel's heart went out to these poor people and as she looked around she couldn't believe the horror that had occurred amongst such beauty. For the first time in her life she realised just how fortunate she was. She looked at her parents and thought how lucky she was that they cared for her and she appreciated the relationships she had with both of them.

They spent five days on the island before flying on to Peurto Rico and once again Rachel was enchanted by the scenery of vivid blue sea and white sands. They explored the landscaped mountains, waterfalls and spent a day trekking with a guide in the rain forest.

They also took boats to surrounding islands each as lovely as the last and eventually they landed on St Kitts. Rachel could see her father was mesmerised by it and as he talked to her about their surroundings she could see that he felt the same about the islands as she did about Skopelos. She told him she thought it was perfectly beautiful but that it looked no different to any of the other Caribbean islands they had visited.

He had laughed, 'My God Jelly Bean you are spoilt. Look around you, there is nowhere as beautiful as this.'

'But Dad,' she said, 'it looks just the same as where we've just been. If you didn't know you'd think you were on the same island. It's not like Skopelos where the rugged coastline makes it more interesting.'

They debated the delights of both islands and in the end Roger hugged his daughter as they agreed to disagree, he so enjoyed his talks with his daughter. Catherine too loved the views on the islands and they ended up staying much longer than they had intended in their rented home on the beach.

On St Kitts Catherine went back to spending more time alone taking herself off most days to paint and not returning until dusk. Roger and Rachel spent most evenings at the bar just down from their accommodation where the young girl drank non-alcoholic cocktails. The lady who owned the bar was called Brigitte and Rachel thought she was beautiful with her smooth dark skin and long black shiny hair. She wore bright colours and smiled a lot, laughing with Rachel and Roger.

They would sit at the bar most evenings, Rachel people watching whilst Roger would be in conversation with Brigitte. She would spoil Rachel by overloading her drinks with umbrellas and the other paraphernalia the child loved. She would put large chunks of pineapple on the side of the glass which Rachel would devour with great pleasure as she thought what a lovely lady Brigitte was.

When her mother joined them at dusk they would move to a table away from the bar and Rachel couldn't help but notice that she rarely spoke to the beautiful bar owner from St Kitts.

CHAPTER TWENTY EIGHT

EMINE

To Emine it felt as if she had been in the camp for yeas but it was in fact only five months. She sometimes struggled to remember a time when she hadn't been there but she realised it was probably a form of self-preservation. She understood that these men were trying to break her spirit and she couldn't allow it but she also couldn't think of her life before this because the loss and yearning hurt almost as much as her injuries had.

She had no set plans of escape after her failed attempt and the only thing she could think of was that if Berat went ahead and sold her she would then try to escape from her new captor. She shuddered and tried not to think what she might have to endure before she could secure her freedom.

She didn't return to the dark putrid cell but remained in the room with the bars on the window. Omer would visit her most days and had taken to sitting with her and eating a meal with her in the evening. Sometimes they would talk and sometimes they would just be quiet but however much he showed her kindness she could never forget what he did to her and she would never trust him.

One night a week she would be taken to see Berat who would study her and the last time she was in his room he stood up and came over to her, 'You are looking better,' he said and as he had the first night he circled her looking up and down her body. He squeezed her buttocks when he was behind her, 'Yes much better,' he said and when he came back to stand in front of her she expected him to fondle her some more but he didn't. 'It is nearly time. We will get a good price for you.'

She looked down not wanting him to see the defiance in her eyes. She had no idea what to do as there seemed no answer to her.

Omer would take her outside now most days and sit her in the shade where she would now be secured by a chain which she couldn't budge. She welcomed being able to be outside where she could watch the comings and goings. The days he didn't come other guards would tend to her but would not speak, all but Yusuf who would take pleasure in taunting her.

One day he entered her room and told her it was time to shower but she didn't move as she hated going with him as he would stand watching her. 'Get up,' he shouted but she still refused. He walked towards her and dragged her to her feet. She winced as she had pain when she moved. He slapped her face with the back of his hand, 'Don't dare defy me,' he hissed at her.

She didn't resist as he forced her out of the room and pushed her toward the shower room. She stumbled once and he hit her in the back and she cried out but managed to get her footing again and walked on passing Berat's home.

He was the only man who remained in the shower room with her and she had thought of mentioning it to Omer who was the only one here who showed her any spark of kindness but the last time she had tried to confide in him he had turned on her so she said nothing. She had mistakenly thought of him as an ally until he had beaten her and although she knew that it would have been Berat's decision to punish her in this way Omer had shown her no mercy and expressed no remorse afterwards. She began to think he might have a mean streak running through him.

The first time Yusuf had remained in the shower room she had asked him to leave but he had just smiled at her menacingly and leant against the wall opposite the shower cubicle so he could see her clearly. 'Wash,' he had barked at her and she had hesitated not wanting to take her clothes off in front of him.

He had slapped her again repeating the word 'wash,' and she had turned her back to him and after hesitating for a moment she had removed the kaftan she was wearing and was conscious that she was naked underneath the garment. She had tried not to reveal anything apart from her bottom and had felt his eyes boring to her as she stepped into the shower. She had picked up the big lump of soap and turned on the tap feeling the ice cold water hit her body. She had shuddered and started to shiver and began to rub the soap over her body. She was aware of a movement behind her and she looked over her shoulder to see Yusuf picking up her clothes and disappearing.

She hoped he would bring her a clean kaftan but was grateful that he had left and had taken the opportunity to turn around so the cold water could cascade down her back whilst she washed her more intimate parts. She had heard him coming back with clean clothes and turned just in time to avoid him seeing all her body.

She had washed the soap off and had been aware of Yusuf watching her all the time. He hadn't rushed her to finish as some of the other guards did, calling from the doorway, and she had realised just how much he was enjoying leering at her naked body. He made her skin crawl.

Eventually she had turned the tap off and looked over her shoulder to where he stood and she saw him pick up the towel and drop it on the floor just outside the shower and she knew he was waiting for her to pick it up. She covered her breasts with one arm and lowered her other hand to cover her modesty. She then turned aware of his eyes boring into her and had then knelt, leaning forward she moved the lower hand as the bending at her waist hid her naked parts. She reached forward and took hold of the small towel which was hard and rough as usual and turning around she had stood again and dried herself then backing out of the shower she had redressed and he had started to laugh.

After he had taken her a few times he had started reaching out as she dried herself and running a finger down her back and each time she had shrugged him off but he would just laugh at her. She tried to exit the shower as far away from where he was standing as she could but it was useless because of course he could just move closer to her and each day she prayed that it wouldn't be Yusuf who would come for her.

On this particular day as he pushed her into the shower room she could tell something was different in his mood and she felt fearful. She noticed he had brought the clean kaftan with him so she knew he wouldn't be leaving her alone and she proceeded to undress. She washed herself as usual and when she had finished her shower she looked over her shoulder to see where he had dropped the towel as he always did but this time he was holding it out in front of him. She didn't know what to do.

'Come and get it,' he laughed mirthlessly but she stayed where she was not quite knowing what to do. 'Come and get it,' he repeated however this time his voice was firm but she still hesitated and suddenly she was aware of him moving behind her and then she felt his hand slap her buttocks hard and the sting on her wet skin made her cry out. She covered herself as best she could with her hands and arms and turned around. He stared at her for some time although she knew he couldn't see much.

'Come and get it,' he said once again holding out the towel but still she hesitated. 'Don't make me say it again,' he said with menace in his voice and she stepped out of the shower and walked towards him thinking if she got very close she could snatch the towel from him. As she grabbed it he let it go from his hands and although his eyes were on her body she felt relieved but it only lasted a moment as he then grabbed her and his hands were all over her. He pulled her roughly to him and kissed her so hard their teeth knocked together, his stubble scratched her face and the sour taste of him made her want to wretch.

CHAPTER TWENTY NINE

She tried to struggle away from Yusuf but he held her there cupping her buttocks in his hands with a vice like grip. He stopped kissing her for a moment and she told him to let her go trying once again to pull away and the fight seemed to excite him more as she suddenly felt his hardness pressing against her body.

He knew she was aware of his growing desire and he saw the horror in her eyes and before she could fight anymore he forced her to the floor. She felt the cold tiles beneath her body as he sat on her legs and placed one hand on her body to hold her down. He knelt over her and she could see he was preparing himself, undoing his belt and pulling up the kaftan type gown he was wearing She took a large breath and started to scream but he cut the sound off by slapping her so hard across the face she saw stars and before she could get her breath again he roughly pressed the hand that held her down with over her mouth.

She could hear her own screaming but it was in her head, her heart thumped in her chest in sheer panic and then he was on top of her. He replaced the hand over her mouth with his own mouth again bruising her lips and then his hands were all over her body and she felt her hot tears coursing down her face.

She tried to struggle beneath him but his weight held her where she was as she screamed into his mouth. Suddenly she was aware of him trying to push one of his knees between her legs and she tried hard to stop him but he was too strong and as he entered her body she stopped moving and prayed for death.

Yusuf started to move on top of her but as he concentrated on his own pleasure his hand slackened on her mouth and she took her opportunity to scream as loudly as she could. It was the horrendous scream of a tormented soul that filled the air and within seconds she heard running footsteps outside.

Yusuf didn't seem to hear but as the door flew open he looked up a shocked expression on his face and as soon as he saw

Omer and two other men standing there he jumped up, pulling down his kaftan and for a moment Emine laid still in shock before rolling over onto her belly trying to hide her body and then she started to sob.

It was obvious to the men who had entered the room what had been happening and after a moment Omer turned to the two guards and told them to leave the room. He looked down at Emine sobbing on the ground and could see the hand prints on her buttocks and as she lifted her face to look at him with huge sorrowful eyes he could see the vicious red mark where Yusuf had slapped her and the blood that trickled from her lip and it was apparent to him that she had not been a willing partner.

He moved forward, picking up the clean kaftan on the chair he threw it at her, 'Cover yourself,' he sounded angry with her and she was confused. She put out a hand and grabbed the gown and pulled it to her as she started to sit up. She saw Omer approach his brother, anger on his face, 'You selfish bastard,' he shouted.

'Oh shut up little brother,' Yusuf sneered, 'just because you're not man enough.'

She thought Omer was going to hit his brother but before there could be any more exchange Berat entered the room and she froze as he quickly took in the scene and what it meant.

He walked over to Yusuf who was refastening his clothes and screamed in his face, 'What have you done?'

'She threw herself on me,' Yusuf said the fear sounding in his voice. His father stood staring at him, 'she begged me to do it to her, I was weak.'

Berat walked over to Emine who was cowering on the floor holding the kaftan to her body. He pulled her up and she clung to the robe in order to hide her nakedness, 'Did she ask you to do this to her?' he jabbed a finger towards her face pointing at the finger marks on her face, 'or this?' he pointed to her bleeding lip. 'Did she beg you to do this to her?'

Yusuf stared at the marks, 'Yes father, she said she wanted it rough,' but his words tailed off as he saw the look on his father's face and the defiance in his eyes was replaced with a look of pleading. His father repeated the question and Yusuf looking terrified started begging and apologising but Emine could see the veins standing out on Berat's neck, he was furious. He called the guards back in and told them to take his son away. He turned to Omer and told him to see to Emine telling him to return her to her room and not let her sit outside.

When they were alone he repeated his earlier command, 'Cover up,' and didn't bother turning around as he usually did as she slipped the kaftan over her naked body. She asked him why he was angry with her and he told her not to speak to him and she sadly complied. He wouldn't look at her as he roughly took her arm and led her back to her room. Once they were inside he turned to leave, 'Omer,' she tried again, 'I didn't beg him to do that.'

He didn't turn around instead he left the room and didn't return that day or the next and she was fed by Mirac who had originally brought her here and who never spoke to her. She cried herself to sleep at night over the horror of what Yusuf had done to her. She found it hard to shut it out of her mind however hard she tried and as she lay in her bed at night drifting off the whole terrifying scene played out in her head.

Two days later Omer entered her room with food and water for her but still refused to speak to her. He returned later but again wouldn't speak to her. The same happened the next day and later in the day when he entered her room and told her it was time for her shower it was the first time he had spoken to her since that night.

He took her to the room where Yusuf had raped her and she held back not wanting to enter, 'I don't want to go in there,' she said.

'You are safe,' he said, 'I won't do anything,' and then he pushed her into the shower room.

He waited outside as he had before and she showered but she couldn't shut out the horror, the memory of Yusuf moving on top of her in this room filled her head and she hurried in the shower wanting to get out of the room as quickly as possible and went out to where Omer was waiting.

He didn't speak to her and led her back to her room. She asked if she could sit outside but he ignored her and taking her arm propelled her towards her room. He saw her in and as he turned to leave she asked why she couldn't sit outside.

'No man in camp wants to look at you,' he answered.

'I don't understand,' she cried and begged him to listen to her but he left the room and she started to cry hard. He returned within half an hour with water and food and put it down and immediately went to leave and once again Emine begged him to talk to her and she saw him hesitate by the door.

'Omer Yusuf forced himself on me,' she said, 'I didn't want him.' He looked at her and she could see loathing in his eyes which she shrank away from, 'Omer, please, don't hate me. Your brother forced me. He raped me Omer.'

'You tempted my brother with your body,' he said and she didn't understand, 'You let Yusuf take you,' he said and she protested but he ignored her, 'you are worthless to us because you have lain with a Yilmaz. No man will pay good money for you because they will not believe you belong to them,' he repeated what Enis had already told her. 'You are no better than the unmarried women who come her every week selling themselves for our pleasure. Like them nobody will pay more than coins for you now.'

She smarted at his verbal attack, 'Omer,' she begged, 'none of it was my fault, please believe me.'

'It doesn't matter what I believe,' he said, 'everyone will know that Yusuf has had you now. My father is very angry. You were valuable to us.' He left the room and she cried again. What were they going to do to her now they no longer thought she was valuable. She felt wretched, not only had she been violated, she was being blamed for it.

CHAPTER THIRTY

OLIVIA

After Jack joined them on the island he moved in and took over Maggie's shifts at the restaurant which meant that he didn't see as much of Olivia as he wanted but she didn't have to work every day and he could help her look after Maggie. At first Maggie was bitter and took it out on Jack but slowly she warmed to his company and Olivia saw her friend come back to life. She wasn't the girl she had started the journey with as she was now somehow harder and definitely more cynical but it was good to hear her chatting and laughing again.

They stayed on the island another three months whilst Maggie grew strong again and Olivia and Jack's love for each other grew more each day until neither of them could imagine life without the other. They all found their lives idyllic on the beautiful island but they knew it couldn't last for ever and the time came when they needed to plan their next step. Jack said he would soon have to leave to take up his position at the hospital in Edinburgh and Maggie who hadn't worked for months said she didn't have enough money left to continue their journey. Olivia who had been subsidising her friend's stay together with Jack couldn't afford to pay for her and felt sad that her travels would have to come to an end.

'I have enjoyed travelling so much,' she said to Jack one night, 'and I am so in love with Greece that the thought of leaving makes me pine.'

'You don't have to stop travelling,' he said.

'Maggie can't afford to go any further and I'm not going on my own,' she answered.

'Come to Edinburgh with me,' he said, There's sea nearby and I know it's not azure blue and there's not too much sun but they all speak with a kind of foreign accent so you'll feel far away from home.'

She hardly hesitated to answer before she agreed and three weeks later she and Jack moved into a small guest house near the hospital where Jack was working. She was so happy to be with him and when they were together everything seem good with the world but it became apparent almost immediately that he would be working long hours and she wouldn't see much of him.

She spent her first few days familiarising herself with the area and then started looking for a flat for them and after scouring the newspapers and estate agents she made appointments to see half a dozen. She didn't particularly like any of them as they were all characterless and the areas they could afford were all pretty run down. She had heard that there was a port town called Leith a couple of miles away and one day she jumped on a bus to travel there.

She walked down to the port and immediately felt at home as she saw the water, it wasn't the Mediterranean but it was pretty enough and she enjoyed walking down to the shore where there were several small bistros and bars. Her heart lifted as she made her way to the town where she located a letting agent and after telling them what she was looking for they gave her the details of two small properties they had on their books.

That night as she waited for Jack to come home she was more than excited and when she showed him the details of the properties he wasn't initially keen, 'It would be better if we got somewhere near the hospital,' he said, 'my hours are so long it would be nice to get home quickly.'

'It's only two miles away,' she said, 'it's really not far Jack, please at least come to see them with me.'

He was about to ask her about what he would do when he worked nights and there was no transport running but he could see how excited she was and he got caught up in her enthusiasm as he had so many times before and agreed to go to see the flats.

They were both on the outskirts of the town which Olivia pointed out would make travel to Edinburgh easier but when they entered the first one her heart sank. It was a basement flat, dark and smelling of damp and as they walked around Olivia knew that she didn't want to live here. They left quickly and made their way to the next flat which was at the top of an old Victorian house up three flights of stairs. The street it was on was tree lined and seemed peaceful and Olivia particularly liked the large front door with the stained glass panels. They walked into a large tiled hallway where there were a couple of bicycles leaning against the wall and made their way up the stairs.

Olivia unlocked the door and they entered a large, light, airy room which was furnished with a small sofa, armchair and drawers and sat at one end of the room was a small table and two chairs. There was even a television which Jack commented on as they made their way through to a tiny kitchen and then through another door into a small but adequate bathroom. The bedroom was like the lounge a fair size but the thing that sold if to Olivia was the view from the bedroom and living room windows. As it was at the top of the house there was a clear view across rooftops to the port and it made Olivia's heart sing.

Although they both agreed that it was lovely she could see Jack was still unsure but as they walked down the stairs and reached the hall he tapped one of the bicycles and said they would have to find the money to buy him one.

In fact they both ended up with their own bikes after moving into the flat four days later. Olivia had trouble finding work and for a while worked in a bar four evenings a week down on the harbour before securing a job at a book store in Edinburgh. It wasn't why she had studied at University but she enjoyed helping people find the books they wanted and it meant that she was home in the evenings when Jack came home.

They didn't have a lot of money as their living costs took most of their earnings but when they had anything spare they would treat themselves to a night out at a local pub that had live music at the weekend and a small club that had open mike nights which they enjoyed but never participated in and when they were particularly flush which wasn't often they would visit one of the small bistros on the harbour

The rest of the time their outings were restricted to walks on the harbour when they would sit and picnic on food they had taken with them and talk of their dreams. She loved being with Jack and he with her but the humdrum of everyday life slowly sapped her energy and Jack saw the vibrant girl he knew fade before his very eyes.

When Olivia would get home she would enjoy preparing a meal for them and would look forward to Jack coming home watching through the window looking to the street for him to come into view. When he got home each evening his face would light up when he saw her and because of the way he swept her up in his arms she never doubted how much he loved her. They would chat about their day as they ate together but within half an hour of leaving the table Jack would fall asleep in the chair exhausted from being on his feet all day and the length of the hours he worked.

Her heart would sink as she watched him sleep and she would busy herself tidying up whilst dreaming of the adventures they had shared, the sunshine and the vivid blue seas around Greece and she would find herself standing at the window looking out to the port at the lights twinkling down at the harbour.

She felt stifled most of the time as she wanted to be free but realised that life wasn't like that and Jack reassured her that when he finished his training and moved up a level he wouldn't work such long hours. They had lived there for a year when he told her that a position had come up in Newcastle to work under a Paediatric Surgeon and she could see how keen he was to go.

CHAPTER THIRTY ONE

When they agreed that Jack should accept the position in Newcastle she suggested that they live on the coast as it wasn't far for them to travel into the city. She wanted to continue her love affair with the sea but he said it was too far as he would sometimes be on call. She had reluctantly accepted what he said and they found a small one bedroom flat on the outskirts of the city but she had not settled in Newcastle as her heart wasn't in it. She didn't enjoy city life and longed for open views and the more she craved them the more her desire to return to Greece grew. She had fallen in love with Greece, its white and blue buildings and clear seas and she particularly loved Skopolos despite the drama.

She had found a job at a publishers without much trouble and she quite enjoyed it and particularly liked the people she worked with but she felt that there had to be more to life. Jack worked long hours and they spent little time together but somehow when he put his arms around her and cradled her as she went to sleep all her worries would fade away for a while.

One day she had broached the subject of moving back to Greece with Jack and he had immediately dismissed the subject but she persevered and he had fought her as he could not follow the career path he wanted to pursue in a foreign land. She had pointed out that there were hospitals all over Greece but all he could see were obstacles such as the language barrier but in reality he actually didn't want to leave the hospital he worked in as his mentor was helping him so much towards achieving his goal.

They loved each other deeply but couldn't agree on the subject and it was impossible to find a compromise. They started to argue and it broke his heart to see Olivia so unhappy but he couldn't give her what she wanted.

Olivia heard little from Maggie who seemed to have gone back to blaming her for everything that had gone wrong with Jason and the baby despite all that she had done for her. Olivia thought it was probably more of a pride thing. A year after they had moved to

Newcastle Maggie suddenly contacted Olivia out of the blue and asked if she could visit. Olivia was delighted as the thought of company thrilled her and she wanted to see her friend and could hardly contain her excitement as she waited for her train to pull into the station.

Maggie looked no different but there was something about her persona that had changed. She greeted Olivia with a hug but there was little warmth there and as they walked to the flat they chatted but Olivia felt none of the previous closeness they had shared.

They could only offer her a blow up bed in the small sitting room but she seemed happy with that and didn't even seem to mind that Olivia had only been able to take a couple of days off to spend with her. The first night she stayed she asked if they could go to a nightclub and Olivia had felt obliged to take her.

Jack said he could only come for a couple of hours as he was on shift early but he was happy to tag along. Maggie spent all the time he was there outrageously flirting with him and although Olivia was initially amused after a while she didn't like it and when after two hours he said he was leaving Maggie kissed him on the cheek and then turning to Olivia with a big smile she said, 'Right let's look for some talent.'

Olivia assumed Maggie wanted some male company and was happy to keep her company whilst she flitted between groups of men until Olivia said she was going to the loo and Maggie said she would meet her by the bar. Olivia was about ten minutes as there was a big queue in the Ladies and when she returned she saw there were two men standing with Maggie.

'Here she is,' Maggie said to the two men who were several years older than the two young women, 'this is Olivia.' With that she turned to one of the men and left Olivia standing awkwardly with the other. Olivia made polite small talk with the man she had been left with but after a while he made a lunge for her and she told him curtly that she had a boyfriend and with that he walked off. Maggie didn't seem to notice that Olivia was standing alone as she was so engrossed with her companion. After an hour she tore herself away from the man and asked Olivia where her date was. Olivia explained and Maggie turned to the man she had been flirting with, asked for his number and then said they were leaving.

As they walked home Maggie said, 'When did you get so boring?'

'If you mean by boring that I don't want to cheat on Jack,' Olivia answered, 'then you're right I am boring, I happen to love Jack.'

'Oh come on,' Maggie laughed.

'What's that supposed to mean?' Olivia asked but Maggie just said 'nothing' and wouldn't be drawn on the subject.

Olivia told Jack the next day that Maggie made her feel uncomfortable without actually telling about the man her friend had matched her with. She told him she particularly didn't like the way he and Maggie had been flirting but he just laughed at her dismissing her saying he was trying to be nice to her friend. Over the next few nights the flirting continued and Olivia certainly was no longer amused even at times feeling like she was the gooseberry.

The days turned into weeks and Maggie was still staying with them, she regularly asked to go clubbing but Olivia would only go if Jack could come too and when he couldn't Maggie would go on her own. One night she didn't come home and Olivia had sat up all night worried sick until Maggie had stumbled in mid-morning and fallen ono the sofa.

'Where have you been?' Olivia asked 'I've been worried sick.'

'Who are you,' Maggie asked, 'my mother?'

'Maggie, I was worried, anything could have happened to you,' Olivia said.

'And things did happen to me,' Maggie laughed, 'I had a great night.'

Olivia snorted, 'What happened to you? You are so different.'

'Different?' Maggie said, 'you mean I never want to be a doormat again. It's my turn to use men instead of them using me.' She saw the look of disgust on Olivia's face and said, 'it's you who's changed. You have got boring. You think you have it all don't you? But look around you, you live in a tiny space with a man who's never here and you work in a boring job. What happened to your enthusiasm for life?'

'It's on hold,' Oliva said, 'Jack is working hard to progress and once he gets where he wants to be our life will change.'

'Do you believe that?' Maggie asked and Olivia thought she wasn't sure. Maggie read her expression and she laughed 'no you don't do you? You say Jack is working but have you ever asked yourself about all the pretty nurses he works with?'

'What are you saying,' Olivia protested, 'Jack wouldn't cheat on me, we love each other.'

'Get real,' Maggie said, 'every man would cheat. Jack's no different.'

Olivia was unhappy with her friend's words and left the room thinking about what she had said but she was convinced that Jack and she were strong.

CHAPTER THIRTY TWO

RACHEL

Rachel had been used to her parents spending their time apart and it had become a way of life that she thought as normal but before arriving on St Kitts she had noticed a difference as they spent more time together and talked more. They even laughed together and she realised that it had been a long time since they had all felt so close.

That seemed to change in St Kitts and she didn't understand why. The first few days it was the same as they explored the island which to Rachel was similar to Antigua and Catherine decided on the areas she wanted to paint. They had visited Brigitte's bar the first night they had arrived and then the following few nights but then something happened that Rachel didn't understand. Her mother started spending time alone again as she had before on holidays and she once again heard her parents raised voices from time to time.

One evening Catherine said she thought it was time to move on to the Haiti but much to Rachel's surprise Roger protested, 'It's beautiful here and I think we should stay longer,' he said.

'I thought you wanted to go to Haiti Dad,' Rachel said.

'I do Jelly Bean,' he replied, 'but I didn't know how lovely it would be here and I'd like to stay.'

'Rachel's right,' Catherine said, 'we came out here mainly so you could visit Haiti. It's time to move on.'

Rachel had been shocked by her father's tone as he snapped, 'No. We are staying.'

That night Rachel laid awake as she could hear her parents arguing in loud whispers. She crept out of bed and leaving her bedroom slipped down the corridor stopping where she could clearly hear what was being said.

She listened as her father said, 'For years you've done exactly as you pleased on holiday. Most of the time I might as well be away with our daughter on my own. This time I want to do what I want.'

'And what exactly is it that you want?' she heard her mother say. Her father didn't reply and then she heard her mother say, 'Perhaps I should rephrase that. Who exactly is it that you want?'

Rachel had no idea what she meant but heard her father's angry voice replying, 'Don't you dare even go there unless you want to talk about who you've wanted over the years.'

She heard footsteps coming towards her and she ran back to her room where she jumped back into bed and closed her eyes tight as she was aware of one of her parents being at her door. She heard the door close quietly and then lay awake most of the night trying to make sense of what her parents had been saying.

They spent another five days there before flying on to Haiti for the last leg of their holiday. She was aware that things were cool between her parents but they were the same as always with her and she thought that whatever had upset them would blow over soon as it had before.

Rachel was surprised that her father didn't seem to have much enthusiasm for the island that he had dreamed of visiting. To Rachel, even though there were some nice bays the island didn't seem as pretty as others they had visited and there seemed to be a lot of armed soldiers around and she thought that her father was a little disappointed.

She was pleased that they spoke French and she could practice on the locals whereas on most of the other islands they had visited on the break they had spoken English.

She read that the island had first been inhabited by the Taino people but had been invaded many times over the centuries which had moulded its culture. First there were the Spaniards when Christopher Columbus arrived thinking he had found India or China. His boat ran aground and he ordered his men to take what they could from the ship to the island where they created the first European settlement. In the 17th century the French claimed the western portion of the island, importing slaves to develop their own sugar cane plantations.

Rachel shuddered when she read this remembering what she had read about slavery previously but was pleased to learn that during the French Revolution slaves and free people alike on the island revolted which culminated in the abolition of slavery and the island became independent.

She was fascinated by the history of the island and whenever they weren't exploring she would read all she could about it. She learned that the French tried to regain control of the island in 1792 and built an alliance with the people who favoured the French more but eventually the United States, a new republic at the time, provided support to the native Haitians in the hope that they would reduce French influence.

The remaining Spanish and British invaders were driven out and in 1825 the French once again tried to regain control of the reunified island which had declared its independence from Spain in 1821 when the revival of the struggling agricultural economy began. The French agreed to recognise the independence of the island but enforced a payment on them which damaged Haiti's economy for a long time to come.

Rachel struggled to understand why one nation would want to take over another and the barbaric practice of enslaving their people. She read that in 1957 Dr Francois Duvalier became President and the people called him Papa Doc and he had proved popular initially until he wiped out the tourism due to his unstable government. The tourism returned when his son Jean-Calude succeeded him after his death in 1971 but the Duvalier regime was ousted in 1986 and the island was now run by the military.

She asked her father about this and he explained about what was happening on the island and that changes were coming which he was right about as a few years after their visit there was a coup d'etat which overthrew the elected President Jean-Betrand Aristride, a former Catholic priest and with the intervention of the US in 1994 democracy was restored to the island.

This had yet to happen and for the present it helped Rachel understand the presence of the armed soldiers that she saw everywhere they went. It was something she was very uncomfortable with even at her young age.

They returned home and things appeared to go back to normal but one night things hit an all-time low when she witnessed her parents arguing aggressively in front of her for the first time.

They were sat at the dining table having their evening meal when Roger announced that he thought they should return to St Kitts for their 'October' half term holiday. Catherine said it was too far to travel for a ten day break but Roger stood his ground. Their voices rose as they each argued their point and Rachel was stunned into silence a she witnessed the anger that emanated for both of them. It upset her deeply and eventually she begged her parents to stop arguing. They both looked at her in shock as they had been so wrapped up in their own anger that they had forgotten she was there.

After a few moments Catherine said in a calm voice, 'If you insist, go but I will not come with you,' and that is what happened when Rachel travelled with her father and without her mother for their second trip to St Kitts that year. She had been sure that her mother would change her mind but this didn't happen and she felt an incredible sadness and had she been older she would have understood the terrible dread that she felt.

CHAPTER THIRTY THREE

For Rachel it didn't seem right going away without her mother and during the day leading up to the break she had tried to persuade Catherine to go with them but she remained adamant.

When she arrived in St Kitts with her father it had been a long day and she was grateful to fall into her bed in the same bungalow they had stayed in before on the beach. Her father had let her know that he was going to the bar two doors away in case she woke and needed him. She slept through and woke to a glorious day with her father which they spent on the beach and swimming in the warm ocean.

That evening they made their way to Brigitte's bar and the beautiful woman whom Rachel liked a lot gave her a warm welcome. They sat at the bar where Roger fell into conversation with Brigitte and Rachel looked around her. It was almost dark but she could make out the shape of one of three distinct volcanic peaks that was visible from where they were staying. Knowing that it was a volcano made the shape of the high peak against the darkening sky look eerie to Rachel. She knew that there hadn't been a volcanic eruption on the island in over a thousand years but she had read about the devastation caused by the ensuing lava flow and it unnerved and fascinated her in equal parts.

The volcanoes formed the interior of the island which was too steep for habitation and a ring road runs around the perimeter of the island which Roger and Rachel had driven on before exploring the smaller roads that branched off. Roger said he would like to revisit Brimstone Hill Fortress and Rachel readily agreed but was surprised when Brigitte joined them.

She liked the woman and didn't mind, she just found it strange but any misgivings soon disappeared when her father told her that Brigitte hadn't visited before and he asked her to be her tour guide for the visit. Of course Brigitte had been before but she was happy to play along as it was a good way to include Rachel.

'The fortress was designed by British military engineers,' she started, 'and built by African slaves. It is the largest fortress built in the Caribbean and one of the best preserved in the Americas.'

Roger beamed and Brigitte smiled at the young girl who sounded so knowledgeable and showing a professionalism way beyond her years.

'The first cannons were mounted on the hill in 1689 during the Nine Years' War when the French used them to capture Fort Charles on Nevis island from the English who in turn used them to recapture the fort a year later. The English continued to use the hill as a fortress until 1782 when the French once again attacked and the British finding themselves cut off and outnumbered surrendered. A year later the Treaty of Paris restored St Kitts to the British who worked on strengthening the fort so that it could never again be taken from them by enemy forces.'

'Wow,' Brigitte said you really know your stuff.'

Rachel smiled proudly and thanked her then continued to tell her audience that the fort was disbanded in 1854 and it started to fall into disrepair until restoration works took place in the early 1900s. She told them that Prince Charles reopened the restored area in 1973.

She walked them over to a displayed plaque and flourished an arm in its direction, 'Finally may I bring your attention to this plaque which was unveiled in 1985 by no other than Queen Elizabeth herself naming Bristone Hill as a National Park.' Roger and Brigitte clapped and they all laughed together.

Rachel and her father spent another couple of days exploring places they had visited previously but Brigitte didn't join them again although the majority of their time was spent sitting on high stools at her bar. One morning Roger announced that he had to go somewhere and that he wanted Rachel to stay with Brigitte. Rachel protested but Roger insisted and was vague about where he was going. Later she asked Brigitte if she knew where her father had gone but she said she didn't although Rachel wasn't convinced.

Roger was missing for most of the daytime and returned in the late afternoon when he found Rachel sitting on the beach in front of the bar. The rest of the holiday flew by and it didn't seem long before they were sitting on the plane home. During the journey Roger turned to Rachel and asked, 'Do you think you would like to live on St Kitts?'

Rachel felt a little alarmed as she didn't think she would like it and was suddenly scared that the family were moving there, 'I wouldn't like it at all,' she answered and she saw her father looked sad but he put an arm around her and squeezed her tight.

A few weeks later when Rachel was sitting in her mother's studio she asked if they were moving to St Kitts and her mother who obviously knew nothing about such a plan questioned her in such a way that Rachel felt awkward and as she squirmed in her chair she wondered if it had been a surprise for her mother. She hoped her father wouldn't be cross with her for letting the secret slip.

At dinner that night her mother brought up the subject and her father looked alarmed and then said he had no plans to move the family to the Caribbean island. She thought this was the end of it but she heard her parents arguing that night and she hoped that she hadn't caused the row by bringing up the subject.

The subject never came up again but even at Rachel's tender years she sensed a change in the atmosphere at home. It was subtle and she couldn't put her finger on what it was but she knew that something was definitely different.

Christmas arrived and Rachel received the usual abundance of gifts but she noticed that her parents didn't exchange presents and she asked why they hadn't given each other anything.

'Oh,' her mother said, 'we are saving up for something special.' She stared over to Roger as she said it but didn't smile.

Four days after Christmas Day Catherine called Rachel into the kitchen where her father was sitting at the dining table. Catherine was just sitting down at the end of the table and she motioned Rachel to take the seat opposite her father. When she was seated her mother said, 'Your father has something to tell you.'

Rachel suddenly felt very scared as the atmosphere together with the looks on her parents' faces told her that it was not going to be anything good. Her father started to speak, 'Jelly Bean you know that I love you more than life itself?' she nodded without speaking. She was holding her breath as he continued, 'You are everything to me however I have been offered a job at a Medical University in St Kitts and I have decided to take it.'

Rachel didn't understand, 'We are moving to St Kitts?' she sounded alarmed and her father reached out putting a hand on one of hers, 'No Jelly Bean I am going alone.'

Rachel was confused and lots of muddled questions fell from her lips until her mother slammed the table and everything went quiet until she said looking at her husband with a stony face, 'Be honest Roger,' and then turning to her daughter she added, 'Your father is leaving us to move to St Kitts. It's true that he's got a job there but the real truth is that he has chosen the beautiful, exotic Brigitte over us.'

CHAPTER THIRTY FOUR

EMINE

Nothing changed for the next two days and however hard she tried she couldn't get Omer to have another conversation with her. That day he entered her room and told her she could go outside but this time rather than taking her to the shade of the shelter where she was usually chained up she was secured to the post outside Berat's home. She turned grateful eyes to Omer and thanked him but his expression didn't change.

There was little a little shade but as the sun moved around she sweltered in the heat. Omer brought her water and bread but refused to move her and she thought she would pass out. Men came and went and she could hear various conversations they had with Berat and she could tell they were planning something.

Late in the day Omer brought her more water and then entered his father's home where he was followed soon after by Mirac and Mustafa who was hobbling after his punishment beating. Neither man looked at her as they passed and when the men started their conversation she heard something that made her ears prick up.

From what they were saying she could tell they were talking about her and she heard Berat say she was worthless to them and they might as well let her go. They all protested but Berat said, 'No I have made up my mind, tonight after we have dealt with Yusuf take her as far away as possible so she can't find her way back.'

Her heart sang and then she heard Mirac say, 'It is dangerous father,' but Berat dismissed his concerns telling him that it was his decision. She heard footsteps coming from the room towards the door and she closed her eyes pretending to be asleep as she didn't want them to think she had heard them but instead of anyone coming out the door was closed firmly.

She could hear them speaking in hushed tones and wondered what they were talking about. The door opened about ten minutes later and the three brothers emerged from the house. Omer came over to her and untying her he told her it was time to shower.

As he led her to the shower room she decided to risk telling him what she had heard, 'Are you letting me go,' she asked.

'Be quiet,' he said but she told him she had heard them talking and he said, 'I told you to be quiet. It would do you good to listen to my words.'

'Listen to me,' she said but his face looked angry as he replied, 'No you will listen to me and do as I tell you.'

She didn't understand the meaning behind the words but she could see a steely determination on his face. He waited outside and she showered pondering on his words she was surprised when she heard a noise behind her and as she turned she saw Omer entering the room carrying a clean kaftan. She turned her back to him quickly but not before she saw him looking at her body. For a moment she was scared but realised that he was leaving the room and although relieved she was surprised by his actions.

He walked her back to her room but told her he would be back for her in an hour and that she needed to be ready. She asked him what she needed to be ready for but he didn't answer. She thought that maybe tonight they would let her go and she realised it was the first time she had had any hope of leaving this terrible place. She hardly dared believe that she was about to be free and spent most of the half hour allowing memories of the past flood in.

She had tried to shut them out as they made her feel more hopeless in this place but for once she allowed herself to remember the better times and as she felt happy and excited tears rolled down her face but then she heard voices outside and they brought her back to the present. She went to the barred window and peered out where she could see the men gathering and she was scared and scolded herself for allowing her guard down.

She watched the men outside and saw Omer break away from the group and walk towards her room. She felt panic in her body as the door opened and he entered, took her arm and led her outside. Most of the men didn't look at her but those who did looked away as soon as she caught their eye. Omer held onto her arm but said nothing and they all stood waiting but what were they waiting for she wondered?

The men were chattering but then a silence descended and she turned to see Berat emerge from his house. He waved towards a group of men who broke away and she watched them walk towards the building she had been imprisoned in for the first few weeks she was here. They unlocked the door and entered, emerging a few moments later dragging a man towards the waiting men.

The man struggled to walk but Emine could see he was weak and as he lifted his head she saw it was Yusuf and moved closer to Omer. He glanced at her for a moment but then turned his look back to his bother. The men dropped Yusuf to the ground, Berat moved forward and his son looked up at him with pleading eyes.

'You are my first born but from this moment you are no longer my son,' Berat said and his voice sounded steely.

'Father, please,' Yusuf begged his father.

'Don't call me father,' Berat said coldly, 'you have disgraced the name you're not fit to bear. You are no longer a Yilmaz.' He turned to the men around him saying, 'No-one here will ever call this man Yilmaz again. He is against the cause. His actions have cost us and no-one can ever speak to him or their fate will be the same as his.'

Yusuf started to beg again but his father looked at him coldly, 'Be quiet,' he shouted, 'Tonight is the last time you will set foot in this camp, you are to be banished, never to return. If any man here sees you anywhere near the camp they will kill you.' He turned to his sons, 'Mirac,' he said and Emine saw him give Berat the same baton that Omer had used to beat her.

Berat raised it and struck his son hard across the body and the man on the ground groaned. He then handed the baton to Mirac who also struck his brother and then he handed the baton to Mustafa and so it went with every man in the camp striking Yusuf.

He grunted and groaned as the baton struck his body and eventually he laid motionless on the ground battered and bleeding.

Mirac and Mustafa moved forward and lifted their brother off the ground carrying him to one of the trucks where they deposited him roughly in the back. Men started to pick up their rifles and follow them and Omer pulled on Emine's arm leading her after the men. He pushed her into the same truck where Yusuf lay and Omer followed her pulling her down into a sitting position.

The trucks set off and travelled for about half an hour. Emine took notice of where they were going as she wanted to familiarise herself with the area. Eventually they came to a halt and the men started jumping out of the trucks. Omer pulled Emine to her feet and after jumping out of the back of the truck he helped her down.

Mirac and Mustafa unloaded Yusuf from the truck and laid him on the ground. The men stood looking down at him and then in turn they all stood over him and spat on his body and then they all returned to the trucks. Emine was scared that they would leave here with the badly injured Yusuf as she felt sure that they had brought her with them to release her as Berat had said.

'You are the cause of this,' Omer said to her and she thought he was going to strike her but was relieved when he once again helped her into the back of the truck and as they set off she remembered Berat saying they had to take her far away and she now held her breath as she hardly dare hope that at last she was going to get her freedom. They set off and then her hopes were dashed as they turned onto the track they had just travelled down and she realised that they were heading back towards the camp. She wanted to scream that they were going in the wrong direction but she saw Omer staring at her and the look on his face instilled her with fear.

CHAPTER THIRTY FIVE

They returned to camp and Omer helped her down from the truck and as they walked back towards her room she saw that everything was quiet after the earlier horrendous event. He led her into her room and she turned to him saying, 'I don't understand I thought you were letting me go.'

He looked at her with no expression on his face, 'I have lost a brother tonight and all you think of is yourself.'

'Omer, I'm sorry,' she tried to appeal to his softer side which he had shown her previously although she hadn't seen this side of him for some time.

'Get some sleep,' he said, 'tomorrow is a big day.'

'What do you mean?' she asked but he left the room locking the door behind him. She couldn't imagine what he meant and thought about it as she lay down to rest. Perhaps tomorrow was the day they were letting her go. She thought about it for a long time until she thought it couldn't be anything else and she fell asleep and had some lovely dreams.

She was awoken by Mirac as he entered the room with food and water for her and as usual he didn't speak. She ate eagerly and then went to the window and saw the men sitting around talking. The children were helping the baker and he seemed to be very busy today. She was surprised to see that there were two women in camp and they were busy cooking on a big fire in huge pots.

She had no idea what was happening but all she could think about was her release. She heard noise outside and once again went to the window where she could see men passing her building walking towards where the trucks were parked and then she heard the vehicles starting up and driving away. Her heart sank as she thought they were probably going to fight somewhere as they had before and she wondered how much longer she would have to stay here.

Some time later she heard the vehicles returning and saw through her window the men returning but saw they were accompanied by the women. Her door opened and Esin and three other women entered her room carrying a brightly coloured kaftan which looked to Emine like it had been tie dyed with the colours of the rainbow. Esin had a bag in each hand one of which she placed on the floor. Mirac followed the women in and taking Emine's arm he led her from her room towards the shower room with the women following.

He pushed her inside and took his position by the door guarding the room whilst the women followed inside. Esin opened the bag and took out bottles and cloths and then turned to Emin and told the women to undress her.

'What are you doing,' Emine asked pushing them away, I can undress myself,' but she made no move to do so.

'Emine you must get ready,' Esin said 'we are here to help you.'

'Get ready for what?' Emine asked and then realised they were talking about her departure and her heart started to sing again and before Esin could answer her she pulled off her kaftan and walked into the shower. One of the women moved forward, picked up two of the bottles and as Emine wondered what she was doing followed her into the shower fully clothed. Emine was a little alarmed but turned on the water and started to wash herself as the woman opened one of the bottles and poured some of the liquid on to a cloth which she started to lather Emine with. She smelt the aroma of the sweet smelling shower gel and it made her feel better immediately, 'I can wash myself,' she said pushing the woman gently away. She saw the woman look towards Esin who nodded and the woman handed the soapy cloth to Emine which she accepted gratefully.

She wasn't aware of the woman opening the other botte and pouring another liquid into her hand until she felt her start to wash her hair. Her first reaction was to tell her to stop but the feeling of the fingers massaging her head and the fragrances wafting around the shower room relaxed her and she was happy to let her continue.

When they had finished and she stepped out of the cubicle Esin smiled at her and the women started to dry her. They pulled a clean kaftan over her head, placed new soft shoes on her feet and took her back outside where Mirac guided her back to her room. The women followed her in and two of them lifted her kaftan over her head. She tried to hang on to it but they laughed and Esin told her to lie on her tummy on the bed. She stared at them without speaking confused but could see they weren't going to harm her and so she did as they asked.

Two of them started to massage her skin with delicious smelling oils and she began to relax. Her muscles which had become tense over the months were teased out of their knots as they were kneaded and stroked. The combination of the long gentle stokes together with the scented oils relaxed her so much that she found herself drifting off.

She was aware that the massage had finished and opened her eyes to see Esin smiling at her. Although she understood why the woman had given her up to the guards when she was in the women's camp she found it hard to forgive her and could never trust her.

She sat up and the women wrapped a sheet around her and then one of the women started to apply make-up to her face and another put jewelled clips in her hair. Then Esin took one of her hands and started to paint a design on her skin with henna. An awful thought struck her as brides got the same treatment, 'Esin why are you doing that?' she asked.

Esin didn't answer but instead she smiled as another woman moved forward and put long earrings in her ears and bangles on her wrists. She went along with it all as it was nice to be dressed up for once but a fear was growing inside her.

When they had finished they asked her to stand and two of the women took the sheet that she was wrapped in and Esin lifted the brightly coloured kaftan from the chair and with the help of another woman they lowered if over her head to cover her naked body which now smelt delicious.

The women left the room leaving her alone and she sat down, the calm and relaxed feeling she had had was slowly fading but she ignored the feeling and closed her eyes, but she couldn't ignore the growing worry and opening her eyes she looked down at her brightly coloured kaftan, the henna tattoo and the bangles on her wrists and thought she was right, she looked like a Turkish bride but she couldn't be. Panic started to rise in her body and she tasted bile in her throat. 'No don't be ridiculous,' she told herself she was going home.

It was dark when Miran accompanied by Esin returned to the room and walked towards her, 'Esin,' she said, 'tell me what's happening.'

She saw the young woman look towards her husband and then back to her, 'It's your wedding ceremony,' she answered.

'No,' Emine cried like a wounded animal, she had been right, 'I'm not getting married to anyone.'

'Come on,' Esin said ignoring her protests, 'it's time.' She went to take her arm but Emine shrank away from her. 'Please,' Esin said.

'Enough,' Mirac said roughly pushing his wife out of the way and reaching down to grab Emine and then he had her on her feet. She started to fight him as hard as she could, kicking and scratching but he slammed her against the wall of the room knocking the wind out of her, 'Leave us Esin,' he said. The woman hesitated but he was angry, 'Get out,' he snapped.

Esin left as Mirac turned back to face Emine who he was holding her in a vice like grip against the wall, 'There's been a mistake,' she pleaded, 'your father said he was going to let me go.'

'You have no value to us so he was,' Mirac said his voice icy cold, 'if it was my decision you would have been passed around the camp and made to live with the goats but he wants to marry you.'

'Who wants to marry me?' she asked and then knowing the answer she added, 'don't I get a say in this?'

'My father has spoken and you are to be married,' Mirac didn't loosen his grip on her.

'No I will not marry,' she said, 'I will die first.'

'You dare to insult the Yilmaz name,' he almost spat in her face, 'you will face worse than death if you do not comply.' She stared at him, fear in her eyes and he continued, 'After every man who wants you has used your body, I will cut the skin from your body tiny piece by tiny piece. It will be a long slow death and you will beg me to end it.'

She started to shake, 'Every day I ask for Allah to forgive me for bringing you here,' he said, 'you have brought torment on my family.'

She stumbled when he let her go and then roughly taking her arm he took her out of the room but she didn't struggle as his words had struck terror into her. All she could do was go along with what was happening but she would never stop looking for an escape route.

As they emerged from the room Esin was waiting and took her other arm and she could see the whole camp was there watching her as they walked forward. At the head of the group she saw a man who was obviously a holy man and standing next to him was Berat who was looking towards her. 'No, she couldn't marry Berat' her mind screamed and she stumbled but didn't fall as Mirac and Esin caught her. She couldn't take her eyes off the fat old man as she neared him and saw his eyes all over her body.

CHAPTER THIRTY SIX

OLIVIA

As time passed Maggie would often not come back to the flat at night or would stay in bed on a morning and Jack and Olivia found themselves spending more time in their bedroom. The kitchen was tiny and did not offer space to sit in. Maggie would walk around the small flat half-dressed and Olivia knew she had to tackle her as to how long she intended staying. Jack didn't mind as he worked long hours and thought it was company for Olivia and misread her objections as her thinking of his comfort having her friend there all the time.

One night Olivia had had to work late and was surprised when she got home to find the flat in darkness. Jack should have been home but she assumed he had had to work a double shift. She went to bed and was woken about two 'o'clock when she heard laughter coming from the sitting room. She got up and found Jack and Maggie giggling together on the sofa.

'Oh sorry sweetheart,' Jack said, 'did we wake you. We've just got back from the club.' Olivia was shocked and her anger grew as Maggie gave her a sly knowing smile. She stormed out of the room back to her bedroom and heard Maggie laughing behind her.

Jack came into the bedroom almost immediately, 'What was that about?' he asked.

'Why are you going to clubs with Maggie?' she heard her own accusing words and hated herself as she found jealousy ugly.

'What are you suggesting?' Jack asked and when she didn't answer he continued, 'I'm looking after your friend and you're what,' he hesitated, 'accusing me of getting up to something with her?'

Olivia felt foolish, 'No of course not,' she said lamely, 'I want her go now. She's stayed far too long/'

'I thought you wanted her here,' he said, 'I thought she was company for you but if that's how you feel, speak to her,' Jack said.

Jack and she argued much more these days as she was unhappy with her life and Maggie wasn't helping the situation so a couple of days later Olivia asked Maggie outright when she was leaving.

'Is this because of Jack and me?' Maggie asked.

'What do you mean, Jack and you?' Olivia demanded.

'I told you every man would cheat,' Maggie said but before Olivia could respond she continued 'Liv I wouldn't do that to you unless you weren't interested in him anymore.'

Olivia was confused, 'I don't understand what you're saying. Jack and I are a couple and you're wrong about him, he wouldn't cheat on me. In fact I feel sorry for you as you have become so cynical since Jason messed you around. Not all men cheat.'

Maggie laughed hollowly, 'You feel sorry for me? Jack is all over me when you're not here, he can't keep his eyes off me. Wake up Olivia.'

'I want you to leave,' Olivia said as she left the room angry at her friend.

She stayed in her bedroom until Jack came home and she could hear him talking to Maggie in the sitting room. He came into the bedroom, and asked her what had happened but Olivia didn't tell him about her exchange with Maggie instead she said that she thought her friend had outstayed her welcome. He pleaded Maggie's case saying she was lonely and enjoyed staying with them and Olivia didn't understand why he took her side.

Maggie didn't leave and Olivia struggled to be civil with her. Five days after Olivia had asked her to leave Maggie was just emerging from the bathroom in a dressing gown after having a shower, her hair wet when Jack arrived. Jack said he was going to take a shower but Maggie didn't move as he went towards the bathroom meaning he would have to squeeze by her. Something about the look on her face made him feel awkward and he was shocked when she opened her dressing gown exposing herself to him. 'Behave Maggie,' he said trying to take control of the situation.

'Oh come on Jack, you know you want me,' she said.

'Liv is right,' he said, 'it's time you went home.'

She laughed and moved out of his way but didn't bother to close her gown He ignored her and disappeared into the bathroom. As she walked to the sofa fastening her gown she heard the water running and then heard the sound of a key in the door. She moved fast, running to the bathroom she opened the door quietly and she could see that the shower curtain was pulled across so Jack couldn't see her and waiting by the doorway she unbelted her dressing gown again.

She could hear Olivia calling out and smiled as she waited. Olivia appeared and Maggie stepped from the bathroom, tying her belt and pulling the door to behind her. She stopped staring at Olivia in mock surprise on her face and then she smiled at her, 'We didn't expect you,' she said.

Olivia pushed past her and entered the bathroom, she pulled the shower curtain back to Jack's utter surprise and she started to scream at him accusingly as he stood silently watching her in horror. She stormed out of the bathroom and entered the sitting room where Maggie was sitting looking smug and she screamed at her, 'Get out, get out!'

Olivia then went to the bedroom and sat on the bed shaking. She had never felt like this in her life and it scared her. She was shocked as she had lost complete control of her emotions and there had been nothing she could do to stop the tirade. She had never experienced all-consuming anger like this before and she had felt as if she could actually have killed both of them in that moment. She didn't recognise herself and breathed deeply trying to calm down.

'Olivia,' Jack was in the room, 'what on earth was that about?'

She looked at him with hatred written all over her face, her anger simmering below the surface, 'You tell me.' He looked at her not knowing what to say, 'I know you've been shagging my best friend?'

He stared at her looking confused, 'What the hell are you talking about Liv?'

'I caught you Jack,' she spat at him, 'I saw her coming out of the bathroom putting on her dressing gown.'

'I have no idea what you're talking about. She wasn't in there with me,' he protested.

'Liar,' she screamed, 'I saw her.'

'She wasn't in there with me.' he said sounding confused, 'if you saw her coming out of the bathroom, I didn't know she was there. I promise you nothing has happened.'

She looked at him accusingly and he could see she didn't believe him and why would she if that's what she saw? He pleaded and begged her to believe him and continued to reassure her that he only loved her and wouldn't do such a thing but she wouldn't listen.

'I have given up my dreams for you,' she said, 'I followed you here where I don't want to be and now you've done that. Is it only about you?' she sounded calmer but now was monotone.

'I don't know what else to say to convince you that I would never cheat on you. There's nobody else for me. I thought you understood that,' he tried to talk her around. They sat for a while, Jack declaring his undying love and Olivia feeling numb when the door opened and Maggie stood there smirking. Jack looked up at her saying, 'Maggie will you tell Olivia that nothing has happened between us?'

'Why would I tell her that?' she asked and Olivia let out a small cry which made Jack's head turn to her and his heart ached. He then looked back at Maggie, 'Tell her that because it's the truth. Can't you see what this is doing to her?'

'But Jack,' she said, 'you have wanted me since the first day I arrived. I warned Olivia but she wouldn't listen.'

'You're mad,' Jack protested, 'tell her the truth.'

Maggie laughed, 'I'm off then,' she said, 'I'll leave you two love birds to it. My work here is done!' and in that moment Olivia knew that Jack was telling the truth.

Maggie had done a lot of damage to their relationship and it took weeks for them to get back to any kind of normality. Olivia couldn't shake off how scared she had been by her loss of control and Jack was hurt that she had accused him of cheating.

When eventually life went back to their daily routine Jack seemed to make more effort to pay attention to Olivia but for her something had died. She still loved him with all her heart but things had been said that couldn't be taken back and the discontentment she had felt for some time grew and she felt as if she was going through the motions of living.

Four months later Maggie contacted Olivia to apologise, she said she had been in hospital and from her words Olivia understood she had had some kind of breakdown but Olivia said that she needed more time to forgive her. She told he friend that she had damaged their lives and she wasn't sure they would ever recover.

Two days later Jack came home to find her gone and his world stopped spinning at that moment. She had left him a letter expressing how he was her soul mate and although she couldn't imagine life without him she couldn't exist living as they were now. She said that although it broke her heart she had come to realise that they wanted different things and whilst she had tried to support him it was killing her. She said she thought they would end up destroying the love they had for each other.

CHAPTER THIRTY SEVEN

Olivia didn't have a plan when she left the flat she had just known that she had to go. She missed Jack the moment she stepped through the door but she believed that if she stayed their relationship would die before her eyes and she couldn't bear that. They wanted different things and it made her feel guilty as she didn't blame Jack but she felt like a prisoner. She knew she was being selfish but in her mind she had no choice as the feeling she had of being suffocated was eating away at their relationship but she knew that if she raged against it and told Jack how she felt that too would damage what they had.

Against her better judgement she had agreed to put her own ambitions on hold when they had moved to Edinburgh and then Newcastle in order for Jack to follow his dream but she wasn't sure she'd done the right thing. She loved Jack so much and couldn't believe her luck that he felt the same but her job didn't fulfil her and she was struggling to stifle the feeling that she was wasting her life.

She had become so miserable with her life that she spent more time thinking about her own desires giving less time to thinking about how Jack felt. Had she thought clearly she would have known that it wasn't just her choice and she owed it to Jack to talk to him so that he could understand. He knew that she was treading water whilst he progressed in his career but he had made it clear to her that once he was established and he felt close to that end he would support her in chasing he dreams. . It was clear that she wasn't thinking straight because Jack would have done anything to find a compromise to make her happier as she was his life.

It wasn't a quick fix for her as she still harboured the wander lust and still had so many places she wanted to visit and she thought this wouldn't fit in with Jack's career. Had she given him another year of experience he would have been happy to go travelling with her in the knowledge that he would have found another position more easily when they returned.

She had kept her feelings at bay for a long time but what Maggie did had started the cracks. She was more than sure that Jack hadn't behaved inappropriately and whilst the momentary belief that he and Maggie had been carrying on hurt her deeply it was nothing to what her doubt had done to Jack. When she had accused him he had looked as if she had slapped him and it had confused her as she had seen Maggie coming out of the bathroom where he was showering, fastening up her robe.

She pushed the thought away and thought about what she was going to do. She had an idea but first there was something she needed to do. She wanted to see Maggie and make things right between them. They had been such good friends at University but things had gone awry when Jason had come into their lives.

She understood that people came and went in life and some arrived for a purpose and then they were gone and she knew that when they left it didn't mean that the friendship hadn't been valuable. It could be something they had to do for you or something you had to do for them but once their purpose had been served it was time for them to leave your life and trying to hang on to that kind of friendship didn't work.

She believed that Maggie and she had been meant to be there for each other through University and they had done that well however there was really no friendship left between them and Olivia was ready to let go but she wanted it to be on pleasant terms.

She made her way to the station and boarded a train for Birmingham where she would change to a train to Bristol which would take her to Cardiff where she would get the local train to Penarth where Maggie lived. It was a long journey and as she settled down next to a window she stared out as the train set off. She watched as the scenery passed by but she couldn't stop her thoughts flooding in and so she started the autopsy on the dead friendship. 'Perhaps she had never really known Maggie,' she thought. Her friend had had a few relationships at Uni but none had lasted beyond a few weeks and every time Maggie had been down for some time after.

Maggie had met Guy in the last few months of their final year and had immediately fallen for him. Olivia was used to her friend being keen so quickly and had been pleased when the relationship appeared to be lasting longer than previous ones. A few weeks before they finished Uni and four months into their relationship Guy finished with Maggie and she was distraught.

Olivia had been surprised at the strength of her distress as she hadn't realised that it was so serious and eventually struggled to help her friend who was inconsolable. That was when Olivia suggested that Maggie join her travelling around Europe and after a few days her friend agreed to go with her and then she saw her spirits lift.

Of course Maggie had fallen hard for Jason, it was in her nature. Olivia imagined that she was searching for something but she was unsure why she was like this however she hoped that one day she would find what she was looking for. One thing that really worried her about Maggie was that when she lost her baby Olivia hadn't been sure whether her friend had also intended to kill herself. Maggie had insisted it was just the baby she wanted to kill but Olivia wasn't convinced and if it was just the baby she struggled not to dislike Maggie for what she had done.

She wasn't sure she could ever abort a baby but she wouldn't know that unless she was faced with the dilemma so although she couldn't condemn Maggie for her choice she abhorred her reason, that being that she blamed the baby for Jason leaving and had been shocked at the pure hatred her friend had felt for it especially as she insisted it was created through love. It was as if she taken her revenge on the unborn child for driving Jason away.

She shuddered now at the thought and for a moment came out of her day dreaming but she soon returned to her thoughts. If she was honest with herself she had to admit she wasn't sure she even liked Maggie, well at least not the later version of her. She had gone out of her way to try to split her and Jack up and although she had apologised it didn't alter the fact that she had deliberately tried to damage their relationship. It was as if she hadn't cared about their friendship either even after Olivia had cared for her in Skopelos.

She had fetched and carried for her and subsidised her financially and whilst she hadn't minded too much as she wanted to help her friend she had hated how mean Maggie was with her. She put it down to a mixture of the misery of losing Jason, perhaps some guilt at aborting her baby and the frustration of not being able to see to herself but now she thought that perhaps that mean spiritedness had always been there.

She didn't want to be friends with Maggie anymore but she did want to let her know she forgave her so that both of them could forget about the pain that had been caused and get on with their lives. She didn't believe as some people preached that it was necessary to forgive to move on as she thought there were things that could never be forgiven and those things needed to be put in their own compartment and not allowed to ruin your life but what Maggie had done wasn't one of those things.

She had twenty minutes to wait in Birmingham before her connection for Bristol arrived and she grabbed a quick coffee. The train was quiet and she had the pick of where to sit and went for another window seat. She took out her phone and looked at it seeing she had a message from Jack. He wouldn't have got home yet and wouldn't know that she had left she thought as she read, 'I'll be home on time. Spag bol for tea. I'll cook. Love you x' 'I love you too,' she thought and a tear escaped down her cheek.

She pushed away thoughts of doubt of whether she was doing the right thing. Their life was slowly killing her and eventually she would have taken it out on Jack and he didn't deserve that. She imagined him coming back to thier empty flat, the realisation that she had gone hitting him and her heart constricted as she felt his pain.

She changed at the small station in Bristol for the train to Cardiff and once there didn't have to wait long before getting on the train to Penarth. The journey had taken almost six hours and she was stiff and tired but she would go straight to Maggie's. She exited the station into the lower part of the town and started to walk. She had been once before with Maggie and as it wasn't a big place she could remember how to get to her house. She passed the tennis courts and park, crossing the road to Church Road where her friend lived. The house was at the far end of the road and when she reached it the walk had only taken five minutes..

She rang the bell and waited for a couple of minutes before the door was opened and Olivia saw Maggie's mother, Jean standing looking at her. They had only met once and Olivia could see she didn't recognise her so she reminded her and the woman said, 'Oh you're that friend,' and then she invited her in with a strange look on her face.

She sat Olivia in the living room feeling a little uncomfortable after the remark Maggie's mother had made. She had gone away to make coffee and Olivia noticed how tidy it was, not a thing out of place. She saw there were lots of family photos around the room, on the walls, on the fireplace and there were more of Maggie than anyone else. When Jean joined her she asked where Maggie was, 'I was hoping to see her,' she said.

She saw that look cross the woman's face again and didn't know what it meant. 'Maggie passed away a few months ago,' she said.

'No', Olivia's voice was a cry, 'how? what happened?'

'Maggie took her own life,' Jean said and sat looking at Olivia without speaking anymore.

'I didn't know,' she said, 'I would have…' she tailed off. What would she have done? She asked herself, what could she have done?

Jean cleared her throat and Olivia could see that her eyes were misty, 'I thought you might have some answers.' Olivia felt a little guilty when she shook her head and Jean continued, 'After she got back from galavanting around Europe with you she was different. Something happened, what was it?'

Olivia had to make a quick decision, she could see that Maggie's mother didn't approve of their travels and the tone she had used was as if she was accusing Olivia of something. She didn't want to add to Jean's pain by telling her that she had also lost a grandchild so she said, 'She had her heart broken.'

Jean nodded as if she understood, 'She always felt things deeply. She gave her heart too freely. She became a bit wild and her father and I had to read her the riot act which made her take off, to yours I believe.'

'Yes,' Olivia said, she stayed with us for a few months.'

'Us?' Jean queried and then a light came on, 'of course you live with a man.' She said it in such a judgemental way that Olivia wanted to retort that it wasn't the nineteenth century but bit her tongue.

Jean sniffed and continued, 'Anyway it didn't do her any good. I suppose you encouraged her wild behaviour,' Olivia tried to protest but Jean ignored her and continued, 'when she returned she was exhausted and ended up having a mental breakdown. She spent some time in hospital and when she came home again she was withdrawn but we thought she was getting better.' She was quiet for a few moments, 'I found her. Her father and I had been away for the weekend and when we came back she had taken an overdose. The Coroner said that she'd been dead for at least twenty four hours.'

'I am so sorry for your loss Jean,' Olivia said.

'I'm sure you are,' Maggie's mother said making Olivia feel very awkward and so she rose, told her once again that she was sorry and left.

'Poor Maggie,' she thought and wished she had realised how tortured she was because maybe if she could have seen past her cruel behaviour she might have been able to help her.

She thought she knew what she was going to do next

CHAPTER THIRTY EIGHT

RACHEL

Her father's words tore through her and she felt physical pain wracking her body. She sobbed and begged her father not to go and for the first time in her life she saw her father cry whilst her mother sat looking on stony faced. Eventually she fell exhausted into her bed and the fear and sheer hopelessness she felt completely overtook her until she fell into a fitful sleep.

When she woke the next morning it took less than five seconds for her to remember what had happened but initially she thought it was a nightmare but it took only another three seconds for her to realise it was real. She jumped out of bed and ran downstairs in her pyjamas in order to speak to her father again.

She searched around, calling out but she couldn't find him. She saw the door to her mother's studio was shut but she turned the handle and entered. She found her mother standing by the window staring out and it was obvious she hadn't heard her daughter enter.

'Where's Dad?' Rachel asked and her mother turned to look at her and she was alarmed by the look in her eyes. She looked as if she was in a daze and the light had gone from her.

'He's gone,' was all she said.

Rachel screamed out and begged her mother to tell her where he was as she needed to speak to him but her mother told her that he had left and wasn't coming back, 'He's made his choice,' she said with bitterness in her voice..

Rachel spent most of the day crying and would run to the window at any noise believing that her father had returned. She had no doubt that he would change his mind and come back. After all he had always sworn to her that he would never leave her, that she was his life and that he loved her more than anything else in the world. She had never doubted him for a moment as he had always made her feel safe and she adored him. She couldn't imagine her life without him and she didn't believe for a moment that he wouldn't return.

She told her mother that her father wouldn't leave her but her mother reaffirmed that he had and wasn't coming back.

'But he loves us,' Rachel protested.

'Unfortunately he loves Brigitte more,' her mother said in a matter of fact manner.

'No,' Rachel protested that couldn't be true. Her mother insisted that it was and that Brigitte had deliberately stolen him from them. Her mother bitter at the rejection told her that her father had been idyllically happy with them but Brigitte had set about breaking up their family because she decided she wanted him. Rachel listened and not knowing any better her young heart suddenly hardened toward the woman she had liked and trusted and the feelings she had had for her turned to pure hatred.

She blamed her for everything and her mother was more than happy to feed this hatred as she was angry at her husband for leaving her. Rachel asked how he could have left her behind and Catherine told her that Brigitte had not wanted her with them and that her father wanted the Caribbean beauty so much that he willingly gave up his daughter.

None of this was true as Roger had fought bitterly with Catherine trying to persuade her to allow him to take Rachel with him but Catherine had been adamant that she was staying with her. It was not that she particularly wanted her daughter with her but that she wanted to punish the man who dared to leave her and she knew that this would cause him the most pain. He was aware that his daughter didn't want to move but he couldn't bear the thought of leaving her behind. It was the most difficult decision that he had ever made and he wished that it hadn't happened until she was a little older.

Things had been bad between him and Catherine for years and when he had met Brigitte he had no thoughts of romance but her gentle way and kindness had enchanted him and before he knew what had hit him he had fallen hopelessly in love. It had totally surprised him and he doubted the feeling because he had only known her for a couple of weeks and he thought it was probably that he wasn't used to being treated so kindly by a woman. She looked at him with desire in her eyes and initially it had stirred old feelings in him, the feelings he had had for Catherine all those years ago.

When they had returned home from their summer in St Kitts he could think of nothing else but Brigitte. Was it possible to fall in love so quickly he asked himself? Perhaps it was just lust or the novelty of being desired again by a beautiful woman. Eventually unable to push the thoughts away he had written to Brigitte expressing his feelings. He had received a speedy reply from her telling him she felt the same.

He knew he had to return to see if his feelings were real and was excited when he took Rachel back in the October. He had never considered being unfaithful to his wife despite his strong belief that she had cheated on him but on the first evening in St Kitts as Rachel slept he and Brigitte cemented their relationship. He had desired her more than he could even remember wanting Catherine and he was surprised that he had no feelings of guilt as nothing had ever felt so right.

After a great deal of soul searching on the part of Roger and Brigitte over the fact that they were breaking up his family and the effect it would have on Rachel by the time he left the island Roger had already made plans with Brigitte to return permanently hopefully with his daughter. Brigitte felt guilty about taking her from her mother but she loved the child almost as much as the man and knew how sad he would be to be without her. She could see how determined he was to return to her however her happiness was tinged with a little sadness due to the circumstances.

He had visited the University of Medicine and Health Sciences on the island and secured a position in Research which included a few hours lecturing and planned to leave as soon as possible. His resolve waned when he arrived home to be faced by Catherine who had not been happy at him going away alone. It was November and he decided to wait until after Christmas so that they could share one last seasonal break as a family but his plan was scuppered when Rachel had asked her mother about moving.

He had been surprised how angry Catherine had been as he had been aware she hadn't wanted him for years. He told her that he knew she didn't love him and she had screamed at him that it had nothing to do with love. He was her companion, her child's father and together they were a family unit and how dare he split them up. He in turn told her he wanted more than companionship in his life and he had found love with Brigitte. This just inflamed Catherine more.

They argued all night. He had told her that he intended taking Rachel with him and she had spat the words, 'Over my dead body,' at him. She cared for her daughter but if she had been honest with herself she was using her as leverage.

After days of arguing Catherine had had to accept that Roger wouldn't change his mind however much she tried to persuade him. She veered between kind words of love, reminding him of their past, and insulting him especially about his virility telling him that he was only good for keeping a roof over their head. On one occasion she tried to seduce him and reeled at his rejection hurling the worst insults she could think of.

After Christmas she told him to go and he informed her that he would book into a hotel nearby so he could see Rachel before he left a he didn't want her to think he had left without speaking to her.

Catherine resolved that he would never see his daughter again and started her onslaught of character assassination of her errant husband. She slowly turned her daughter against the man she had adored telling her that he had never really loved her. She conveniently forgot her extra marital liaisons and put the blame for the breakdown of their relationship squarely at Roger's door who had allowed himself to be seduced by the Caribbean beauty.

Rachel couldn't believe that her father had left her, it completely broke her heart. He loved her, how could he leave her? She just couldn't fathom what had happened to her and when her father failed to contact her everything he had ever said to her became a lie in her mind. She felt totally betrayed by the man she loved above all others and she never really recovered.

Roger tried to see Rachel before he left for St Kitts but Catherine told him that she was heartbroken and didn't want to see him. Roger protested telling her that he would come round to the house to explain and as she didn't want him getting their daughter on his side she said that he needed to give her time and that she was sure she would come around.

He phoned the house the night before he left begging Catherine to let him speak to Rachel and Catherine said she would ask her. She didn't move away from the phone as she had no intention of asking her daughter if she wanted to speak to her father and then lied to him saying that she didn't want to speak to him. He rang regularly from the island once he had arrived but Catherine never told her daughter. It was a time before mobile phones so Roger couldn't call her directly. He continued these phone calls for six months until one day the number was no longer obtainable. He wrote letters to his daughter regularly but they were all returned.

His life with Brigitte was more than he could have hoped for as he had never known that such contentment was possible and the lifestyle the island offered was idyllic. The only thing that marred it was the absence of his daughter which broke his heart.

It played on his mind constantly and now he couldn't contact her and after living on the island for almost a year he returned to England for a visit as he had to see his daughter. When he arrived at the house, he rang the bell and a complete stranger opened the door. She told him that Catherine had sold the house to her six months ago.

Roger contacted the bank to see if they could help but although he transferred money to her account every month they wouldn't give him Catherine's new address. He visited the University where she had taught but she didn't work there anymore. He didn't know her friends or where to find any of her arty crowd and eventually he had to return to St Kitts crestfallen with no idea of how to reach his daughter.

CHAPTER THIRTY NINE

Rachel and her mother moved around quite a lot as Catherine tried to evade Roger as she was determined that he wouldn't find them. She wanted to punish him for rejecting her and taking away the lifestyle that she enjoyed. She had many arty friends across the country and although at first Rachel hated moving around eventually she took to the nomadic lifestyle.

Her mother always seemed to have a lover and Rachel didn't bother to get to know them as they came and went but one day she realised that one man had been around for some time. He was a handsome older Greek man named Stalios and Rachel found she actually liked him. She practiced her Greek on him and found him fun and now a young teenager she could see he was very handsome with his long, dark, curly hair sometimes hanging over his shoulders and other times tied back. Rachel was fascinated by him studying his big moustache as it moved when he talked and how white his teeth looked when he laughed and he laughed a lot.

He was very tactile and would gently pinch her cheek or sometimes he would lift her off her feet and swing her around. He wasn't anything like her father but he was fatherly to her and she learnt to care deeply for him. He was always hugging her mother and she could see that he made Catherine very happy. She would hide her head under her pillow at night as she heard their noisy love making which seemed to go on for a long time and took place most nights.

Rachel knew about the birds and the bees but knew nothing of the emotions that went with it and didn't know why it took so long. She hoped that they wouldn't make a baby as she was too old to have a baby sibling. She didn't like to think about what they were doing and would try to shut out the pictures that came into her mind when she heard the noises coming from her mother's bedroom.

One day Catherine announced that they were moving to Greece to live with Stalios and Rachel was very upset. She had tolerated her mother moving her around the country even growing to like seeing the different places but to move abroad that was another thing. She loved Greece but it was too far away from everything she knew.

She could tell from the talk she had no choice in the matter and only warmed to the idea one night when she was talking to Stalios about his home, 'Where in Greece are you from Stalios?' he asked.

'I am from the beautiful island of Skiathos,' he answered, 'Wait until you see it Paidi mou,' he used the term of endearment that literally meant 'my child', and which he always called her.

She remembered, 'But I have seen it,' she said, 'you're right it is beautiful and the best part is that it's close to Skopelos.'

She told him about her visit there and he could see how excited she was when she spoke of the island and he smiled his big smile, 'The ferry goes there many times a day, we can go often.' He had sold the idea to her.

As the days grew nearer to them moving 'Rachel grew more excited, she had said she would return to the island of Skopelos and now she would be able to go there whenever she wanted.

The move went well and Rachel fell in love with the area all over again. Stalios had a lovely white painted villa there with olive trees growing in the garden and a wonderful view of the sea. She hadn't realised that Stalios was wealthy but it was obvious by the opulence of his villa and they began to live very comfortably. Her mother had money from the sale of their house but she had not spent it freely as she had not known how long she would have to make it last.

It wasn't long before Stalios took her over to Skopelo and he was happy to sit on the deck of the ferry with her as she searched the ocean for the dolphins that played in the warm waters. As they approached the island she excitedly pointed and called out to him and he put a protective arm around her shoulders. They drove off the ferry and made their way away from the main town and as they drove around the island she couldn't hide her joy at being back there.

They climbed the steps to the tiny chapel on the island as she had done before with her father and they enjoyed the view from the top. When they got back that night she excitedly told her mother about the island although she had been there herself and Catherine smiled over her head at Stalios grateful that he was so good with her daughter.

Catherine had been looking for a studio where she could work and she told them that she thought she had found the perfect place. They all went the next day walking up the cobbled street and Catherine stopped outside a rundown looking shop front. The windows were filthy and the wood frames and chipped door had cracked paint. She smiled at them as she could see that they weren't impressed and unlocked the door to expose a large area inside but that too was dirty with broken bits of furniture all over the place.

She wouldn't listen to their objections and took herself off every day to her new studio but she wouldn't let them accompany her. Rachel was worried that she had found another man due to her disappearances but she could see how happy her mother was when she was with Stalios. She had never seen her so happy not even with her father.

Two months after they arrived Catherine announced that her studio was ready and as they followed her through the town later that day, they turned onto the cobbled street they had been on before and as they approached the studio both stopped in their tracks. Stalios let out a whistle as Rachel said, 'Wow'.

Before them was a shop front painted a bright, shiny white with clean gleaming windows. The stone work beneath the windows had been tiled in traditional blue and white Greek tiles and the door had been replaced with French windows which were opened in by huge blue, pot knobs. They walked inside to see an immaculate wooded space which was bright and airy. There were several of Catherine's canvases which she had had shipped over on display and at the back of the studio they could see several canvases waiting to be painted on.

They were both so happy for her and it proved to be a huge success with Catherine selling many pictures and taking commissions to paint more.

Rachel had been enrolled in a school where she made some friends but all the spare time she had was spent exploring Skopelos. They spent two happy years living like this before it all changed.

She came home one day from school to find her mother sitting at the dining table looking ashen. She held her breath as she asked her what was wrong and saw her mother turn old eyes to her, 'Stalios is dead.'

CHAPTER FORTY

EMINE

Berat who had been watching her walk towards him with lust in his eyes looked hard at her as she reached him, 'You are here for a great honour. She looked away from him, her skin crawling, so tempted to scratch his eyes out, she shuddered as her mind went to what was about to follow. She loathed this man and now she was about to marry him and then what, 'no' she wouldn't let her mind go there.

He turned to the people crowded in the camp, 'The past is in the past,' he said, 'this woman's sins will never be spoken of again. Yusuf paid a high price for her to stand before us with a fresh start. He no longer exists as a Yilmaz but tonight we will welcome a new Yilmaz. Now let's get on with the ceremony.'

The men cheered and made noises of appreciation as he took her hand and she shrank away but he didn't seem to notice as he turned her to face the holy man and then she saw Omer whom she hadn't noticed before standing close by and now she stared at him as his father moved away and he took his place.

She realised that she was about to marry Omer and although a better option to Berat it was still something she didn't want. She turned to him speaking quietly so nobody else could hear, 'Omer, please I don't want to marry you.'

'Do not speak,' he said but she ignored him and begged him to stop the ceremony, 'you will not disgrace me,' he said, 'do not speak again.' She didn't listen and started to protest in a whispered tone in his ear whilst Berat bent forward and spoke in the other ear telling him to control his bride.

Omer pinched her arm hard and she winced and she saw the steely look in his eyes, 'You have bought shame on yourself but you will not bring shame on me. Do not make me beat you before we marry.'

Emine stopped speaking and turned back to the holy man and she felt Omer kneel beside her and taking her hand he pulled her down next to him. She didn't listen to any of the words being said but knew when Omer pulled her to her feet and gave her a ring that they were married. Berat moved forward and taking her face between his hands he said with menace in his voice, 'You now belong to my youngest son and you will do as he bids, do you understand?' he didn't wait for an answer before kissing her roughly as did Mirac but Mustafa hardly touched her cheek and the only tenderness she felt in the embraces from the family was from Enis but it just made her think of Judas.

When all the embracing was over Omer moved away and Enis took her hand and led her to follow her new husband to a building much bigger than the one she had been living in. Omer opened the door and as they entered she saw a small living area with table, chairs, drawers and an old sofa but they didn't stop here instead Enis led her through to another room. She saw immediately it was a bedroom, a double mattress on the floor and another battered chest of drawers under the window. There was a hanging area and standing next to this was an old woman.

Emine understood that this was the consummation ceremony in the nuptial chamber and she was equally shocked and surprised as she didn't think anyone did this anymore. In times past families would want proof of the new wife's virginity by seeing the bloody sheets after consummation but this was outdated. She knew that the ceremony had continued even after the proof was no longer expected but even this had stopped as far as she knew. It appeared she was wrong.

Enis left them and the older woman following tradition asked Omer and her to hold hands Omer performed his ritual prayer and then reached inside a pocket in his gown and took out a pretty flower hair clip which he presented to Emine. In bygone days this would be the point where the bride would remove the veil from her face in response to the gift but as she wasn't wearing a veil she thanked Omer.

The old woman left them and she was left alone with Omer, 'Omer I don't want to be married to you,' she was pleading with him.

'It's too late,' he said 'it is done.'

I won't sleep with you,' she said.

'You are my wife,' he said moving towards her.

'No,' she snapped, 'I might have to accept that you have forced me to marry you but I will not sleep with you.'

He stopped in his tracks anger on his face, 'You continue to bring shame on the Yilmaz name.' She looked back at him with defiance and she felt the sting on her cheek as he hit her with the back of his hand, 'I am your husband and you will not defy me.'

She put her hand to her face where he had hit her and they stared at each other for moments and then she saw his face soften a little, 'I will be patient,' he said, 'you were not prepared. I will give you time.'

She relaxed a bit but when he told her to sit down panic filled her face, 'We must wait,' he said, 'I will not be shamed by going back outside so soon.' She understood that he wanted the camp to think they had consummated the marriage.

They returned outside and she could see that people were sitting around sharing food. They clapped and cheered when Emine and Omer emerged from his home and she felt herself blush. They went towards Berat where they sat down to join him to eat whilst he leered at her, grease on his chin and then slapping his son on the back he laughed out loud imagining he knew what had gone on in the house.

She looked around their group and saw Enis and Mirac were sitting together eating and the young woman smiled at her. She wasn't hungry but Omer insisted she ate and when the food touched her lips she realised just how hungry she was after the trauma of the day. The men started to get drunk but when she asked for a drink Omer told her that the women were not allowed alcohol. She challenged him saying that it was double standards as the men shouldn't be drinking either according to their religious laws.

He looked as if was going to be angry again but instead he smiled and putting down his drink he said, 'Then I shall not drink either.'

When the group finished eating, Enis stood and taking her hand she led her to an old sofa that had been brought outside and covered with a sheet. She sat down but Enis didn't join her instead she sat nearby.

She looked over to where Berat and his sons were sitting talking, laughing and drinking and she saw that Omer was being teased into drinking the alcohol in front of him. She saw Berat say something whilst leaning forward and grabbing his son's groin and she heard the raucous laughter of the family and could only imagine what was being said.

The men stood and Omer came over to her joining her on the old sofa, 'He whispered in her ear, 'You must kiss me now in front of everyone so the men can start their celebrations.' Before she could answer his arms went around her and he closed his lips over hers and she tried not to pull away. It wasn't the most terrible thing that had happened but it was unwelcome.

She could hear the men cheering again and then Omer let her go and she saw Mirac take Enis' hand and lead her into a building she imagined was his home.

She sat watching as the men started to grab the women around them, pulling them down on to their laps. She shuddered as she saw how they mauled them grabbing at their bodies. She saw Berat watching nearby and then he walked over to a girl who looked no more than a teenager and taking her arm he steered her into his home.

Her heart went out to the young girl but she was even more shocked to see one man push a woman to the ground and climb on top of her and proceed to have sex in front of everyone. She turned her head away but was confronted by similar scenes around the camp.

Omer saw her distress and stood up, taking her hand he led her to his home and once inside he continued through to the bedroom which was lit by several candle lit lanterns. He turned to her and she could see anger on his face again, 'Never question my actions again in front of the men,' she realised he meant her comment about him drinking alcohol, 'your name may mean fearless and courageous but let's see how fearless and courageous you are if you shame me again.'

She needed to get him back on side, 'I'm sorry Omer,' she said lamely but he ignored her words and proceeded to undress until he was standing naked before her. She turned away but was aware that he was getting into bed under the sheet. She stood looking at him wanting to run but he looked at her with a blank expression on his face, 'I have told you I will be patient.'

She hesitated and then started to take off the jewellery she had been wearing and then went to the bowl of water on the side and washed the make-up off her face that the woman had put on earlier. She went around the room blowing out the candles until all that were left were the two on Omer's side of the bed.

She didn't remove her dress as she walked over to the mattress and went to lie down next to Omer he said. 'It's usual to remove your clothes before getting into bed.'

She ignored him and sat on the mattress, 'I am your husband,' he said in a stern voice, 'I have said I will be patient but you will do as I say. Now undress.'

She stood up and asked if he would blow out the candles in the lanterns next to him but he ignored her not taking his eyes off her. She knelt down next to the mattress, turned her back to him and pulled the kaftan over her head and then lifting the sheet slipped under the sheet keeping her back to Omer. She heard him blow out the candles and she felt his arm go around her, his hardness pressing into her, 'You smell so good,' he said, 'now let's sleep.'

CHAPTER FORTY ONE

The morning after the wedding Omer woke her and for a moment she reeled in shock before remembering the day before. He rose from the bed not trying to hide his nakedness whilst she pulled the sheet on the bed around her. He went to the hanging space and produced a plain robe for her and then after he had washed and dressed he left the room allowing her privacy.

When she emerged into the living area he was waiting for her at the table with food and he invited her to sit with him. They ate in silence and when they had finished she asked, 'Will I stay here in this house with you now?'

'You will stay here for our three week honeymoon period and then it will be decided if you will be taken to the women's camp.'

'I don't want to go there,' she protested.

'There are no other women in this camp but you may be able to stay as the wife of a Yilmaz,' he said, 'it will be up to my father.' He was lying as it was up to him but he was keeping that knowledge to himself.

'Didn't he allow Esin to live here?' she asked referring to the wife of Mirac who had betrayed her.

'Mirac chose for her to go there,' he said, 'his love is for the cause and he wants no distractions. If you are taken to the women's camp you will be brought here once a week with the other women and I can visit you when I want.'

'But if Mirac was allowed to choose for Esin to go to the women's camp can't you chose for me not to,' she asked in desperation but she saw a shadow cross his face. ,'I want to stay with you,' she lied and she saw him look at her curiously. She was used to this camp and continuously planned how to get away. He told her to come outside with him and was surprised when he secured to a post outside their home.

'I thought now we were married you wouldn't feel the need to treat me like a prisoner,' she protested.

'You are my wife,' he said, but you cannot be trusted. You would bring great shame on me if you ran away and I would be punished like Mustafa or worse banished like Yusuf. She saw the pain in his eyes as he spoke of his brothers and understood that he blamed her for it all.

Each day would be the same, they would rise, eat their breakfast, he would secure her to the post in the shade visiting her throughout the day with water and at lunchtime he would sit and eat bread with her. Each evening he would untie her and he would sit with Berat and his brothers and eat his evening meal whilst she was seated close by on her own.

The second night had been the same as her wedding night as he watched her undress but she still kept her back to him and had slipped under the covers. He had tried to turn her towards him but she resisted and he didn't force her instead he put his arm around her pulling her towards him and then he would cuddle up pressing himself into her back.

They would go through the same thing every night and each night she would resist him trying to turn her towards him. He took her to the shower every other day as he had before but now he would remain in the room but she steadfastly kept her back to him as she had with Yusuf. He had given her scented shower gel the first time he took her to shower after they were married and she was grateful as she was for the kindness and friendship he showed her throughout the day.

On the fifth night they went to bed and went through the usual ritual of him watching her undress, her backing into bed, him trying to turn her over, her resisting and his arm going around her but this time he rested his hand on her beast and she froze before moving his hand away.

She felt him stiffen behind her and then she felt the pain as he pinched her bottom so hard it made her yelp, 'Do not try my patience,' he said to her in a less than gentle voice replacing his hand on her breast and this time she didn't object as she didn't want to anger him enough to force himself on her. It was the same the next night but the night after he undressed but didn't get into bed waiting for her to undress. She turned her back to him but she was very aware of him standing behind her and after she had removed her robe she felt his hands on her as he spun her around.

She shrank back and tried to cover her nakedness, he moved towards her and kissed her hard but she did not respond and pulled away, 'Leave me alone,' she shouted and then she felt the sting as he slapped her face hard and she fell back.

'My patience is running out,' he said, I am your husband and yet you continue to insult me. When I touch you, you behave as if I disgust you.' He looked at her with raw anger in his eyes and then turning he got into bed telling her to join him. She hesitated scared of what was about to happen but the look on his face indicated she had no choice so he slowly made her way to the bed and got in. She expected him to force himself on her and was surprised when he turned his back on her and went to sleep.

The next day he didn't speak to her and didn't visit her through the day. In bed that night he again turned his back to her and behaved the same the next day. He took her to the shower and stayed in the room as usual but said nothing to her. In bed that night he watched her undress as he had before and she went through the usual ritual of backing into bed.

She hoped that he would again turn his back on her as he had the last two nights but this night she felt him move close to her and she felt her body going rigid as he started to stroke her buttocks. He didn't speak and after a few moments he tried to turn her as he had before but she resisted and so he threw his arm around her and as usual put his hand on her breast but this time he started to caress her. He fell asleep like this but she struggled to sleep at all that night, she must get away..

It had been eight days since they had married when Omer told her that she was to be trusted to help around the camp. He took her over to the baker who set her to work and then she was given washing to do. She accepted her chores gratefully as she was bored stiff just sitting outside her new home. This became a daily event and she was also given the chore of making the evening meal for the camp.

The bedtime ritual continued and one night they had a repeat of the night he assaulted her but this time he slapped her face so hard she fell back and he continued to slap her body several times before saying angrily, 'Better men than me would have taken you by now and I feel shame every day that I am not like other men. You continue to insult me and I'm not sure I have any more patience.'

The next day she expected him not to speak to her but instead at breakfast he asked, 'Is it such a disgusting thought for you to lie with me?' She looked at him not sure how to answer and then she tried to use a gentle voice, 'Omer I never wanted to get married. I understood that your father was going to let me go. Mirac said you wanted to marry me. Is it true? Did you stop your father letting me go so you could marry me?''

'No other man would have you after you laid with Yusuf, he had not been softened by her tone.

She protested, 'Yusuf raped me, I didn't want him,' she stopped herself adding the word 'either'.

'And yet it happened,' Omer said, 'you laid with him and yet you cannot lie with your husband.'

'What are you saying?' she said, 'are you suggesting that I encouraged him in some way?'

'I do not know,' he said, 'all I know is that you gave yourself to my brother and yet you resist me, your husband.''

'I promise you I didn't 'give' myself to him, I didn't encourage him' she said.

'Do you know what the other men would say if they knew I hadn't laid with my wife?' he snapped at her, 'do you know what my father would say?'

'Is that all you care about, what the others would say?' she snapped back at him, 'what about me, what about what I want.'

She saw his face harden, 'Do not question me? You have already tried my patience.'

They sat in silence for a few moments and then he spoke to her in a cold voice, 'In a week our honeymoon period will be over. I will ask my father to agree for you to be taken to the women's camp where you will stay.'

She almost felt relieved as she wouldn't have to face this daily barrage until he said, 'My father spoke to me about you going there. He doesn't want you here but he allowed the final decision to be mine as in the women's camp you would need to be locked up all the time as he cannot spare men to guard you twenty four hour a day.'

'I don't want to be locked up again,' she said but he cut her words off. 'my father had all the locks in the other camp broken apart from one building which is similar to the one you spent your first days in and that is where you will be kept.'

'Omer, please I don't need to be imprisoned, I won't try to escape again,' she lied.

'And still you lie,' he said standing up, 'In four days you will be taken to the women's camp.'

Whilst she went through the motions of her chores that day her mind racing as she thought of nothing but escape she had no idea that Omer had no intention of sending her to the women's camp. His father had wanted to take her far away and release her as he felt she had brought bad luck to their family but Omer had wanted her for himself. His father had resisted but then he had said if that is what Omer wanted that it was fine.

They hadn't discussed Emine going to the women's camp as it was Omer's choice. Few of the other men were married but those who were didn't want their women with them but Omer chose to keep her here, partly because he was afraid she'd escape and partly because he wanted her close so he could control her and take her whenever he wanted. He had tried kindness and violence but neither seemed to be working so now he was using the threat of being imprisoned in the women's camp in the hope that he would eventually break her.

CHAPTER FORTY TWO

OLIVIA

Jack was totally devastated when Olivia left but he didn't know what to do about it. He didn't know where she had gone and didn't know where to start looking for her. He visited her work but her boss told him she had handed in her notice with immediate effect the day before and had not said where she was going. Her parents were dead and apart from Maggie she had no friends. He had been her life. He didn't know how to contact Maggie but doubted she would have gone to her anyway.

His world spiralled into despair and he walked around like a zombie. He missed Olivia so much, she was his best friend as well as his love and he mourned the loss of her. His mentor spoke to him about his condition and told him he must sort himself out or she would be forced to rethink his position in the department. Her harsh words seemed like a slap which brought him out of his despair and he began to accept that Olivia was right and that they wanted different things.

He continued at work another six months and didn't realise that he was on automatic pilot and his mentor once again spoke to him commenting that he seemed to have lost his passion. He didn't agree but noticed that she no longer chose him to join her in theatre.

He had been drinking but didn't realise how dependant he had become on alcohol to get him through the days and started to make mistakes at work which were unacceptable. One day his mentor took him on one side and told him to clean up his act. She told him that this was his last chance to prove himself worthy of a place on her team.

It hit him hard and was like a wake-up call as he examined his recent behaviour and realised what his life had become and he was disappointed in himself and desperately unhappy. What was he doing? What did he want from life? He awoke one night and sat bolt upright as it suddenly dawned on him what he actually wanted and that was to be with Olivia. His life was pointless without her in it. He was sure she had gone to Greece and he knew what he had to do. If it meant he had to go to study in Greece for a while in order to work there that's what he'd do. He could no longer function without her.

He had a mobile phone number for her but it was unobtainable as was Maggie's. He had tried it in the vague hoping that she might know where Olivia was. He handed in his notice and his mentor didn't try to dissuade him.

He travelled to Skopolos and started his search. The island is small and everyone knew what was going on on their small island but could find no trace of her. He visited the restaurant she had worked in and saw the owner who had been their landlord but he hadn't seen her. Positive that she would come here he took a room over the bakery opposite the ferry arrival point and spent hours watching ferries coming in but Olivia was never on any of them. He was at a loss as he didn't know what else to do. He then moved across to Skiathos and started studying Greek, regularly returning to the island of Skopolos but she was not to be found.

After six months his money started to run out and he had reluctantly had to give up swearing that he would return as often as he could until he found her. He travelled back to Norwich where he started working in a hospital where he had secured a position with the help of a very kind reference from his mentor in Newcastle and before he knew where the time had gone eight years had passed. Knowing that Olivia had studied there made him feel somehow closer to her. He had even had a relationship that lasted almost a year but his heart wasn't in it and how could it be when Olivia carried his heart with her wherever she was.

He worked closely with an older doctor, Marcus Reid, who one day suggested that they set up a private practice together but Jack wouldn't commit himself initially as he had still not given up on finding Olivia. He returned to Skopolos when he could but the visits had grown fewer over the years. Eventually he agreed to go into partnership with Marcus and soon found himself very busy in private practice.

The internet was growing and someone had told Jack about a site called 'Friends Reunited' and he searched for Olivia on there but he had no joy. He did however find Robbie Nixon, his old friend he had travelled with but with whom he had lost touch. They exchanged messages and talked about their travels. Robbie mentioned that he had kept in touch with Maggie for some time after their return but that she had stopped answering his letters. Jack felt a glimmer of hope as he asked for her address and Robbie gave him it telling him it was her mother's address.

Jack travelled to the address in Penarth and found Maggie's mother at home the first time he called. He explained that he had been a friend of Maggie's and her mother looked sad but after a few moments hesitation invited him in.

She made tea for them and then sat down opposite Jack, 'It's nice to meet Maggie's friends. How did you know her?'

'We met when she was backpacking after she finished university,' he answered and saw a shadow cross the woman's face.

'I don't know what happened when she was away but she had changed completely when she came back. Do you know what happened to her?' she asked.

Jack hesitated, 'We had a wonderful time but she was badly let down by a guy I knew.'

'It must have been more than that,' her mother said, 'she was so withdrawn when she came back, her character seemed to change completely.

'I'm not aware of anything else happening,' Jack lied.

'She was never the same again,' her mother said, 'she had a breakdown and spent some time in an,' she hesitated before saying the word, 'institution.'

Jack was shocked, 'I'm sorry,' he said.

'She was up and down after that,' she said, 'and then she went away, to visit her friend in Newcastle I think,' and Jack thought about when Maggie visited them.

'Yes,' he said, 'she came to stay with us.'

Maggie's mother looked at him a bit confused, 'She was away months but when she returned she sank back into depression and had another spell in hospital.' She sighed, 'when they released her she was on medication which made her like a zombie. She wasn't in a good place and then a few months later she took her own life.'

'Oh my God,' Jack said, 'I'm so sorry, I didn't know.'

Maggie's mother smiled weakly at him, 'I told all this to Olivia when she visited years ago, didn't she tell you?' then she hesitated before adding, 'I'm sorry for your loss too.'

Jack thought it odd that Jean would offer her condolences to him but didn't feel it appropriate to tell her he wasn't that close to Maggie however he was surprised about what she had said about Liv, 'Olivia was here?'

'Yes,' Maggie's mother said, 'Olivia, the friend who died.'

CHAPTER FORTY THREE

Stunned into silence by Maggie's mother's shocking words Jack stared at her without speaking for a moment and then in a choked voice said, 'Olivia isn't dead.'

'Oh,' she seemed surprised, 'that's what the paper said.'

Jack had so many questions that came incoherently tumbling out, 'What paper? How? Was she sure?' and loads more.

'It was three or four years ago,' Jean said, 'that earthquake that happened in Athens. Her photo was in the paper, I recognised her straight away. Didn't you see it?' she asked although he obviously hadn't.

Jack said he hadn't and she continued, 'It was on the news too, I'm surprised you didn't see it. When the earthquake happened she was reported missing and they had a photo of her. She looked just like she did when she came here. I followed the story and eventually they announced that she was dead.'

'How could I have missed it?' he asked himself and once again asked Jean if she was sure. 'She sat here, where you are now, about ten years ago, I know it was then because it wasn't long after we lost Maggie. I'd know her anywhere. She had come to see Maggie but of course she was gone by then.'

'Did she say where she was going from here?' Jack asked.

Jean looked at him quizzically, 'I don't think so, it was such a long time ago,' she sat thinking, 'No,' she said, 'I'm sure she said nothing about her plans but I assume she ended up in Greece.'

He couldn't and wouldn't believe what he had heard and as he walked to his car in a daze he shook his head. He was staying at a hotel in Cardiff overnight and when he checked in he asked if they had WiFi but it was a long shot as not many hotels had it at that time and this hotel didn't offer that facility. He asked if there was an internet café nearby and he was told that there was but that it would be closed now and he realised he'd have to wait until he got home to Norwich. He was tempted to set off straight away and not bother staying at the hotel but it was a long journey which he had already done today and he felt as if he had been put through a wringer.

He went to his room and tried to settle but it was impossible as his emotions were all over the place and he ended up going for a walk around the city centre. He saw nothing as he walked as all he could think about was Olivia and for the first time in a long time he found himself praying. He prayed that Jean was wrong and that he could find Olivia and that they could be together again for ever.

He didn't think he'd sleep that night but he managed a few hours although they were full of dreams of Olivia and he woke up in a sweat when he dreamt he could see her struggling under a street covered in rubble calling his name. His heart was pounding hard and he fought to get his nerves under control He looked at the clock, it was five in the morning and he knew he wouldn't sleep anymore so he rose, showered, checked out and started his drive home.

There was no traffic for the first two hours and he made good progress but it still took him almost five hours to get back to Norwich. All the way home his mind was full of Olivia and he could feel the frustration growing inside him. At one point as he waited in traffic he started to slam his hands into the steering wheel as he raged against what might be. She couldn't be dead, she just couldn't.

His outburst hadn't helped calm him at all and memories of her flooded in, he remembered the times they had spent travelling and the experiences they had shared, he could see her face clearly smiling at him and his heart constricted, he remembered her enthusiasm for life and then he felt the pain of her leaving again. He had seen her light fade whilst living in Newcastle and it was his fault. He had fooled himself that she had been okay with him following his career but how could she be? She had her ow dreams.

They had discussed it and agreed that she would shelve her dreams until he got where he wanted but they had been kidding themselves because they wanted to be together. He had no doubt that she had loved him but to put a free spirit like Olivia in a small flat in the middle of a city with no views to feed her soul, for her to work in an office, tied to a desk it had slowly killed her spirit. He had wanted to treat her but he didn't earn enough to take her places but then he thought about the times she had suggested that they got on a bus to the coast so they could just go for a walk and he had dismissed it because he was tired.

He had tormented himself for the past eight years about his part in Olivia's departure but it suddenly struck him that wealth and position weren't important to her, she had just wanted them not to waste their lives and enjoy what freedom they had. He had been a fool and now she may be gone for ever. He pushed the possibility out of his mind.

He remembered the very first time he had set eyes on her in that bar in Barcelona and how disappointed he had been when she disappeared. As their eyes met something passed between them and she had stolen his heart at that moment, he knew it then and he knew it now and he remembered how happy he had been when he saw her at the port. He was sure that she had known he loved her but he had never told her that he had loved her from the first moment he had seen her and he didn't know why he hadn't. He had scolded himself so often over the years for not looking after her love well enough and he had paid a high price.

He drove straight to his practice where they had WiFi installed and his receptionist was surprised to see him as he had booked time off. 'I'm not here,' he told her and she nodded understanding. She could see something was wrong and that there was an air of urgency to his manner.

He entered his office and locked the door, sitting down at his desk he switched on his PC and waited whilst it loaded. It always seemed to take an age but today it was definitely tormenting him with the time it was taking.

Eventually after all his icons had loaded he opened a search engine and searched for 'Athens earthquake'. Articles appeared about earthquakes in Greece and then he saw 1999 Athens Earthquake and he clicked on the link. It was an article about the quake and stated that it occurred on 7th September at 14:56:51 local time near Mount Parnitha in Greece with a moment magnitude of 6.0 and a maximum Mercalli intensity of IX (Violent). It went on to say that there was widespread structural damage mentioning several towns that had been affected. He scanned the details until he got to the bit that stated that 143 people had been killed but none of them were identified in this article.

He searched for an article on casualties and clicked on each one regarding this subject but the majority talked about the number with no identification of them.

He was getting frustrated as he searched and stopped for a moment trying to think of another way to find out what he needed to know. He had a thought and typed in 'Olivia Weber' but nothing came back that related to Liv. Unlike present days not everything could be found on the internet then and he struggled to think of another way to find the answer to his question.

He tried to search Newspaper Archives but after an hour he had still found nothing and he was totally stressed. He sat thinking about it and decided he would go the local newspaper and see if they had any archives on the subject. He thought that Maggie's mother had been wrong but until he had the proof he wouldn't rest.

He was loath to turn off his pc but in the end gave up and watched as the screen eventually went blank. He sat for a while in torment when he decided that he would try some more not prepared to give up.

He waited for his pc to load up again and this time it seemed to take even longer than the last time and as it loaded he thought of the type of questions he should ask to get the information he wanted.

'British woman missing after 1999 Athens earthquake,' he typed and within a moment various links appeared. He clicked on the first one and there were photos of people who were reported missing after the quake. Despite the search criteria they were not all British and he scrolled down the screen until he stopped in total shock. There staring back at him was a photo of Liv just as she had looked the last time he had seen her.

So she had been reported missing. He clicked on other links and her photo kept reappearing with headings such as 'Still Missing'. So she was missing and not dead he thought so she could still be alive but then he clicked on a link that dashed any hope he had as there was the photo of Liv with a statement that she had died in the rubble created by the earthquake.

An inhuman cry escaped his lips and within a moment there was a knocking at his door. The receptionist asked if he was okay and he shouted back that he was just before he totally broke down sobbing.

He lay in bed that night numb and as he drifted he suddenly sat up in bed with a thought, 'What was she doing in Athens? Who had reported her missing? She must have been identified, but if so who had identified her?'

CHAPTER FORTY FOUR

RACHEL

Stalios had been killed in a car accident when a delivery truck had smashed into his car. Catherine had told Rachel the shocking news in a monotone voice and the girl ran to her mother and hugged her crying but Catherine didn't respond as she sat like a statue.

Things didn't get better as Catherine fell deeper and deeper into depression and Rachel couldn't get through to her. She had a few days off school and tried to care for her mother who appeared to be locked in her own misery.

The funeral was three days after Stalios had died as was usual in Greece and Rachel guided her mother into the small Greek Orthodox Church where the ceremony was taking place and all eyes turned to look at them. After the initial staring nobody looked at them again and nobody spoke one word to them. It was as if they weren't there. Rachel was confused as Stalios had loved them and they had all been happy together but she didn't know that none of his family approved.

Rachel had listened to the words of the priest who referred to Stalios as a good man who had been a loving husband to his late wife Alexandra and he said that now they would be reunited once again. Rachel had been shocked as she hadn't known that Stalios had been married but when she thought about it he was quite a bit older than her mother so it shouldn't have surprised her. The priest mentioned his children, Salomao, Castor, Anastasia and Elina and Rachel wondered who they were. She looked to the front pews of the church and saw various people with their heads bowed crying and thought that some of them must be his children.

She was surprised to see they were all adults and she suddenly felt a pang of guilt as she realised that she hadn't known a lot about the man who had treated like his own daughter, the man who had shared her adventures and whom she had loved like a father.

She wanted to protest when she heard the priest say that Stalios had been lonely and spent the last few years alone pursuing his love of the arts. He hadn't been lonely or alone she wanted to shout, he had been with them and he loved them but she sat in silence.

Catherine didn't seem to hear any of the words and didn't notice people ignoring them and sat with her head down during the ceremony and allowed herself to be led outside and home again by her daughter as she was in a daze.

Rachel was worried as Catherine didn't cry, didn't speak or respond to anything she said to her. She wouldn't eat and Rachel had had to insist that she at least drank something. She made milkshakes so that she was getting something inside her and would sit watching her drink them, encouraging her until they had gone. Apart from that Rachel had no idea what to do and she had nobody to ask. Her school friends wouldn't know what to do and Catherine had few friends here because unlike back in England she had been totally content with Stalios as company and had not sought the company of others. Those friends she had made through her studio didn't come around and Rachel didn't know where to turn.

Rachel would leave her mother each morning as she left for school and would often return to find she hadn't moved. She would have to make her bathe and change and put her to bed at night and she despaired.

One day when she had arrived home from school she had been pleased to find her mother sitting on the verandah and saw that she had made herself a sandwich. She sat with her and talked about her day and saw a mild response when her mother nodded a few times.

There was a knock at the door and when Rachel opened it she saw one of the men she had seen at the funeral standing there.

She looked at him curiously and he stared back at her unsmiling, 'I am Salomao Karakostas ,' he said, 'Stalios was my father.' She invited him in pleased that he had come and hoping that he may make her mother feel better but that was not to be.

He explained that he and his siblings were claiming their father's villa and that Rachel and Catherine had to move out. Catherine said nothing but Rachel protested exaggerating that they had given up their home to travel here with Stalios but telling the truth when she added that they had been a family'.

'My father only had one family and that was my late mother, my siblings and myself,' he said in a cold voice.

'No,' she said, 'we were a family, he loved us and we loved him.'

'I'm sure you loved his money,' Salomao snapped.

'That's unfair,' Rachel said, 'we have our own money. He was like a father to me and my mother loved him very much, look at her, she's devastated at his loss.'

He snorted, 'You may have thought he was like a father to you but he was my actual father and as for your mother,' he looked at Catherine who didn't seem to hear what was being said, 'I don't doubt she had feelings for my father but I'm sure her greatest loss is the lifestyle he offered you both.'

'Please go,' Rachel said fighting back tears as she followed him to the door.

Salomao's parting words were, 'You have a week to move. If you're not gone we will have you forcibly removed.'

Rachel went back to where her mother was sitting and asked her what they should do not expecting her to answer but she said, 'He's right. We weren't married and we have no claim on this villa. We will have to move.'

Rachel's heart sank, she loved this home they shared and to have to leave it on top of losing Stalios broke her heart. Even though Catherine had acknowledged they had to leave she did nothing about it and it was left to the sixteen year old Rachel to find their new home.

She had no idea where to start and didn't know what they could afford but wandered around the town until she found a lettings agent. She found a cheap two bedroomed apartment on the outskirts of town which was gloomy and seemed so grim after the opulence of Stalios' villa. Catherine who had appeared to be improving slipped backwards after the news that they had to leave the home she had shared with Stalios.

She didn't seem to care where they lived after that and took no interest in the apartment and stopped going to her studio. Rachel continued to try to get through to her and slowly she saw a semblance of her mother returning but it was only a shadow of her former self.

She would sit in the apartment with the tv on but wouldn't be watching it, she no longer made any attempt with her appearance but was eating now which Rachel was happy about and even joined in conversations with her.

Rachel took her to the studio in the hope that it would spark something in her but Catherine had stood in the space looking blankly around as if she hadn't seen it before. Rachel pointed out the artwork and led her to a canvas she had started on before the tragedy but she just turned away from it. She couldn't get her mother to show any interest and started to take her for daily walks and slowly she returned to version of the old Catherine. The spark in her eye had been extinguished and she didn't laugh often but she started enjoying their walks and conversations. Rachel even hoped that she would soon return to her studio.

Six months after Stalios' death things changed

CHAPTER FORTY FIVE

Rachel had taken her mother for a walk by the harbour where they had sat and had cold drinks and as they walked back out of town to their dark apartment Rachel saw a man standing on the pavement outside the door to the building.

He looked at them as they approached, and asked her mother if she was Catherine who had known Stalios Karakostas. Catherine looked at him suspiciously not answering and Rachel looked from one to the other before answering, 'Yes she is. We lived with Stalios.'

He smiled at her, 'I am Dado Chalkias. I was Stalios' solicitor,' and then turning to the door he asked if they could go inside.

They all walked up the stairs in silence and Rachel let them into their apartment asking if she could get him anything but he said that was not necessary. He sat down opposite Catherine and opening the case he had been carrying took out some papers. He started to speak, 'Before Mr Karakostas passed away he came to see me and asked me to draw up a new will which included a provision for yourself and your daughter.'

Catherine and Rachel stared at him waiting for what more he had to say, 'He left you his villa and individual allowances for you both to enable you to live comfortably.'

'Wow,' Rachel said,' that's wonderful,' but Catherine didn't speak.

The solicitor looked at her and asked her if she understood what he had said and she nodded. He looked a little confused and Rachel said, 'Stalios' son made us leave the villa, he said it belonged to him and his siblings.'

The solicitor looked a little awkward, 'Mr Karakostas' children believed that was the case but they acted hastily'. He waited a moment and then sighed, 'I must be honest with you they have objected to these provisions in the strongest terms but there is nothing they can do, Mr Karakostas made sure of that in the way he had me write his will.'

'Thank you,' Rachel said and he smiled at her. He turned back to Catherine who was still sitting silently, 'On another matter, I believe you rent a studio in town?' he asked reading out the address from the document he was holding and when Catherine nodded he said, 'Mr Karakostas had instructed me to buy the building for you and the sale had gone through two days before he died. He wanted to give it to you as a gift.' He handed Catherine a document, 'These are the deeds to the building,' he said and then he handed her another together with some keys, 'and these are the deeds and keys to the villa.'

Catherine took the papers and stared at them and then looked back up at the solicitor. He asked her to sign some papers and she said, 'I don't want them'.

He was visibly shocked as was Rachel. He asked her why and she said that she didn't want them if she couldn't share them with Stalios. Rachel tried to talk her around but she seemed resilient and the solicitor explained that this was what Stalios had wanted. He said he thought she would be foolish not to accept the provisions and spent an hour advising her on her options. Eventually she agreed to think about it.

Rachel kept telling her every day that it was the right thing to do, that it was because Stalios loved her that he wanted her to have his home and money for them to live well. Catherine insisted that she didn't need his money and didn't want the villa as she would be surrounded by memories. Rachel insisted that they needed the money and pointed out how much better it would be to live in the villa rather than this dismal apartment. She reminded her of the views and the light airy rooms.

She felt that she was flogging a dead horse when three weeks after the solicitor's visit Catherine suddenly agreed with her. Rachel had no idea what had changed her mind and she didn't care she was just happy to be leaving the apartment.

That evening they walked to the villa and saw a car on the drive. Catherine unlocked the door and they walked into the home where they had been so happy. It didn't look any different and there didn't seem to be anybody about but then they heard the sound of voices drifting in from the verandah. Catherine marched across the living room and Rachel followed. As they stepped through the doors that led outside the voices stopped abruptly.

Salomao was there with three other adults whom Rachel recognised from the church and she wondered if they were Stalios' other children. None of them spoke but she was aware of her mother straightening her back and then she said in a cold but firm voice, 'Get out of our house.'

The four people stared at her and Salomao started to protest but Rachel could see that he knew he had no argument to make and they left and then Catherine broke down and cried for the first time since Stalios' death. She sobbed uncontrollably in Rachel's arms for almost an hour before she stopped. She spoke no words but got up and made her way through to the bedroom she had shared with the man she loved and when Rachel looked in on her later she was sleeping soundly.

Rachel was happy to be back in the villa but Catherine seemed restless and so very sad. She talked more to Rachel but there was no joy in her anymore and she didn't return to the studio which concerned Rachel.

They fell into a way of life that Rachel thought was good and she lived in hope that the spark would eventually return to her mother.

A few months after they had returned to the villa Rachel made her way home not knowing what was awaiting her. It was just a normal day and she was oblivious of the bombshell Catherine was about to drop.

She let herself into the villa and was surprised that her mother already had some food ready for them as they usually ate later in the evening. She started to eat and then her mother announced her that she was sending her back to England. Rachel was shell shocked and started to protest but Catherine was unmoving. Rachel begged her not to do it but no matter how much she pleaded and protested Catherine stood by her decision. She told her that she had already found her a sixth form college in Leeds, a family to live with and that she would send her allowance to her monthly.

Rachel was heartbroken when she left Greece but she settled into her new school and found the family she lived with nice enough. They included her in everything they did but Rachel didn't always want to join in and they didn't push her. They never asked questions about why she had moved from Greece and Rachel assumed they knew of her circumstances.

They lived in Roundhay a lovely part of Leeds near the park which was very large and Rachel found it her solace as she walked there and found peaceful places to sit and get lost in her thoughts. The people she lived with seemed to accept that she enjoyed her solitude and didn't intrude.

She received her allowance monthly but didn't hear from Catherine and worried about her so as soon as the first school holiday came around she travelled to Skiathos to see her.

She went to the villa but saw a car on the drive that she didn't recognise. Her mother must have bought it she thought but when she knocked on the door it was open by a woman she didn't know who told her that she and her family had bought it from Catherine the month before.

She was so upset as she loved the villa and as she walked away tears of disappointment in her eyes she justified Catherine's decision to sell their home telling herself that she knew her mother had struggled with the memories there. For the first time she understood how much her mother had loved Stalios, how much she must miss him and realised that her mother, the woman who had had so many lovers, had lost her soul mate when he died.

She would find her mother at her studio she was sure and as she turned down the cobbled street she was disappointed to see the studio was closed. She despaired as she approached it wondering what to do if her mother wasn't inside and then she thought what if her mother was still suffering so much she hadn't come back at all. Her despair was replaced by horror when she looked through the window and saw the space was totally empty.

She went into the other shops on the street in a panic but nobody could tell her where Catherine was. They told her that she had closed the studio over a month ago but didn't say where she was going. She tried everything she could think of to no avail.

Her mother had gone and she didn't know how to get hold of her.

CHAPTER FORTY SIX

EMINE

She thought of nothing but escape and as she laid in bed that night next to Omer he turned his back on her and she thinking he had given up on her tried to plan but it was hopeless. Omer didn't speak to her over the next few days and hardly looked at her and when he did it was with a coldness that cut to her very soul. She didn't want this marriage and knew that it wasn't legal anyway but she knew that if he sent her to the women's camp to be locked in a dark cell, her chances of escape would be even less than here.

She would try to speak to him through the day but he would walk away and at night he just wouldn't answer her. Once in bed she had turned over pleading to his back for him to speak to her but when he turned around to face her she had quickly turned away and no words were spoken.

She had come to the realisation that the only way to stop him sending her away was to succumb to his advances but the thought made her insides shrivel. Three days before she was to leave she was surprised when he put an arm around her and as he had before placed his hand on her breast. Her mind was racing and suddenly she came to a decision she hated herself for and forced herself to turn around to face him and even though she couldn't see his face she could sense his surprise. She moved towards him and after a moment's hesitation he started to kiss her but she couldn't stop herself from cringing inside and remained stiff as he caressed her but he didn't seem to notice as he continued to touch her body and when he pushed her on her back and climbed on top of her she gritted her teeth in the dark.

In the morning he sat outside with breakfast for her and she smiled at him but he didn't return her smile. 'Sit,' he said. 'We will eat together until you go to the women's camp.'

'But I thought,' she said but he cut her off, 'You thought that if you laid with me I'd let you stay here.' She didn't answer as she was unsure of the right words to say. If she answered yes then she was admitting she had only slept with him so she could stay and if she protested then he would see she was lying.

'You don't have an answer,' his words were accusing as he tormented her, 'you who have so much to say. Do you not think I could tell you didn't want me? I could lie with any woman of my choice in the women's camp and they would show me more warmth than you. You are my wife and yet you refuse to give yourself to me.'

She protested, 'It was our first time,' she said, 'I was nervous.'

'And you lie again,' he said, 'did you show more passion when you laid with my brother? Was he more of a man for you?'

'He was an animal,' she said angrily but she could see him shutting down so continued, 'Look Omer it's true I don't want to be here and I don't want to be married.'

'At last you speak the truth,' he said, 'You are married to me but I can grant your desire not to be here. You will go to the women's camp in two days.'

'Please give me a chance Omer, please,' she pleaded, 'you are my only friend.' He turned away so she wouldn't see the cruel smile on his face.

She spent the day doing her chores and Omer kept to his word eating meals with her. He took her to the shower but she couldn't bring herself to turn around and wash before him and when they left the shower room he said, 'We have lain together and yet you still hide your body from me.'

'I didn't think you wanted me now,' she said playing for time and he answered non-committedly, 'You are my wife, it is my right.'

That night he didn't blow out the candles after she had backed under the sheets. She lay as she usually did with her back to him and then she felt him stoking her buttocks. She turned around to face him and he kissed her deeply and then pushed her on her back but instead of climbing on top of her he pulled the covers from her exposing her to the dim light. She lay still and closed her eyes so she couldn't witness him exploring her body with his eyes and then his hands but she knew she had to appear to want him and taking a deep breath she made herself respond to his touch and gave herself to him in the way he wanted with a passion she didn't feel.

The next morning he rose and dressed but waited whilst she rose before leaving the room but she couldn't help but turn away from his gaze.

When she emerged from the bedroom he asked her, 'Was last night an act?'

'No,' she lied convincingly, 'I am just shy of you.'

'I am your husband,' he said and however many times he said those words she wouldn't accept it, 'Give me time,' she said.

'Time is short,' he said, 'tomorrow you leave for the women's camp.'

'Please,' she ran to him and knelt next to his chair, 'please let me stay with you.'

He looked at her with quizzical eyes, 'It doesn't suit you to beg.' She smarted at his words, 'We will spend your last day here together.'

After breakfast he took her outside and suggested they went for a walk which surprised her greatly. He laughed lightly at the look on her face enjoying the power he over her feelings and taking her hand he walked her out of camp but in a different direction to the one she had taken when she had escaped. They walked like two lovers hand in hand not speaking for some time. She thought about running but where would she go? She could see a wooded area ahead and Omer led her in that direction.

He walked her into the woods holding her hand and after a short way she was surprised to see a small patch of greenery as the area was so dry and then she saw a small, shallow pond with a trickle of water coming into it. He sat down on a tree stump and pulled her down next to him. The sun broke through the trees and had she been with anyone of her choice this would have been a romantic moment.

'This is such a peaceful place,' he said, 'this is where I come to think.'

'What do you think about?' she asked trying to appear interested.

'I think about how my life is and I think about the cause,' he answered.

'Is that what you wanted your life to be?' she asked.

'This is what I was born into,' he said, 'I must do as my father wishes.'

'But,' she started to question him however the look on his face stopped her. They sat in silence for a few moments, 'Have you killed anyone for the cause?' she asked.

'Of course,' he answered solemnly, 'Did you imagine me incapable to taking life?' but before she could speak he continued, 'life has to be spent for the cause. We must be taken seriously.' He looked at her his face serious and then he smiled at her, 'enough talk of war.'

They sat like friends talking and she was lulled into a false sense of security when she decided to broach a subject that had been on her mind for a long time, 'Omer do you think you could get my passport from your father?'

His head spun around, 'Why do you need your passport, you're not going anywhere.'

She could see the suspicion in his eyes, 'No, of course,' she spluttered, 'but as we're married you should have it.'

He was not smiling when he took hold of her face in one hand squeezing her cheeks and hurting her, 'Don't take me for a fool,' he said in an icy voice. She pleaded with him with her eyes as she couldn't speak as he still had hold of her face, 'we are married and yet you still think of leaving.' She shook her head, her eye full of fear and he let her go and her although her face hurt she didn't turn away from him. 'If I can't trust you our marriage means nothing. You mean nothing.' His face remained stern but the anger left him, 'Last night I thought you had accepted our union. Were you lying when you gave yourself to me?' he hesitated, 'am I mad to believe in you?'

'No,' the word came out in strangled cry. She didn't want him to turn against her again, she knew that if she went to the women's camp she would never escape but she didn't know what to say afraid that she may choose the wrong words so she just repeated the word, 'No. I just thought it would be something you would want.'

He studied her face as if searching for the truth and then she saw his face soften, 'I also think of this when I am here,' he said leaning forward and kissing her hard. He continued to kiss her and started to run his hands over her body and she forced herself to kiss him back and then he stopped as suddenly as he had started, 'Look how you tempt me,' he said.

They got up and walked some more before returning to camp where they ate some bread and then he helped her make the evening meal saying they would eat early as the women were coming to the camp that night.

. They spent the afternoon talking and when he took her for a shower she thought she wouldn't turn from him but she couldn't help herself. She couldn't bear to see him staring at her body. When she stepped out of the shower and started to dry herself, he turned around but she couldn't resist covering herself with the towel.

'And still you are shy of me,' he said but he was smiling. She smiled back and said his name in appreciation but he took this as an invitation and moving forward he took her in his arms and started to kiss her. She tried to kiss him back aware that she didn't have long to change his mind about sending her away.

He stood back and started to strip off his gown. She was horrified, 'Not in here, please,' she said and she saw the anger so added, 'Yusuf.' He looked as if she had slapped him and turning away he picked up her gown and almost threw it at her. She tried to talk to him but he as usual when he was annoyed with her he ignored her. She preferred that to his anger when he hurt her but she needed him on side.

He ate with his father that night whilst she sat with the women and she saw Berat leering over at her as usual. The men started calling over to the women and she saw Omer beckon her over. She went to stand by where he sat and Berat asked her, 'Will you be returning with the women in the morning?' she looked towards Omer who didn't answer and Berat laughed.

Omer didn't ask her to sit and she stood patiently behind him whilst the men continued to chat. Eventually he stood up and taking her hand led her without speaking to their bedroom as soon as the men started grabbing women.

Tonight was her last chance to dissuade him from sending her to the women's camp and so she didn't hide herself from him as she undressed and she put a fixed smile on her face. She climbed into bed and this time didn't wait for him to touch her before she went to him enthusiastically.

When she woke up Omer was not in bed and when she emerged from the bedroom she saw him sitting at the table with breakfast.

'Sit,' he said and she sat down looking at him not knowing what to expect. 'Last night was pleasurable but you must wait for me to initiate intimacy,' his voice was scolding.

'I wanted you so much,' she said not knowing what else to say but even to her ears her words sounded desperate.

He looked at her and she could see he wasn't sure she was telling the truth, 'Maybe,' he said, 'but it is a husband's place to lead in the bedroom.'

Her hopes were dashed and her heart sank as she realised that what she had thought was a good move had angered him, 'Am I leaving with the other women?' she asked.

'I have thought long and hard about it and the way you behave makes me think it's the right thing for you to go. My father wants you to be with the women,' he lied.

'Omer, please,' she pleaded, 'I will behave, I promise. I'll do whatever you want.' She hated the whining in her voice and the words she was saying but she was desperate.

He looked at her as if he was considering her words and then said, 'You are my wife and your place is here with me.' She jumped out of her chair as he continued, 'you will obey me or I will reconsider my decision.'

Before he could say anymore she threw herself at him, hugging him and thanking him with genuine gratitude. He pushed her away and she fell to the floor, 'Please act appropriately,' he said but inside he was jubilant as he mistakenly thought he now had total control of her.

As he looked at her fearful face as she cowered on the floor he felt the power he had over her and he felt his desire growing. He stood up, pulled her up from the floor and led her back into the bedroom.

CHAPTER FORTY SEVEN

Life continued with Omer in the pattern that had started during their 'honeymoon' period. She would help around camp through the day, they would eat together and at night when he let her know he wanted her she would go through the motions.

If she challenged him about anything he would threaten her with the women's camp and slap her. The slapping happened often now and she began to understand that he enjoyed punishing her as she noticed that his desire for her was heightened after he had hurt her. He now drank with the men and would send her to their home and come back smelling of alcohol and would throw himself on her.

One night when the women came he called her over to the table where he was with his father and she stood there for some time before he looked at her with a smirk on his face, 'Go to our bedroom and wait for me there.' The men laughed raucously and Berat slapped him on his back. She was humiliated and stood her ground glaring at him. Anger flashed across his face, 'What are you waiting for?' he demanded, 'go and prepare yourself for your husband.'

She could hear the anger in his voice and saw Berat staring at her so she thought better of challenging him any further and turning on her heal she almost ran to their home.

She was in bed when he returned and had blown out all the candles but she she heard him stumbling around the room as he relit them. His face was contorted with pure rage as he took off his clothes and then went to the drawers and fumbling about in one of them he pulled out a leather strap. She felt sick and fear coursed through her body as he advanced on her. He tore the bed sheet off her naked body and started to whip her.

Each stroke stung and tears streamed down her cheeks as she tried to make herself into a ball but it didn't stop the pain as he continued, 'You dare shame me in front of my father, in front of the men?' He stopped striking her and she felt relief although her body was in pain. ,'Look at me,' he said and when she didn't, she felt another lash of the leather strap, 'Look at me,' he screamed at her.

She sat up and looked at him standing naked before her and she could see how aroused he was. Her face filled with hatred and she heard his usual words, 'I am your husband. You will show me respect.' Then he was on top of her taking her so roughly she cried out in pain but this only made him more excited.

He didn't speak to her for over a week but that didn't stop him climbing on top of her every night and she would be grateful when it was over and he turned his back on her.

The beating had been so severe the welts on her body were still raised a week later when he entered their bedroom just as she was undressing and he looked at them and she saw his face soften. He left the room and returned with some massage oil and started to gently rub her wounds without speaking and that night he was more considerate with her.

This became the pattern for their life, most of the time he would be gentle with her in bed but at least once a week he would find a reason to be angry with her and slap her but she knew it was because it turned him on. He hadn't hit her with the leather strap again but it was a threat he hung over her head. She accepted that the sex was something she had to bear but on his part Omer insisted on taking her every night as he felt it was the only time he had complete control over her.

They had been married almost a year and she hadn't yet found a way to get away as Omer rarely took his eye off her. She had noticed that there were a lot of meetings going on in Berat's building. She assumed they were planning an attack but when she broached the subject with Omer he wouldn't discuss it with her telling her to remember her place. He enjoyed talking down to her but had noticed that she wasn't as feisty as she used to be. He liked the feeling of control over her but also enjoyed the odd spark he saw in her as it gave him the excuse to punish her because what followed gave him the greatest pleasure of all.

One day after a meeting she saw the men running around and Omer came over to her quickly, 'Get our things together, we're leaving.'

'Where are we going?' she asked.

'Don't question me, do as I say,' he said but he didn't hit her as he usually did when he thought she was overstepping the mark, 'hurry,' he snapped.

She could see men coming out of buildings carrying bags and she ran inside. She knew there was a battered suitcase in the hanging space and she started to stuff it with their clothes and possessions. The bedroom door was open and she saw Omer in the living room filling a large holdall with pots, pans and anything else he could fit in it before calling to her to come quickly.

She dragged the case from the bedroom and when he saw her struggling he took it from her and ushered her out, 'Please Omer what's happening?'

He looked at her as if he wasn't going to answer but then said, 'We have to leave the village, our location has been discovered.'

'Discovered?' she said, 'won't we come back here?' He said that they wouldn't and she stopped in her tracks, 'your father still has my passport. We can't leave without it. Ask your father.'

'My father has gone and the militia are on the way to arrest us and who knows what else and all you can think about is your passport,' he shouted at her.

'Please Omer,' she begged, 'it's important. Let me go look in his house.'

He slapped her hard across the face and putting his fist in her face he said, '.If you don't move now I will leave you here bleeding for the militia to find you and if you think the men here are animals with women they are nothing compared to the men who are coming.' She knew what he was saying was the truth and after a moment's hesitation she reluctantly stepped forward and he pushed her towards one of the waiting trucks where he threw their bags and helped her to climb into the back.

Some other men joined them and when all the trucks were full they set off. They drove for about an hour before one of the trucks broke away from the convoy and soon after they stopped in a village where some of the men climbed out of the trucks. They stopped in another two villages and more trucks left the convoy and had driven for about another hour before their truck stopped on a wide road and Omer stood and threw their bags onto the road. He helped Emine down and the trucks drove away. In front of them was open ground which went on for as far as the eye could see and when she turned around she saw a stone wall edging a dry field and sitting at the far end of the field in front of a small wood stood a house.

There was a gap in the wall and Omer dragged their bags through it and told her to follow him and they made their way across the field to the house. Outside there was a table and chairs and nearby there was a wood burning oven like the baker had used in camp with a huge pile of chopped wood standing by it. She could see a well and a small outbuilding just behind the house and on entering the building she saw that it looked like someone lived here, there was a sofa, a double mattress on the floor and a table set for a meal but on closer inspection she saw that the food was covered in flies and was rotting. Her stomach turned as she looked around and thought it looked like the owners had left in a hurry.

'Whose house is this?' she asked and he answered that it was theirs. She asked whose house it had been and he answered the same and she could tell from his face that she shouldn't ask anything else and in that moment she knew that he was fully aware of what had happened to the people who had lived here and she was sure that it wasn't a good thing.

He told her to unpack and clean the house and she started by dragging the case she had packed to the bedroom which was similar to what theirs had been in camp with a double mattress, hanging space and a set of drawers but when she went to the drawers they had the personal belongings of the previous occupants in them. She removed everything and replaced it with their own things.

She couldn't help but wonder what had happened to them but knew better than to ask Omer again. She hoped they were okay especially when she found children's clothes in one of the drawers. This explained the other mattress in the living area she thought. The children's clothes were not the traditional Turkish robes that made up most of the garments in the other drawer for the parents but dresses for a girl of about eight years old and vests, trousers and shirts of a young teenage boy. Looking at them she thought some of these boy's clothes would probably fit her not that she could imagine when she would need them unless she managed to escape and perhaps that was a possibility now they weren't in camp.

There were two pairs of jeans, one looked bigger than the other and she tried the smaller pair on first, trying to pull them on under her robe but they wouldn't go over her thighs so she tried on the second pair which she got on but couldn't fasten. She put them to one side thinking that she could cut some rope to use as a belt which would hold them up if she could find something to cover the open zip and buton. She slipped off her robe and tried on a vest which fitted snugly and then tried a shirt on but it was too tight. She noticed there was an adult man's checked shirt in the pile of clothes which she tried on. It was big on her but would cover the top of the jeans and she put it with the jeans and vest in their empty suitcase which she took out to store in the cupboard she had seen in the living room.

She asked Omer to help her carry the mattress from the living room into the bedroom as she thought they could put them on top of each other to make the bed more comfortable. He looked at her in a disinterested way but said he would come in shortly. She made her way back into the living room and unzipped the large holdall Omer had packed. She removed the pots and pans and saw their bedsheets which she pulled out. Something fell on the floor and she saw it was the leather strap he had beaten her with.

She bent down to pick it up and heard the door opening and knew that Omer was coming in. She quickly picked it up and threw it back in the bag, 'What are you doing in that bag?' he sounded angry.

'I'm unpacking,' she said but he pushed her out of the way picked up the bag and told her to leave it alone. She thought he hadn't wanted her to find the strap and was glad she'd put it back for now as she felt sure he would check. He turned back and half carried, half dragged the mattress into the bedroom where he threw it on top of the other one that she had stripped of bedding.

She followed him in carrying the bedding and he asked what the pile of clothes was. She explained that she had removed them from the drawers and he told her to fold them as they could sell them at market and then he left the room. She made the bed and folded the clothes and put them in a pile in the corner of the living room. She thought about what he had said about selling the clothes and wondered if this meant they were going to leave the house at some point.

Then she went to investigate the outhouse and found it was a washroom with a large stone sink where she washed with water from the well and as she returned to the house she saw Omer coming out of the bedroom and he looked a little furtive and she immediately thought he had been hiding the strap. Later when she went to bed before him she quietly searched quickly for it and found it pushed to the back of the second drawer she looked in. She had been right she thought and taking it out she looked around looking for somewhere to hide it. She settled on pushing it under the bottom mattress and that night they lay on top of it on a different mattress but in their sheets and she was relieved that Omer didn't come near her.

The next day two men from the camp arrived with food for them and sat with Omer talking for a while before leaving. She unpacked the food and took some bread out for her and Omer to eat. They hadn't eaten for over twenty four hours and sat in silence sharing the bread. She could see Omer was preoccupied but didn't care enough to ask him what was on his mind.

This went on for days with Omer hardly speaking to her and the men returning every two days with food for them. One night when they were eating she asked, 'Are we staying here?'

He looked at her as if he had forgotten she was there, 'Until it's safe for us all to be together again,' he answered, 'and that might be a long time. Do you think you can be happy here Emine with me?' She lied telling him she could and he smiled.

She had an idea and taking advantage of his softer mood she asked him if he could ask the men to bring flour and yeast so she could make bread in the oven like the baker had in camp.

The next time the men came it was late in the day and they sat outside drinking with Omer and she was worried that when they left he would force himself on her as he had before when he was drunk. He hadn't touched her since they had arrived and that suited her but as she lay in bed that night she held her breath as she heard Omer stumble in an was happy when he just fell on the bed and slept.

A couple of days later the men returned with her ingredients and excitedly she lit the oven and whilst it got hot she mixed the bread as she had with the baker many times before and covering the bowl left it outside to prove. She had seen the baker make different breads although it was usually flat breads but that night they dined on a fresh crusty loaf.

Omer watched her all the time and when they had finished eating he told her he had a present for her and produced shower gel and shampoo telling her he had filled the sink for her and she thanked him and ran to wash. When she emerged from the washroom she felt clean and fresh and Omer passed her smiling as he went in to wash.

That night as he lay in bed watching her undress she saw the look in his eyes and resigned herself to what was to come.

CHAPTER FORTY EIGHT

OLIVIA

When Olivia had left Maggie's mother's house she hadn't had a clear plan of what to do next but she was desperate to see Jack. She felt so guilty about Maggie and shouldered the blame for what she had done and she needed him to talk to and to comfort her. She loved him so much and realised how lucky she was to have him in her life. She was being selfish wanting to be free, he loved her and she should be satisfied with that.

She decided to spend some time in Cardiff so she could get her thoughts in order before returning and after booking into a hotel she wandered around the streets everyday not understanding why she didn't hurry back to Newcastle and Jack. She had made her decision but something was stopping her going back straight away and she thought it was the freedom she felt. She had escaped the humdrum everyday life they had in Newcastle and the only thing making it bearable was Jack and the love they shared. He texted her and rang her but she ignored his calls although she desperately wanted to talk to him she knew that if she did he would want her to go back immediately. She wasn't ready and thought he deserved better than her half-hearted agreement to return. She was wracked with guilt over Maggie and wasn't sure she deserved the happiness she could have with Jack.

After a week she couldn't wait any longer to see him and decided she would ring him that night and return the next day but as she took her final walk around Cardiff she came upon a travel agents advertising holidays to Greece. The window was full of photos of the islands she loved so much and as she stood staring the resolve she had made to return to Jack melted and she made a decision. She walked into the travel agents and bought a flight to Athens in two days' time. She was going to visit the islands she had planned to visit before Maggie had lost the baby and they had stayed in Skopelos.

She called into WH Smith's and bought a guide and that night pawing over the book reading about Santorini, Mykonos, Paraos, Naxos and more, her excitement grew as she planned to pick up where she had left off in Greece but this time she would do it alone. She considered ringing Jack to tell him but couldn't bear to hear the rejection in his voice as it would break her heart and it might make her change her mind again.

She arrived in Athens and made her way to the ferry port where she travelled to Santorini where the houses are all painted white and the streets are cobbled and steep. She found work quickly there and absorbed herself in the culture trying to put Maggie and Jack to the back of her mind.

She stayed there six months before moving on to Mykonos where she spent another six months. Over time she managed to come to terms with what had happened to Maggie although she didn't free herself of total guilt she learnt to accept that her friend had been troubled and although she had contributed to her anguish she wasn't totally to blame.

Jack was a different prospect as she couldn't forget him and many times was tempted to call him. She would pick up the phone thinking what she would say but then would wonder how she could ever explain away the hurt she had caused him. As the years went by she realised that she had left it too late to contact him and thought that he would probably now be happy in another relationship and perhaps even married. When she imagined this her heart would constrict but she had made her choice and it was only right she let him get on with his life.

She spent the next three years living and working on the Cyclades islands and although she loved her life she always felt that something was missing. She had a few relationships but nothing worked as none of them were Jack and she thought that she would always be alone.

She decided to travel north to the Skiathos area where she would revisit Skopelos in order to finally banish the mixed feelings she had about the events that had occurred there but as soon as she stepped on the island she felt at home.

She spent a few weeks there reliving the memories of happier times and she realised without a doubt that he place was with Jack. She had matured and although the wander lust would never leave her she came to the conclusion that none of it was worth anything without Jack. She realised that he may have moved on but she had to take the risk as she had to give their love a chance, she had to find out.

She had one more place she wanted to visit before leaving and happily made plans to leave for Newcastle in three weeks' time however she would regret the next decision she made for the rest of her life.

She had wanted to visit Turkey as she had never been and as she was so close she thought she'd do it now. She didn't want to spend a long time there but rather just get a flavour of it so she planned to take a ferry and then return on a ferry to Athens where she could fly home to see Jack.

She didn't like Turkey very much because although she found the people very friendly she found the men a bit too familiar especially with a young woman travelling alone. She decided to return to Greece earlier than planned and immediately started to feel nervous about facing Jack but then the unthinkable happened.

As she sat on the ferry going to Kos she tried to sort out her thoughts trying to make sense of what had happened when she had walked into a nightmare.

She had hurried down the paved streets of Bodrum making her way to the ferry port when she stepped into a small alley. She played out the scene in her mind reliving the experience. She saw the man's lifeless body lying on the ground and then her mind skipped back a few reels seeing the scene playing out before her. She saw him attacking her and the pure hatred on his face and he cursed at her, he knocked her off her feet and then she saw him on top of her a knife raised above his head ready to take her life. They struggled and he dropped it and then she saw her trying to get away but as he lunged at her trying to stop her she had stabbed him. He had fallen on her and he had pushed him off and that was when their eyes had met and she found herself staring into the woman's eyes full of fear and anguish and she froze. The whole event had only taken seconds and yet it would affect the rest of her life. She was unsure what to do and then it was as if they both came out of the daze and the reality of the horror started to sink in.

She started to run trying to put distance between herself and the man lying in the alley. She was terrified at the thought of facing the Turkish police as she was sure they would never believe her nor understand.

She felt like a fugitive as she boarded the waiting ferry wanting it to set off quickly wishing to get away from Turkey as soon as possible. She had spent the time praying that they would land in Kos soon and that she could put the picture in her mind behind her.

When she went to disembark she stopped in her tracks as she came face to face with the woman from the alley. They stood for a moment staring at each other and then something passed between them bringing them clarity as they recognised understanding in the other's eyes and they smiled weakly at each other knowing that they didn't pose a danger to each other.

.

CHAPTER FORTY NINE

After Jack learned of Olivia's death he wasted no time in travelling to Athens to find out who had identified Olivia as he couldn't accept that she was dead. He wasn't sure where to start but arrived late and checked into a hotel where he couldn't eat and struggled to sleep. In the morning he asked where the British Embassy was as he thought that that might be a good place to begin.

He spoke to a guard at the entrance gate telling him that he wanted to speak to someone about someone he had lost in the 1999 earthquake and the man went to a booth and Jack could see him on the phone. The guard came back and told him that someone could speak to him in three days' time if he wanted to make an appointment. He was very frustrated but however much he pleaded his case the guard gave him no choice and so he made an appointment for ten o'clock in the morning in three days' time.

He spent the rest of the day kicking his heals wandering around but he couldn't concentrate on anything. Then he had the idea of calling on the police because surely they would be able to help. He returned to the hotel and asked for directions and then made his way to the police station.

His Greek was limited and he couldn't make himself understood but one of the policemen signalled for him to sit in the waiting area where he sat for nearly two hours before a man dressed in uniform stood in front of him asking in English if he could help him.

He told the policeman that he wanted to know who had identified the body of a British woman supposedly killed in the earthquake. The policeman told him that he wasn't sure that they would have that information but told him that he would look in the files and if he returned the next day he would tell him what he had discovered.

When he left the police station Jack saw that night was drawing in and made his way to a small restaurant where he ate without tasting the food he put in his mouth. He sat for a while lost in thought before a waiter approached him asking if there was anything else he could get him. Jack jumped as he had been so lost in his own thoughts but thanked him, paid the bill and made his way back to the hotel.

He slept fitfully and was back bright and early at the police station where he asked for the policeman he had seen the night before only to be told he wasn't in until the afternoon and once again he felt the frustration that was facing him at every turn.

Later in the afternoon he returned to the police station where he didn't have to wait long before the policeman he had come to see appeared. He sat next to him holding a piece of paper in his hand.

'I have found the list of those who were reported missing and the name Olivia Weber,' he said looking at the paper, 'was on the list for those missing in Ano Liossia. I have searched and there is no record of her being identified and as far as our records are concerned she is still missing.'

'But I was told that she had been identified, 'Jack said but deep down he felt hopeful.

'That may be the case,' the policeman said, 'but we don't have that information. As she was British I suggest that you visit the embassy. They may have more information for you.'

'But wouldn't you have the information if she was dead,' Jack asked grasping at straws.

'That is not the case,' the policeman answered.

'Where is Ano Liossia?' Jack asked and the policeman told him it was a village in the district of Athens and Jack asked how he could get there.

The policeman gave him directions but told him that there was nowhere there he could get further information and then said, ''I cannot help you further.'

Jack hung back not wanting to leave somehow hoping that the man would suddenly produce evidence that Olivia was alive but the man stood up to move away, 'Good luck,' he said.

He didn't care what the policeman had said he would go to Ano Liossia, 'but what then?' he asked himself. He decided to wait and spent the rest of his time wandering around Athens not that he remembered anything he saw until he could visit the embassy.

He sat in his room thinking about what he was doing, he was trying to find out who identified Olivia and it suddenly struck him that if he was successful it would mean that all hope was gone and that she was dead.

The day arrived for his appointment at the embassy and he felt anxious as he made his way there. He was escorted through the gates and shown into an ante room where he was told to wait. He didn't wait long before a man walked into the room, 'Hello,' he said, 'my name is Miles Stewart, how can I help?'

Jack introduced himself and told him what he wanted. The man smiled at him, 'If you leave me your name and address I will forward any information we have,' Miles Stewart said, 'it might take a week or so.'

'No,' Jack slammed his hand on the table he was sat at displaying all the frustration he had felt building 'I have spent years looking for the only woman I have ever loved only to be told she perished in the earthquake. I don't believe it but it is tearing me apart. I must know for sure, don't you understand.'

Miles looked a bit shocked and didn't speak so Jack continued, 'You must have files on your computers with the information.'

Miles sat for a moment staring at the man sat before him and he could see how upset he was, 'Wait here,' he said, 'I will see what I can find out'.

He returned half an hour later carrying papers, 'I have found out what you need to know,' he said. 'Olivia Weber was reported missing in Ano Liossia.'

'Who reported her missing?' Jack enquired.

'I believe it was her mother,' he answered.

Jack sat stunned before saying, 'That's impossible, her mother's dead.'

'Well I don't know about that,' Miles said, 'but according to our records it was her mother who reported her missing but it wasn't her who identified the body. That was done by a friend of Olivia's mother so perhaps the information was recorded incorrectly.'

'I don't understand,' Jack said and then asked who it was who identified Olivia.

Mile gave him the name of a man called James Ridley and an address for him in Ano Liossia.

He left the embassy and jumped in a taxi giving the driver the address of James Ridley and they set off driving out of the city. Jack left confused, if Olivia's mother was still alive then why had she told him she was dead? He didn't understand why she would lie to him and was confused as he thought he had known everything there was to know about Olivia.

The driver pulled up outside a bar fifteen minutes later and Jack got out and entered the building where he saw a few locals sat drinking. He walked towards the bar where a large man with long straggly hair and stubble on his face stood. Jack guessed he was about fifty years old as he gave him a friendly smile, 'Well I think I can recognise a fellow Brit,' the man behind the bar said in an accent that suggested he was from around Liverpool.

Jack asked him if he was James Ridley and the man answered, 'That's me, welcome to my humble abode, what can I get you?

Jack launched straight into why he was there, his words tumbling out and making little sense.

James studied him and then said, 'Sit down. They call me Jimmy by the way. What can I get you to drink?'

Jack said he didn't want anything but Jimmy insisted and so he ordered a beer and waited for answers. Jimmy put the drink down on the bar in front of him, 'How do you know Olivia?' he asked and Jack explained their relationship and then asked the bar owner the same question.

'I'm a friend of her mother's,' Jimmy said, 'Olivia talked about you'.

Jack didn't ask what she had said about him partly because he wasn't sure he wanted to know but mainly because he had more pressing questions but something Jimmy had said struck him and he said, 'You say you are a friend of Liv's mother?' and Jimmy nodded so Jack added, 'I thought Olivia's mother was dead.'

Jimmy looked awkward, 'It's a spiritual thing man,' he said, 'to me she's still here,' he tapped his heart but Jack didn't really understand. Jimmy continued, 'she left us years ago now and it was very hard on Olivia as she'd already lost her father. She rarely talked about either of them because it caused too much pain. I'm surprised she told you.'

Jack nodded, she hadn't been lying to him he thought and then asked Jimmy what had happened to Olivia. The bar owner looked grave, 'She'd been doing her thing travelling around the islands,' Jack smiled as he knew that was something she loved. Jimmy continued, 'She was staying here with me when it happened,' he looked thoughtful for a moment before continuing, 'it was mayhem when the quake hit, complete mayhem. Olivia was out that day and when she didn't return at first I thought she was probably helping, you know what she was like.'

Jack nodded and after a moment Jimmy continued, 'But when she didn't return that night 'I was naturally worried and thought she had been injured. I went to the hospital but she wasn't there so I reported her missing.'

'The man at the embassy said it was her mother who reported it,' Jack said.

'Don't understand that,' Jimmy said, 'I told them that I was a friend of her mother's when I reported her missing. They must have written it down wrong.'

That was similar to what Miles at the embassy had said so Jack nodded understanding now and Jimmy continued, 'They found her after a couple of days but it was a week before they told me.' He looked lost in thought.

'Are you sure it was her?' Jack asked sounding desperate.

'Jack, I don't know what to say, I'm one hundred percent sure. I'm sorry man.,' Jimmy answered.

Jack was loath to leave Athens but there was nothing there for him but before he returned home he flew to Skiathos and took the ferry to Skopelos where he spent a few days reliving the memories he had of his time on the island with Olivia.

As he stood on the ferry leaving the island he resolved that he had spent enough years pining for Olivia, that however much he wanted her they would never be together now so he must move on. It was a lot easier said than done though as the ghost of her haunted his dreams, his waking hours and his relationships in the following years until one day he accepted that he would never find anyone who would feed his soul in the way she had.

CHAPTER FIFTY

EMINE

Their life became a pattern of Omer sitting outside lost in thought and her cleaning, washing and baking bread and although she accepted this she was bored. She saved the paper that wrapped their food and folded and tore it to make doilies but that didn't fill much of her time. There was nobody to watch here like there had been in camp, nothing much to see apart from Omer sitting outside lost in thought. Vehicles passed on the road but they were soon gone. Although her resolve to run away had weakened as Omer had succeeded in breaking her spirit she had considered approaching one of them to try to get away but how did she know that they weren't men from the Yilmaz camp. She didn't realise it but she had grown to accept that this was her life and Omer had slowly taken control of it.

He would talk to her when they ate together and would draw her to him in bed some nights but it wasn't like before where he was on her all the time for which she was grateful. One night, she had bathed in her gel and washed her hair and felt relaxed as she got ready for bed.

Omer was looking at her but with little interest and she said feigning concern, 'Omer you're not yourself, what's wrong?'

She was shocked by his reaction as he jumped out of bed advancing on her, 'What do you mean what's wrong? Are you so insensitive that you don't know.' She cowered away from him, 'I have lost my family, I'm separated from my people, the cause is inactive, we have no money and there is nobody to talk to.'

She knew she had given him an excuse to take his frustration on her and fearing the punishment that usually followed she wanted to turn it around as she walked towards him, 'You can talk to me,' she reached forward to touch him in the hope she could calm him.

'What can I talk to you about?' he pushed her hand away, 'Do you think I don't know that you're not interested in my life. You think only of yourself. You seduced me with your body just as you did Yusuf before me in the hope that you could fool us into letting you go.'

'No' she protested but the word was hardly out of her mouth when she felt the sting of the slap on her face as he screamed 'Liar' at her.

Although she had not tried to escape as she had no idea where she was she was very aware that there was only him now to stop her. There were no other men outside to chase her down and as he raised his hand to hit her again she went to run from the room not caring she was naked, her only thought was to get away.

He was too quick for her and had his arms around her waist before she had taken two steps. He lifted her off her feet and threw her on to the bed and turning he went over to the drawers and opening the second one started to rummage through it. He looked at her accusingly, 'Where is it?' he shouted at her.

She feigned surprise as she asked him what he was looking for but couldn't keep the fearful look off her face and he screamed at her, 'Where is it?'

He threw himself at her grabbing her by the hair, 'What have you done with it?' and when she begged him to stop again saying she didn't know what he was looking for he screamed at her 'Liar, tell me what you've done with the strap.'

She didn't answer and he slapped and punched her and she cried at the severity of the attack but then it stopped as suddenly as it had started and she opened her eyes and saw that the anger of his face had been replaced with the lustful look that had followed the violence towards her in the past and she whimpered, 'No,' as he climbed on top of her.

As in the past he didn't speak to her for days as she hobbled around injured but he didn't come near her in bed and for that she was grateful. A few days later as they sat eating he presented her with a bangle which matched the ring he had given her when they married, 'Emine let's be friends,' he said and when she didn't answer he added like many abusers before him, 'It's your fault I get angry, don't give me cause to beat you again.'

She wanted to say that she knew he enjoyed it but instead just nodded. That night he pulled her to him however this time he was gentle with her but it made no difference to her. She would take her mind to somewhere else as he moved on top of her so that she wouldn't anger him by shrinking from his touch. At one point she was aware of him grunting and she shuddered but he took that as a sign she was enjoying it and said her name before kissing her.

She sat the next day watching the vehicles as they drove by and had a thought, 'Omer you said we need money, what about me baking more bread and selling it at the side of the road to the passing vehicles. He looked at her suspiciously but then said, 'It sounds like a good idea but first we are going to market tomorrow to sell those clothes. Bake some bread to take there and we'll see how it sells.'

She was excited waiting for the men to arrive early the next day,' I trust you,' Omer said as she saw the truck pull up on the road. She knew what he meant but she wasn't sure she had the energy to try to escape. They climbed in the back of the truck and it started to move and after about half an hour they arrived at a village where there was a square where people were selling fruit and vegetables.

They set up a stall but Omer hardly left her side as they sold their wares. It was very early in the day and the market was only open until lunch time and the time passed quickly as she watched the comings and goings and she actually felt happy for a while. She talked to an old woman on the next stall who told her the market was held every day except Wednesday and Saturday, their holy day, so people could buy fresh produce.

She noticed a dolmus, a large people carrier type vehicle that served the Turkish people as a bus, and wondered where it went. She saw it leave and return about an hour later and when Omer left her once to visit the toilet she asked the woman on the next stall where it went. She told her it travelled to and fro from the coast road.

They did well that day selling everything they had taken, her bread going first and on the way home Emine asked Omer if they could go again to sell bread and he said that maybe they could but he thought her idea of selling her bread at the side of the road was a better idea. She felt disappointed but the next day she put a sheet over the old wheelbarrow which had been abandoned on the field, filled it with freshly baked loaves and flat breads and wheeled it down to the road where vehicles stopped and bought it from her within an hour of setting up.

It became a daily event and she came to recognise the people who stopped and never saw any of the men from the camp. She noticed that most of people who stopped were on their way to market as they had their trucks loaded with fruit and vegetables.

A vague plan had started to formulate in her mind after she had seen the dolmus and although it wasn't a clear idea she knew she would need money if she was to try to escape again and so for every third loaf she sold she slipped the money in her pocket for herself. It would take a long time to save enough to get her away but she had waited this long and she could wait as long as it took as her courage wasn't as strong as it used to be.

The men would come with their food and Emine suggested to Omer that they bought their own fruit and vegetables from the trucks that stopped but Omer dismissed the idea. He enjoyed the men calling as it gave him someone to discuss the cause with and every now and again after they had visited he would present her with a small gift of such things as oils, shampoo and more bangles which jangled on her wrist. She knew what each gift meant and that she would pay for them in bed the night they were given.

The gifts were preferable to a beating and at least she knew what was coming unlike the nights he took her by surprise. He didn't come near her often these days which she was glad of as she hated him touching her but she knew there was no point in refusing him. Apart from him making her skin crawl she was always fearful of getting pregnant and thanked God each month when she knew that there was no baby on the way.

One evening, when they had been at the house for almost a year, after they had eaten he said he had a gift for her and she expected the usual shower gel or bangle but he produced something from behind his back that brought memories flooding back. It was the handbag she had had with her the night Mirac had kidnapped her. She took it with shaking hands and stared at for a moment. It was a very large soft brown leather bag with a long strap which she used to pass over her head so she could wear the bag across her body.

There was a large press stud which brought the leather edges together hiding a thick zip beneath it. She opened both now and looked inside, reaching her hand in she took out a pair of sunglasses which she placed on the table and her wallet which was made of black leather. She opened it but it had been emptied of the money she had had and the photographs she kept in it. She knew better than to ask where they were and instead reached in again and found a tube of hand cream, a bottle of sun cream which she could see was out of date but which she would keep, a packet of wipes which were bone dry and a lip gloss which she smeared her lips with.

She reached in again but the bag was now empty and as she rummaged about she stopped for a moment as she could feel something inside the lining. It felt like a pen or something similar and as she fumbled about she found a hole in the lining and slipping her finger in she pushed the shape towards it. She stopped as a memory came to her like a thunder bolt and she tried not to show any emotion on her face. Her finger had touched something else and the realisation of what it was filled her with excitement. She had used this hole in the lining to hide money in case her purse was stolen and she knew that was what she was touching now.

Omer looked at her suspiciously and asked her what she was doing reaching forward for the bag but she kept a grip on it, smiled and produced the pen that had also been in the lining. 'I have a pen,' she said hoping that he wouldn't question her any further, 'I'll be able to write.'

'What will you write?' he sounded annoyed and she told him she liked to write poetry and draw then she smiled at him and thanking him for her present put all her belongings back into the bag.

The gift had really lifted her spirits and that night as she waited for Omer to join her for his reward she put her finger through the rip in the lining and felt the paper hidden there. She eased it out and saw it was several Turkish lira notes folded together but she quickly put them back when she heard Omer moving around. That night for the first time in a long time she actually felt as if she could start planning her escape and this was made even more possible a few days later.

CHAPTER FIFTY ONE

Omer had noticed her mood had lifted and it made him happier too and he started to chat to her again. She collected some dry washing one day and as she walked towards the house she saw the men arriving. They sat with Omer and she could see they had brought alcohol with them. She put the food away and took the clothes into the bedroom to put them away placing the pile on the chest of drawers. She opened each drawer placing the clean washing away and when she picked up the last piece she knocked one of her earrings, a gift from Omer that had been on top of the drawers, on to the floor.

She couldn't see where it had gone and knelt down to look for it feeling about with her fingers. She laid on her belly and peered under the drawers and seeing something shining she reach in but the back of her hand brushed against something on the bottom of the unit. She turned her hand over and felt around and her fingers settled on something stuck there which she pulled at and then she pulled it out and stared at what she had in her hand. It was a passport and when he opened it with shaking fingers she could see it was her passport.

If she had ever hated Omer it was nothing to what she felt now. He had let her believe that the passport had been destroyed but why wouldn't he she thought, he had prevented his father from freeing her because he wanted her as his wife and he had kept her prisoner ever since.

Her mind was set as she resolved to leave as soon as possible and suddenly she felt her strength returning as hope filled her very being. She went into the living room and looked outside where she could see Omer deep in conversation with the men outside and she then went to the cupboard. She quickly opened the suitcase and took out the clothes she had saved that had belonged to the previous owners and putting the suitcase back she ran to the bedroom and stuffed them in her large handbag together with her passport and hid it in the living room cupboard.

Omer was drunk that night and when he entered the room she expected him to fall on her as usual when he'd been drinking and was pleasantly surprised when he fell into bed instead and went to sleep.

The next day was Wednesday, so she knew she couldn't leave then but she would leave soon. The following day she cut a length from the washing line and put it in the pocket of her gown. She later hid it in the cupboard and went out to eat with Omer.

He hadn't spoken much to her that day and she noticed that he seemed distracted so that night as they ate and asked him what was wrong. He didn't turn on her as he did sometimes when she questioned him and in his mistaken belief that they were close again he confided in her telling her that the men had told him that they had seen Yusuf in the area. Her blood ran cold at the mention of his brother's name and she understood why he had raged the night before. He blamed her for everything to do with Yusuf but the news only served to make her more determined to leave.

Thursday arrived but Omer told her he didn't want her to leave the house as he was worried about Yusuf seeing her and she was dismayed wondering when he would allow her to go to the road again. A few days later the men said that Yusuf had moved on and he told her she could sell bread the next day and she arose early to bake leaving Omer in bed she collected her bag from the cupboard. She went to the washroom whilst the mix proved and slipping her gown off she put on the vest and then put her gown back on. She couldn't risk putting the jeans on as Omer sometimes grabbed hold of her and then she flattened the bag as best as she could and hid it beneath the sheet in the wheelbarrow.

Later she took another sheet and folded it over the one already there to hide the shape of her bag just in case Omer looked in to the wheelbarrow. She loaded the bread in on top of it and was surprised to see Omer come out. 'I'm coming with you,' he said and when she protested he insisted that it was safer.

'I thought you said the men told you Yusuf had gone,' she said and then she saw a look of suspicion cross Omer's face so added smiling, 'but it would be nice to have your company.'

This was the pattern for the next few days but she went prepared each day thinking he might grow bored and leave her alone but this didn't happen until the following Thursday. The night before after they had eaten he said he wasn't going to accompany her the following day.

She tried to hide her joy but he picked up on her excitement, 'You're pleased,' he looked suspiciously at her, 'I thought you enjoyed my company these days.'

'I do,' she lied, 'but this means you feel safe again and that will make you more relaxed,' his smiled at her taking her words at face value. She tried to calm down but she was sure he would hear her heart beating so hard in her chest. Later as she stood up to go to bed he stood up and followed her. She looked around at him and he said, 'Show me how much you enjoy my company.'

The next day as she sat by the road waiting and hoping that a vehicle would come at the right time, the time when Omer wasn't watching her. Vehicles came and went but each time she looked he was there looking her way. She had been there about an hour when she suddenly heard shouting. She looked around and saw a man carrying a rifle striding across the field towards Omer who was on his feet. As he got close to him she could see it was Yusuf. She dipped behind the wall and could hear the men shouting and then she heard a shot ring out.

She held her breath as she lifted her head to look over the wall and saw Yusuf standing over Omer who was lying on the ground with his hands raised towards his brother beseeching him. She saw Yusuf raise the rife again and shoot four more times into Omer's body. She dropped down again, and panic setting in she pulled the sheet off the wheelbarrow, scattering the bread, grabbed her bag and then she heard her name being shouted as Yusuf searched for her. Keeping bent at the waist she ran as fast as she could down the road. She could see a high wall further on and had often wondered what it was and as she ran towards it now she could hear Yusuf screaming her name.

When she reached the wall she saw it was the side wall of a house that had long since fallen into ruins. She hid behind it and quickly pulled the jeans and shirt out of the bag, stripping off her gown she had never dressed so fast. She didn't want to keep the gown but she was worried Yusuf might find it and somehow realise what she had done. She dragged her hair back into a ponytail with a clip Omer had given her and put the sunglasses on. She had earlier threaded the rope through the jeans and as she hurried off she tied it to keep the jeans up.

She was careful to keep in line with the wall so he wouldn't see her but that would only offer her cover for so far and then to her relief she heard a truck approaching. She was relieved to see it was one of the men she sold bread to and his wife was with him. They stopped and she told them she was going to the market and they offered her a lift. She gratefully accepted and she climbed in the back with the water mellons not looking back and the truck set off. Had she looked back she would have seen Yusuf standing by the wall watching her.

Within an hour she was on a dolmus travelling towards the coast. She knew she stood out in the clothes she was wearing but had she kept her robes on she would have attracted more stares as village women didn't usually travel on public transport alone.

She kept her head down all the time scared that one of the men from the camp would see her but although she drew a few curious looks nobody took much notice of her. She couldn't believe it was this easy and as she got off on the coast road she asked the driver if she could get a dolmus to Bodrum. He pointed to the other side of the road and she waited there for a very nervous twenty minutes before she saw the dolmus she wanted coming down the road.

The journey took almost an hour but when they arrived she alighted smiling and almost skipped into the square she recognised. It had been almost two years since she had been there but it all looked so familiar. Now she was here she wasn't sure what do and she stopped for a drink but kept her eyes peeled.

She went into a church where she felt safe and waited until dusk as she tried to remember her way to the ferry port. She thought about Omer and realised she didn't feel anything about his death. There were times when he was cruel to her and sometimes kind but however he had treated her he had kept her prisoner. His father had been prepared to let her go but he had wanted her so she had been given to him as if she was an object and that is how he had treated her. He had like many abusers before him broken her spirit until she felt as if she relied on him. She believed him that she couldn't leave and had given up on the idea of leaving and it had only been the dolmus she had seen in the market that had sparked the idea of escaping again as she realised there was a very real means to getting away.

She ventured out in the early evening and the night was drawing in as she made her way down to the harbour. She turned down a small alley and had only walked a few steps when she heard footsteps behind her and as she swung around she came face to face with Yusuf and she let out a small cry. 'You think you can escape me?' he asked lunging at her and knocked her off her feet.

She screamed as she fell heavily to the floor and he held her down causing her to have flashbacks of the last time he had held her down. She started to fight as hard as she could and then she saw him draw a knife from his waistband and knew that it wasn't rape he had on his mind this time.

'You stole my family from me,' he was screaming in her face as he raised the knife but as he brought it down she somehow managed to summon up a strength she didn't realise she had as she took him off guard and threw him off. He fell back, the knife falling from his hand and as she turned to get up he caught her leg dragging her down again. He was grabbing at her legs trying to prevent her from fleeing and she turned around and started to kick at him but then she saw he was getting to his feet. She shuffled on her bottom away from him and her hand fell on something, it was the knife.

He was up and once again lunged at her cursing and then without thinking she plunged the knife into him with all her strength. She was sure it had gone straight into his heart as he fell on top of her. She sat for a moment in total shock and then pushed him off sure he was dead as he wasn't moving and she could hear no sound coming from him. It was then she saw a woman standing watching her, She froze and stared at her afraid but the woman didn't move as she stared back. She wanted to explain about Yusuf but realised how crazy it would sound and the woman would call the police and they'd never believe her. She got to her feet and turning on her heel she started to run.

The whole event had taken no more than two minutes and as she ran she thought of what she had done, she had killed Yusuf but it had been her or him she told herself unaware that Yusuf was not dead at all.

She reached the harbour in minutes and saw the ferry port where a large boat was waiting. She ran without stopping to the port and went to the office to buy a ticket. They told her she had to hurry as the ferry was leaving in ten minutes and as an afterthought she asked where it was going. The ticket seller looked at her curiously and told her it was going to Kos and then shook his head as she ran off.

As she waited for the ferry to leave it was the longest ten minutes of her life expecting the police to flood the boat looking for her but only one more person boarded the ferry before it left and when Emine saw her she was alarmed. It was the woman she had seen in the alley and she hoped that she wouldn't see her. Maybe she'd followed her and had already called the police and they were on their way. Eventually she was relieved as she felt the movement of the boat as the ferry set off and the only thing that made her nervous was the woman who had boarded. She sat on deck in a corner almost out of view and as Turkey faded into the distance she felt a mixture of relief and sadness.

Later she stood up and walked towards the railing standing there looking down at the dark sea and the white waves the ferry created as it cut through the water. She looked back and could just make out the fading lights on the harbour in Bodrum but they were almost invisible now.

She looked back down at the water below for a few moments losing herself and then she slipped off the bangles that Omer had given her and one by one she tossed them into the ocean. The last thing she discarded was the ring he had given her on their wedding day and looking at it for a couple of seconds she threw it into the sea wishing she could rid herself of the memories as easily.

The journey only took ninety minutes and when they docked she hung back not wanting to bump into the woman from the alley but as she went to disembark she came face to face with her. She stopped in her tracks as they stood staring at each other for what seemed an age but she felt something pass between them and thought she could feel that there was an understanding between herself and the woman which didn't need words and then she was gone.

She stood alone in the harbour sure that she was safe but then realised that she had gone through too much to put trust in a total stranger and caught the next ferry leaving Kos which happened to be going to Athens.

CHAPTER FIFTY TWO

EIGHTEEN MONTHS AGO

'Oh my God', he thought, 'it couldn't be her, it couldn't.' He pictured her face as it had been all those years ago and thought of the one he had seen today. 'It was her, it definitely was her.' A strong emotion overcame him, the ferocity of which surprised him and his head spun as he tried to get his breath. He felt sick and angry at the same time. He was sweating and his legs felt weak and he staggered slightly as he moved to a seat. He could see people looking at him but nothing really registered.

His day had started badly as he had overslept. When he stirred from his sleep he turned with no hurry to look at his clock and he read the time and laid back then it hit him and he checked the time again and he realised that he had slept in. He didn't know whether he had slept through the alarm or he had forgotten to set it but he didn't have time to check. If he hurried now he may not miss his flight.

He flew out of bed tripping over the covers that tangled themselves around his legs, asking himself why he hadn't booked a wakeup call. He had arrived at the hotel the night before so he would not have to panic about hold ups making him miss the flight.

He had to forego the shower and washed quickly, he couldn't have a coffee. Throwing his toiletries into the washbag he almost ran back into the bedroom where he placed the bag in his case. Luckily he had only been staying the one night and had only taken out of his case what he needed overnight.

He picked up the phone and asked reception to call him a taxi advising them he was running late for his flight. He was dressed and down in reception within ten minutes of waking up. He didn't feel great as he felt disorientated but he was pleased that he only had to wait two minutes before his taxi arrived.

The traffic was heavy as usual in Athens and he was glad he had booked a hotel close to the airport and yet it still seemed to take an age to get there. He grew more and more anxious as the taxi moved slowly through the streets of the capital.

After what seemed to be an age they approached the airport and he was dismayed to see the queue at the drop off area. He said he would get out where they were waiting but the driver said he couldn't put down here and that they would soon be there.

Eventually he was out of the taxi in the drop off area and collecting his case from the boot, he paid the driver and ran to the entry to departures. Once inside the airport he scanned the boards noting the desk where he needed to check in. As he approached the desk he saw that there was no queue but also there was nobody sitting behind the desk.

'No,' he thought, 'he'd missed check in.' Just before he reached the desk an agent appeared and took a seat.

''You're cutting it fine,' the pretty dark haired woman said as she took his passport and documents. She studied them and then checked him in and seemed to take an age and he worried that something was wrong. She weighed and checked in his case and then smiled at him, handing back his documents with a pleasant, 'Enjoy your flight.'

He hurried towards the departure hall and as usual there was a big queue at security but surprisingly it seemed to move quickly and he was through the other side making his way to Passport Control. The man at the desk spent what seemed an age checking his passport and kept looking at him suspiciously. Eventually he waved him through and he ran towards the notice board to check which gate he needed.

As he looked up at the board and saw the word 'Delayed' flashing he heard a voice coming over the speaker announcing that his plane had indeed been delayed and advising to keep checking the boards for boarding information.

He didn't quite know how to feel as he felt frustrated after half killing himself to get here but on the other hand he could go to buy a coffee and try to find some calm. He could start the day again on a better foot mentally.

He bought a coffee and found somewhere to sit as near an information board as he could. He finished his coffee and kept getting up and down to check the board. He didn't particularly take much notice of the people around him and it was only because someone knocked him as they walked by that he actually looked at the woman who had bumped into him.

She was a woman probably in her seventies dressed as if she was going on a beach type holiday. She had a big bag slung over her shoulder and in one hand she held her travel documents and in the other she had a book. She apologised and he watched her walk away and saw her drop the book she had been carrying. He moved forward to assist her by picking the book up but something stopped him in his tracks as it was then he saw her.

At first something stirred, one of those moments where someone looks familiar and then it hit him as he did a double take. Yes she looked older but it was definitely her, he'd know her anywhere, her face was etched on his memory.

He sat now taking deep breaths his mind reeling, 'Of course she looked older, it had been over twenty years since he'd seen her. She had totally affected his life and after what she had done he had spent years searching for her before he had given up. His life was totally different now from when he had known her but she had always been there in his mind.

He shook his head looking to where he had seen her, 'Why hadn't he gone after her? How would he find her? Where had she been all these years? How had she managed to remain under the radar?'

He knew the answer as to why he hadn't followed her was that his legs wouldn't have carried him. He was in total shock as the past hit him hard in the face. He couldn't answer the other questions but there was something he was sure of and that was that must find her.

CHAPTER FIFTY THREE

RACHEL

It had been weeks since she had thought she had seen him and had laid low for days afterwards. She had expected him to knock on her door and confront her but how would he know where she lived? One of the locals may tell him if he asked but they had never told anyone before and she knew that some of her readers had tried to track her down.

It may be a coincidence and she thought he probably wouldn't even recognise her after all these years but she couldn't risk running into him in case he did after all she had recognised him. Even he could recognise her he probably wasn't looking for her she tried to reassure herself, it was possible he didn't know she was even on the island but however much she tried to convince herself in her mind he was searching for her and it scared her.

She had been careful moving around the island for a couple of weeks after seeing him only going out when she needed to using the local shop for provisions. Eventually she decided it was safe and in the end even convinced herself that she had imagined it.

She had been holed up in her villa for weeks now and had been writing constantly to take her mind of her worries and she needed a break. It was a beautiful day and she decided to venture down to the harbour. She drove into town, parked up and strolled along the paved area edging the harbour looking at the boats that were moored there. Some of the people on them smiled at her and said good morning and she responded happy to be out.

She wandered through the cobbled back streets window shopping and even called into a small craft shop where she bought some locally made earrings. She had considered two pairs, both were long and fell almost to her shoulders, one was made up of blue and green stones which were pale and subtle whilst the second pair was made of orange and brown stones. She held them up to her ears but couldn't decide which pair she preferred and in the end decided to buy both.

She looked in a few more shops before returning to the main road calling at the bakery and then the Deli where she bought cheese and cold meats. As she walked back towards her car in the baking sun she decided to stop for a cold drink. She placed her bags under the table trying to shield her purchases from the sun and waited for a waiter to come.

A young man approached the table to take her order and recognising her passed the time of day with her. It was lunch time and she decided to order a glass of cold wine together with water and as the waiter walked away to get her drinks she picked up the menu. She hadn't intended eating but it was such a lovely day and there were a few people about she could watch and so she decided to have a Club Sandwich.

Although tourist numbers had initially swelled after the island was used as the main location for the filming of the blockbuster Mamma Mia the visitors had gone back to a manageable number. This suited Rachel as she hated the thought of the island being ruined by commercialism. She wondered whether it was because the island hadn't really taken the opportunity to cash in on the popularity of the film even demolishing the jetty that the film company had erected for the film.

She thought that in some ways it was a shame for the locals that they hadn't taken advantage of the income it could have brought but for her own part she preferred it kept as it was. There was now a bar on the beach used in the film where the temporary jetty had been and a mobile café set up near the steps to the church which called itself the 'Mamma Mia Café' but apart from those two things the only reminder was the ugly concrete causeway the film crew had laid in order to transport the filming equipment from the main island to the rock where the church stands.

She sometimes thought that because the island could only be reached by ferry or hovercraft and therefore probably put some people off but although there were definitely more visitors not so many that it was uncomfortable.

Rachel had lived here for years now and would hate to have to consider moving due to the island being spoilt and although she knew she was probably being selfish it suited her perfectly. It was the ideal place to write as she found it inspiring and there was nothing better than sitting on her veranda looking out to sea.

Her sandwich arrived and she picked it up and took a bite. She savoured the taste of her favourite sandwich and then took a gulp of water. She finished her sandwich all the time people watching and then picked up her wine feeling totally relaxed.

Someone approached her table from the side and a familiar voice said, 'May I join you?'

Her glass was half way to her mouth when she looked up and she froze. She just stared at the man standing there looking older than she remembered and not waiting for a reply he sat down. She continued to stare whist he ordered a lager but couldn't stop her hand shaking as she put her glass down. No words were exchanged. He looked back at her studying her and when his drink arrived he said, 'You are still as lovely as I remember.'

She found her voice, 'I'm sorry you are mistaking me for someone else. I don't know who you think I am but my name is Rachel Ross and I live on the island.'

'Rachel Ross,' he said, 'the famous author,' it wasn't a question. 'You have done so well for yourself.'

'Thank you,' she said trying to sound polite, 'I enjoy my writing.'

'I imagine Skopelos is the ideal place to write,' he said and as she nodded in agreement he added, 'and to hide.'

She tried to remain calm although her heart was almost beating out of her chest as she knew her very existence was at stake. She was in great danger and she wasn't sure what to do. She kept her voice pleasant as she said, 'I don't' know what you mean. I may be a little reclusive but this island lends itself to that way of life and as I have lived her for almost as long as I can remember I think I probably became that way without realising.'

He stared at her and she continued, 'I am not hiding from anything though,' she hope her words rang true.

He laughed but with no mirth, 'I've never forgotten you. I searched for you for years.'

She tried to keep the fear out of her eyes as she replied, 'I'm not sure what you mean. Are you a fan?'

'A fan?' he echoed, 'for as long as I can remember.'

'If you have a book I'll sign it for you,' she said reaching for her bag and for just a moment she thought that perhaps he really didn't know who she was.

'I'd never read any of your books until a few weeks ago,' he said, 'I saw one in the airport and recognised your photo immediately.'

She had argued with her publisher about putting her photo on her books and in the early days she had managed to obscure her face when the photos were taken. She had said she wanted to appear mysterious but recently a clearer photo had adorned her books. It was over twenty years since her first book had been published and she was older, her hair was different and she didn't think she resembled the young woman who had come to live on the island.

'As I said earlier you are mistaking me for someone else,' she said, 'I don't know you.'

He looked at her curiously and then smiled, 'Of course you know me.'

She asked a passing waiter for her bill and the man sitting opposite her asked her to stay. He said it in a way that she felt she had no choice but she had been her own woman for years now and nobody was making her do anything she didn't want. The waiter returned and she gave him some money to cover the cost of her food and drink but she didn't wait for the change instead picking up her bag she hurried away from the table without speaking another word to the man.

He followed her grabbing her arm, swinging her around to face him but the waiter was at their side almost immediately, 'You haven't paid your bill,' he said addressing himself to the man holding on to her and then looking at her he said, 'Are you ok?'

She said she was fine and he turned his interest back to the man asking him to pay his bill again. He let go of her in order to reach for his wallet and she took the opportunity to turn and leave. As she hurried to her car she heard him call after her,

'I'm begging you, Olivia please wait.'

CHAPTER FIFTY FOUR

She spent days after the encounter like a prisoner in her own home. She didn't know what to do. She considered leaving the island but it would break her heart. When she had thought she had seen Jack in Skopelos town all the old memories that she had put behind her came flooding back. It hadn't taken her long all those years ago to realise she had made a huge mistake leaving him as she knew she loved him with every fibre of her being.

She had been on her way back to him when things changed after what had happened in Turkey. She had been mentally scarred and had struggled to come to terms with what had happened. She had shared that moment with that woman in the alley and once back in Greece she heard talk about the police in Turkey asking for help in finding two women who had attacked a man in Bodrum. They had put out descriptions of her and the other woman and she was terrified of being handed over to the Turkish police as they would never believe her story.

Then she was totally shocked when she read in a paper that he wasn't dead and then she had gone into hiding constantly looking over her shoulder and the years had passed.

She had never forgotten Jack and had dreamt of him often. The man who had sat opposite her in the café bar was older than she remembered but essentially he looked the same. His build hadn't changed, he was still as handsome as she remembered and his eyes were still gentle and interesting.

Even now all these years later she couldn't tell him about her feelings and it scared her how strong they still were when she was confronted by him. She was in danger if her whereabouts were revealed and she wracked her brain trying to think of a way around this. She couldn't tell Jack that she was in hiding.

There were only two other people who knew, her mother and her friend Jimmy. When she had arrived in Athens she had sought help from the only person she knew there, her mother's friend Jimmy Ridley. Catherine had known him from pre Roger days and had always been close.to him. When Olivia had twice referred to him a Jimmy Riddle when she was a child it had caused great mirth and when the joke was explained to her she had been embarrassed but in later years she had shared the joke.

It was Jimmy who had told her that her mother had returned to Skiathos and drove her to the refuge her mother offered. She hadn't seen her for years and had harboured a great resentment towards her for abandoning her but she needed her and when she saw her she had broken down relieved to find safety and told her everything.

Catherine had been horrified by her tale and suggested they call the police but almost immediately said that probably wasn't the best idea as they would probably send her back to Turkey and there she may not be believed.

She spent two months with her mother before taking the ferry to Skopelos from the harbour in Skiathos to start her new life. She was horrified by what had happened but after blaming herself and beating herself up for weeks she realised that she had to somehow learn to live with it.

Catherine had recovered from the great sorrow she had endured after Stalios' death and had returned to being as shallow as Olivia remembered her surrounding herself with the same type of arty people and taking young Greek lovers but they formed a new kind of understanding which brought a closeness and Olivia was grateful for it. It had taken her years to understand her mother but she had accepted her as she was and surprised herself with the realisation of how much she loved her. She never expected her mother to return the same strength of feeling but she would take what she offered. They had agreed that she should go into hiding and as she was afraid to use her passport again it would have to be in Greece and the island she had fallen in love years earlier seemed the perfect place.

They had enjoyed trying to think up an alias for her and eventually Olivia had a thought about her favourite show before she went missing. She along with thousands of others had loved the series 'Friends' and she came up with the name Rachel Ross from two of the characters.

As she was fluent in Greek she quickly found a job working at a restaurant, renting a room in the town and slowly as she recovered she started to write. She couldn't reach out to her publishing connections however her mother knew people and helped her publish her first novel which had some success. She published another three books before she had a best seller and from then on she enjoyed great success. She was able with some financial help from her mother to buy her own villa on the hill overlooking the sea and lived happily in peace and very comfortably. He mother opened a bank account on the island in her name but Olivia was the only person who could access it so she had control over her own finances.

She had struggled with the many thoughts that flooded her mind. She hadn't known what to do about Jack, of course she wanted to tell him the truth but she was scared to do so and as she couldn't risk her whereabouts becoming known even after all these years she would have to continue with the lie. She hoped that he would leave the island and she could go back to her peaceful life.

Ten days later she thought her wish must have come true as she had heard nothing but then she hadn't left her home. She risked going into the town and shopped with no adverse event. She even relaxed enough to stop for lunch before making her way back to her villa.

Ten minutes later she was sitting on her veranda thinking to herself about Jack again. Seeing him had thrown her quiet life into turmoil a she remembered what they had had together and what it might have been if she'd stayed. He was a cloud over any relationship she had and she had come to the conclusion that she was happy being on her own if she couldn't have him. She thought that he must have left by now and it made her feel sad although she wouldn't allow herself to think what might be if she allowed Jack back into her life and consoled herself with the thought that he had probably changed and she might not like him anymore. Her thoughts were interrupted by the doorbell.

She got up and walked back into the house and walking across the living room into the hall she scolded herself and told herself she must try to forget him but when she opened the door, she froze and realised it wouldn't be that easy when he was standing there.

CHAPTER FIFTY FIVE

She stared at him, her mouth turning dry as the desert, 'How did you find out where I lived?'

'I followed you,' he said simply.

'So you're stalking me?' she felt a little scared and it showed on her face.

His heart constricted, 'May I come in?' he asked.

'I'm not in the habit of inviting strangers into my home,' she replied.

'But I'm not a stranger,' he said, 'I'm not going to hurt you Liv,' the pet name almost threw her as her legs turned to jelly.

She stared at him for a moment and then because she would like to spend a little time with him she stood back from the door and allowed him in. He smiled at her and entered the hall of the villa. She closed the door and led him through to the open plan kitchen/lounge where he stood looking around. 'This is lovely,' he said.

'I was sitting on the veranda,' she said pointing at the open door adding, 'would you like a beer?'

He nodded and walked towards the open door and then out on to the veranda. She watched him go and her heart started to melt, despite all that had happened to her she still loved this man more than she could have imagined. She took a beer from the fridge, opened it and then taking a deep breath she hardened her resolve and made her way outside.

Jack was standing looking out to sea, 'This view is amazing,' he said half turning to her, 'if I lived here I would spend all my time here.'

'I do, it's my favourite place,' she answered. He took the beer from her and sat down where she joined him. 'I'm sorry but I don't even know your name,' she said.

'Liv, please,' he said but when he saw the fixed look on her face he said, 'okay if you want to play this game. I'm Jack Lynforth,

I'm a GP with a private practice and I have lived with a broken heart for over twenty years.'

She wouldn't be drawn but she wondered why he had become a GP when he wanted to be a surgeon. 'Why a GP?' she asked, 'Did you never fancy being something more, oh I don't know like say a surgeon.'

He laughed sharply, 'So you remember what I wanted to do. When you left me Liv I lost my way and things fell apart a bit really. My path took a different direction.'

'Look Jack,' she said, 'I know you think I'm this 'Liv' person but I'm really not. My name as you know is Rachel Ross. I have lived on this island for over twenty years and I write books.'

'I came here looking for you when you left,' he said ignoring her words, 'I thought you might come back here because I knew how much you loved it. Do you ever think of the time we spent here looking after Maggie?'

She almost answered that of course she did but she checked herself and didn't speak. He waited a few moments but when he realised she wasn't going to say anything he continued, 'I couldn't find you. In fact I visited here for at least three years after you had gone and came back sporadically over the years in the hope that one day I would find you.'

She couldn't believe her ears, of course she wasn't here for the first few years after she left but it is a wonder that she hadn't bumped into him on his other visits. He continued, 'That was until I was told that you were dead but here you are very much alive.'

She didn't understand, who would tell him that she was dead? 'I'm sorry that your friend is dead,' she said, 'how did she die?'

'I was told that she had died in the 1999 earthquake in Athens by a friend of your mother's Jimmy something, I don't remember his last name now. Why did he lie to me Liv?'

She had no idea and trying to keep any emotion out of her voice said, 'You're wasting your time because I am not who you are looking for. Maybe you just wish she wasn't dead and I look like her,' it broke her heart to say the words but she must persuade him to leave her alone.

'No I wasn't wasting my time because eventually I found you,' he said. 'When you left I was desperate. I searched and searched but didn't know who to ask as your parents were dead and I didn't have details for Maggie. That's why I came here. About eight years after you left I located Maggie's mother who told me she had committed suicide but you already know that because she also told you when you visited her. Then she told me you had died in the earthquake so I went to Athens and eventually found Jimmy. I couldn't accept it, I couldn't let you go Liv.'

She stared at him unsure what to say, she was very confused about why Jimmy Ridley would tell him that she was dead. She couldn't ask the question.

'I gave up Liv so imagine my shock when I was in the airport and saw a photo on a book and I was sure it was you,' he said but of course I had doubts. I looked you up under both Olivia Weber and Rachel Ross and could only find information about Rachel but there didn't appear to be any information on where you lived. I kept searching though and eventually I found a very old article about you when you had your first best seller and it mentioned you lived on Skopelos. I couldn't believe it because I had been here so many times.'

She couldn't believe it either. She knew the article he referred to but she had asked her agent to remove it and she had promised that she had done so. She had checked and hadn't found it herself so she was surprised now. She would sort that when Jack had gone.

'I prefer to keep my location private,' she said, 'I like a quiet life and would prefer it that people didn't come here to meet me.' She thought she sounded pompous but she hadn't known what else to say.

'The other thing that surprised me was that the article mentioned your parents,' he said and he saw a flash of something cross her face. 'Now that didn't make sense because you told me your parents were dead and Jimmy also told me your mother had died years ago. I thought that perhaps it was true as I couldn't find any trace of her but when I looked up your father I found him living in St Kitts. I contacted him but he said he hadn't heard from you in years.'

She had had to stop herself crying out, he had contacted her father? How was he? She had forgiven him years ago when she had learnt the truth about her mother and realised how hard it must have been for him. She remembered the naked man called Mark and when she was older had understood what had been going on. Her actions had however prevented her from contacting him and she often thought of him. She could not ask Jack how he was so instead said, 'You can't have spoken to my father as he died many years ago,' she hated herself for the words she had said.

'You know that's not true Liv,' he said gently.

She ignored his words and asked 'You say you've been looking for this Liv person for over twenty years, why haven't you moved on?'

'Believe me, I've tried,' he answered, 'I have had a few relationships but it's hard to care for someone when you took my heart with you when you left. Perhaps I've been foolish but nobody has ever compared to you Liv.'

'I am not Liv,'' she protested.

'When we spoke at the café I knew it was you,' he said, 'but you were so adamant that I did have my doubts. I couldn't find you and nobody would tell me where you lived. I decided to go home to sort a few things out and come back with a better plan but the strangest thing happened in Skiathos.' He hesitated but Olivia didn't say anything so he continued, 'I couldn't get a flight until the next day so booked into a hotel. I had a wander around that night looking in all the lovely shops on the harbour trying to take my mind off you and there I found a lovely artist's studio.'

She knew what was coming and braced herself so she wouldn't react, 'I went in to look around and the owner was there. Do you know who that is?' he asked but she shook her head without speaking, 'It was a lady called Catherine Weber, your mother.' He waited but she didn't say anything,

She had noticed some missed calls from her mother on her phone but had thought she'd ring her later and hadn't got around to it as she was in turmoil, what a mistake. 'You're mad,' she said, 'I am not this Olivia Weber person and you certainly didn't see my mother in Skiathos because like my father she's been dead for years.'

He ignored her words 'I told her that I had seen you but she insisted that you were dead but I could tell from her face that she was lying. Now I have as you just said either gone completely mad and am seeing the ghosts of you and your mother or you are Olivia Weber, the woman who took my heart with her all those years ago.'

She didn't know what to say and so sat silently and he continued, 'Liv I know it's you. 'I don't know why you insist you are not you and I don't know why you lied about your parents. I don't know what else to say to you except that I have loved you from the first moment I saw you in that bar in Barcelona and that feeling has never gone away. Please give me another chance.'

'You seem very nice,' she said, 'but I'm not her and you need to get on with your life.'

'Let me tell you about the Liv I knew,' he said. 'I was taking a year out from a medical placement when I went travelling across Europe with friends. It was our last night in Barcelona as we were moving on the next day to Italy. I was in a bar and I saw this young woman sitting with her friend and it was one of those eyes meeting across a crowded room moments. That's all it took, one moment and I was smitten. Imagine how upset I was when I turned away for a moment and when I turned back she'd gone. I ran out into the street but couldn't see her and spent the rest of the night kicking myself for not going over to her.'

Olivia was back in the bar in her mind looking at him across the room and wanted to say she had felt the same.

'Do you remember,' he said leaning forward but she shook her head and looked away. He continued, 'I couldn't believe my luck the next day when we went to catch the ferry and there she was waiting to catch the same ferry. I wasn't letting her go this time. We travelled around Europe together, Liv, her friend Maggie, my mates Robbie and Jason and me but I didn't tell her how I felt for a long time and it drove me to distraction. She didn't seem that interested and I wanted her to grow to like me.'

She wanted to laugh out loud, she had been as smitten as him from the first moment and had never known he felt the same. Even when they were together he didn't tell her but then neither did she. She smiled at him which encouraged him, 'Part way through our travels we went our separate ways because Jason had let Maggie down very badly. She was pregnant and he wanted to get away and I shouldn't have gone with him but I did.

I couldn't bear being without you and I came back for you to this very island.' He stabbed his finger at the scenery repeating, 'this very island. This is where I found you then and this is where I've found you now.' He looked at her but she was staring out to sea.

He said gently, 'That is when I told you how I felt,' he had changed the 'she' to 'you' a few minutes earlier but Olivia hadn't noticed as she remembered the moments he was describing. He had realised though and didn't want to spoil the moment and hear her denials again so he reverted to referring to her as 'she'.

'I couldn't believe it when she said she felt the same,' he continued, 'Can you imagine being so completely in love with someone and finding out that they feel the same?'

'It must be amazing,' she said as she fought to stop the tears that were threatening to come.

'It was,' he replied, 'we stayed on the island for months and then when we returned back the UK we moved in together. Like you she wanted to write but the best she could do was get a job in a book shop as she needed to work as I didn't earn a lot as a junior doctor. When I started working in surgery I found a job in Newcastle and we moved there where she found a job in publishing. She was always a free spirit and I could see her slowly dying. The spark was dimming and it broke my heart to know it was because of me. I didn't know what to do and just tried to give her what I could to make her life easier.'

'I'm sure she was happy with you,' she said, 'What happened?'

'She wasn't fulfilled I know but I think Maggie was the catalyst that made Liv leave,' he said, 'Maggie came to stay and I thought that this was maybe what she needed to bring some spark back. She ended up staying far too long and I didn't really like it but I went along with it because I thought it was what Olivia wanted.'

She stopped herself saying, 'I didn't know.' She listened as he finished his tale, 'I even joined Maggie on some of her nightly jaunts so that she wouldn't leave but it back fired as Liv accused me of having a thing with her. I had done everything I could to make sure her friend stayed and maybe I sent out the wrong signals but she deliberately tried to split us up.'

Olivia remembered the pain she'd felt at the time but knew that it had all been Maggie. He put a hand on hers and she didn't pull hers away, 'Maggie went and things seemed to return to a semblance of normality but the damage was worse than I realised.'

'Do you think it was all down to her friend?' Olivia asked

'No,' he said, 'I think she had felt suffocated for a long time, she wanted to write, travel and live here. Maggie was damaged and deliberately set out to split us up and she did a lot of harm but it wasn't down to her. I thought we were strong enough to handle anything together but I realise now that I didn't take enough care of her love.'

'So Olivia left,' she asked.

'Yes she left and I've spent the last twenty odd years mourning her,' he smiled at her, 'mourning you.'

She moved her hand away now and said, 'I'm sorry you lost your love but I am not her.' He started to protest but she put up her hand, 'No you must listen. I know what you believe I am not and never will be her. It's time to get on with your life and forget about Olivia. There's nothing for you here.'

He stayed for a few hours and they talked but whatever he said she denied she was Olivia Weber and he couldn't get her to budge. He could see that she was closed to him and saw no love in her eyes as she looked at him.

It was with a very heavy heart he left her promising that he would be back. She begged him not to return because she was happy here and didn't want to move but she would if he returned.

He felt it was hopeless and returned home the following day to continue his life. It took him a long time to come to terms with the fact that he had lost Olivia for ever especially as he didn't really understand why. He sadly came to the decision that he would leave her in peace and allow her to live the life she had chosen even though it broke his heart.

After Jack had left Olivia had spoken to her mother immediately asking her to come over to the island as she was still nervous of leaving her villa for a while in case Jack was still hanging around. She didn't want to encounter him again because she wasn't sure her resolve would hold. Hearing what Jack had said to her had torn her heart apart.

Catherine arrived and they talked about him visiting her, 'I told him you were dead,' she said.

'I don't understand,' Olivia said, 'and why would Jimmy Ridley say the same in 2002?'

'I have no idea,' Catherine lied.

CHAPTER FIFTY SIX

PRESENT DAY

She was sitting on her veranda enjoying the sunshine. It was eighteen months since Jack had visited and ever since her writing had been sporadic. Her heart was no longer in it. She thought of him every day but scolded herself when she did. She jumped when the doorbell rang followed by banging on the front door. She rushed through the hall feeling alarmed to answer the door as the banging continued together with constant ringing of the bell.

She felt a bit scared as she opened the door and was relieved to see her mother standing there. She pushed her way past her, 'Have you seen the newspaper?' she asked and then answered herself, 'Of course you haven't, you and your reclusive lifestyle.'

'I do read newspapers Mum, just not today,' she answered.

Her mother threw the newspaper she had been carrying down on the table and then opened it at page three, 'there,' she said, 'read that.'

Olivia froze as she saw the headline and then her eyes went to the photograph and she drew in her breath sharply. She sank to a chair and read and then re-read the words as she couldn't believe what she was seeing. She looked up at her mother with tears in her eyes and Catherine said, 'Come on we have a lot to do,'

It took almost six weeks for her new passport to arrive and she was very impatient. She hadn't dared renew it before as the less people who knew where she was the better. During that time she reached out to her father by letter and he rang her as soon as he received it and they talked for hours. Within days he was standing at her door and they had hugged and cried and only broken away to look closely at each other. She had missed him so much and although they could never make up for the years they had lost they would try. He stayed for eight days before he had to return to the Caribbean but they both felt that a huge weight had been lifted from them and promised they would never lose each other again.

Her mother had told her that he had tried to contact her when they first broke up but that she had deliberately moved them around so he couldn't find her. She told her how hurt she'd been when he left but when she realised that it had been wrong to keep him from his daughter it was too late to put it right. She was scared that Olivia would never forgive her but as they had cried and held each other Olivia told her that she loved her and of course she forgave her

She arrived in Newcastle the day after the passport arrived and made her way to the flat she had shared with Jack all those years ago. It had struck her on the way here that he probably didn't live there anymore and since she had last seen him he may have found someone else. She had told him to get on with his own life and at the time she had meant it so she couldn't have blamed him for listening to her. She didn't know what else to do but go to the flat but if he wasn't there she wouldn't give up until she found him and explained her actions even if he didn't want her anymore.

She stood before the door of the flat she had shared with her love all those years ago and it looked no different. She rang the bell and waited with baited breath. The door opened and her heart sand to see a young man standing there.

'I'm looking for Jack Lynforth,' she said with disappointment in her voice.

'There's nobody called Jack living her,' he said, 'sorry don't know him.'

She turned to leave thinking what to do next when she saw a young woman appear next to the young man. She made her way down the stairs to the outside and thought she would look for Doctors in the area because surely there must be some kind of register. She longed for the days when there were phone books on every street corner.

She heard footsteps behind her and a woman's voice, 'Excuse me, Jerry my boyfriend said you were looking for Jack Lynforth.'

Olivia turned and nodded looking at the young woman she had caught sight of in the flat. The girl continued, 'Are you Olivia?'

Olivia was stunned, how did this young woman know who she was. She answered that she was and then held her breath.

The girl smiled at her, 'My Lynforth owns the flat. We rent it off him,' she explained, 'when we moved in the previous tenants told us that if Olivia ever came looking for Mr Lynforth we must give her this,' she handed her an envelope with 'Liv' written on it.

She opened it and saw a piece of paper with an address and phone number on it, 'Thank you,' she laughed, 'thank you so much.'

She hurried away and heard the girl call 'Good luck,' after her.

Should she phone first she thought but no she wanted to see him. She got back on to the main road and flagged down a taxi which took her back to the station.

The journey was going to take nearly five hours and she knew that she'd once again rehash what she was going to say to Jack as she had on the plane journey. She had to change in Peterborough and when she got off the train she could hardly contain her eagerness to get to Norwich. She had to wait another twenty minutes for the next train but afraid that she might miss it she went straight to the platform and sat impatiently waiting for the train.

As she drew nearer to her destination she suddenly started to panic and considered backing out but she gave herself a good talking to and when she arrived in Norwich went straight to the taxi rank.

. She gave the driver the address that Jack had written on the paper all those year ago and suddenly she thought, 'What if he'd moved?' The tenants had obviously passed on the envelope down the years and Jack had probably forgotten he had left it at the flat. Suddenly what had seemed like a hopeful sign lost its meaning.

She sat thinking about what was about to happen. It was Saturday and she hoped he'd be home. She hadn't checked into a hotel as she hadn't known she was coming to Norwich, not that she had done so either in Newcastle as she gone straight to the flat and only had a backpack with her. If he didn't want to see her she was prepared to return to Skopelos immediately and even had a ticket for a flight later that evening in her bag although it was from Newcastle. She thought that perhaps this was a sign that she shouldn't haven't have come.

She hoped there was still a chance for them but expected nothing from him, she just wanted him to understand. She felt she owed him an explanation. The taxi drove out of town and after a short time passed through a small town and then taking a country road he drove a hundred yards and stopped outside a large old cottage. She took his card so she could call him for the return trip.

She stood looking at the cottage and thought how lovely it was with its painted windows and roses growing up the walls. There was a small well-tended garden and she walked through the small wrought iron gate, up the path to the large wooden door. She located the bell and hesitated before pressing it.

Within moments Jack was standing in front her with a look of wonderment on his face. He said nothing so she said, 'May I come in?'

'I'm not in the habit of inviting strangers into my home,' he replied.

'But I'm not a stranger,' she said smiling feeling hopeful.

He took her through to a large kitchen which overlooked the back garden which was wide, long and she thought looked like the countryside.

She sat down and he offered her a glass of wine never taking his eyes off her for a moment. She took a big breath and then started her tale, 'When I left you I went to see Maggie's mother. I felt really guilty and blamed myself for her death and all I could think of was getting back to you.'

He didn't interrupt and sat staring at her so she continued, 'I spent a little time in Cardiff trying to get my head straight but I didn't feel good about myself and then the day before I was going to come back to you I saw an advert for holidays in Greece and I don't know why but I decided to go back there and continue what we had planned to do visiting the Cyclades.

I spent a few years there, I know I should have contacted you but I think I was lost and the longer I left it the harder it was. Eventually I'd got the wander lust out of my system and knew I had to come back to see if you still wanted me. I'd bought a plane ticket to come back to you but had three weeks to wait so thought I'd visit Turkey. It was only a ferry ride away and I'd never been. I didn't really like it but thought I'd kill the time there and even got a job in a bar for a couple of weeks.

I was walking home one night when a man grabbed me and I was taken to a camp of terrorist fighters. They had my passport and knew my name but called me Emine.' She heard Jack suck in his breath and he started to move towards her but she asked him to allow her to finish. She told him the whole sorry story about her life in camp, what happened with Yusuf and afterwards with Omer not sparing a single detail.'

'But when you escaped why didn't you come back?' he asked.

She told him about Yusuf finding her in Bodrum and that she thought she had killed him. She told him about the woman who had witnessed the horror and how she had run away sure that the woman would fetch the police and had been even more afraid when she had seen her get on the ferry. She told him of her encounter with her on the ferry but instead of telling anyone that she was there she had looked at her with great understanding and she had known that she didn't have to fear her.

She thought that she must get out of Greece as the papers were full of stories about her attacking Yusuf, not the other way around so she made her way across Greece to Skiathos where she knew her mother had returned.

She was scared of the police finding her but then her fear had been compounded when she realised Yusuf wasn't dead and knew that he wouldn't rest until he found her. She was scared for her life and didn't want anyone else to be in danger so she became a recluse on the island she loved. She told him she could never reveal her identify not even to him.

When she had finished she could see tears in his eyes, 'My God Liv I can't believe what you've been through. I should have been there.'

She smiled a weak smile, 'I just needed you to know why I didn't come back,' she said.

'Why did you say your parents were dead?' he asked.

'You can't understand the hurt my father caused me when he left. I adored him and I felt totally abandoned. My mother used to tell everyone he was dead and to be honest it was easier for me to handle the pain he had caused by going along with that. When I was sixteen my mother also abandoned me, I shouldn't have been surprised really because she had always been self-centred but she knew she was all I had so she became dead to me. I didn't want to talk about the pain either of them had caused me so it was just easier to say they had died.'

'Why did Jimmy what's his name tell me you were dead?' Jack's mind was spinning.

'Jimmy Ridley,' she said and then smiled as his name had always made her laugh, 'I didn't know about that, that was my mother's doing.'

'You should have told me before,' he sounded angry, 'all these years that have been wasted. I searched for you, you were all I wanted but when I found you, you told me to get on with my life.' His phone rang but he ignored it. He started to speak but his phone rang again. He apologised and looked at the screen telling her he had to take the call.

When he'd finished he said, 'I don't' believe this, not now, but 'I'm really sorry I have to nip out. One of my patients needs some medication. Stay here, Please don't go anywhere. I'll be about forty minutes, we'll talk more when I get back.'

He was gone and she felt flat. She had thought that getting all this off her chest would make her feel better but it hadn't. He had once moved towards her and she had stopped him, he had said that he would have been there for her if he had known but it was all past tense. Thinking about what he had said she realised that he was telling her that he had moved on when he protested that she had told him to get on with his life. She realised that he no longer had feelings for her and with a heavy heart she knew what she must do. She had explained to him what had happened and hopefully that would put his mind at rest and now she must leave. She was too late and it was over.

EPILOGUE

Within three hours of sitting with Jack in his lovely kitchen she was on the plane home. She had been able to change her ticket to fly from Norwich and as she sat on the plane she thought of Jack and cried for what she had lost and then she remembered what had brought her here, it was the day her mother had arrived with the newspaper.

Olivia read the heading 'Turkish Terrorist Dead. 'She wondered what all this was about but as she got closer she saw the photo that accompanied the article and she froze. Her legs buckled and her mother caught her and helped her to a seat. Catherine stood beside her, 'Read the article,' she said and Olivia started to read.

'Yesterday Turkish authorities confirmed that the terrorist Yusuf Yilmaz has died. The man who is suspected of kidnapping and murder many people whilst involved in violent attacks in his homeland died peacefully in hospital after losing his final battle with cancer. It is believed that he was in his sixties but little is known about the terrorist himself. He was the eldest son of Berat Yilmaz the leader of a radical faction who violently battled against the government and who died himself eleven years ago a trusted source has told us.

We have been informed that Yusuf Yilmaz was estranged from his family over twenty years ago but the source told us that he returned to the faction after his father's death and continued leading their reign of terror. It is known that they lived in a remote village but they evaded military forces. Why he was estranged from his family or what he did during the years before returning to the village is unknown.

He had three brothers, Mustafa who died in a Turkish prison after his capture seven years ago, Mirac who was killed fifteen years ago by authorities when he attacked a military building and Omer who was the youngest of the family. The source told us that when the group disbanded for the first time some years ago Omer left his family with his wife believed to be called Emine. Omer was found dead by the authorities over twenty years ago and it is believed that he was murdered by opposing factions. He had been shot several times at his home thirty miles outside Bodrum. It is unknown what happened to his wife but it is feared that she suffered the same fate although her body has never been found. She was not implicated in the shooting of her husband.

Yusuf Yilmaz was involved in an attack in Bodrum in the 1990s when he was stabbed by a young woman whose identity was never discovered. He was buried with no ceremony by the local authorities.'

Olivia looked up at her mother, tears in her eyes and Catherine said, 'It's over,' and then she sat down, 'There's something I have to tell you,' she looked scared. She took her daughter's hand, 'About three years after you came to live in Skopelos Yusuf visited me in my studio'. Olivia felt sick and her mother saw the blood drain from her face and so she squeezed her hand. 'I didn't know it was him when he came but I was surprised when he spoke to me in English as everyone always thinks I'm local. I'd assumed he was Greek but I knew as soon as he spoke he was Turkish and I was immediately suspicious.

He tried to be charming as he talked about the art but he was creepy and when he asked about Emine I knew it was something to do with the Yilmazes. I wasn't facing him when he asked thank goodness or he would have seen the shock on my face and I still didn't know it was Yusuf himself at that point. I told him I didn't know an Emine and he said she was a friend of my daughter Olivia. I told him that I didn't have a daughter. I know he didn't believe me and,' she hesitated, 'he was a bit rough.'

Olivia squeezed her hand, 'He kept coming back over the next few years,' Catherine said, 'Obviously he didn't believe me. When the earthquake happened in Athens I had this idea. I asked Jimmy if there were any bodies not identified after a week if he'd identify one as you and he agreed straight away.'

Olivia looked at her in shock, 'Mother don't you realised, someone somewhere still doesn't know that their loved one is dead.'

'I was desperate Olivia, I had to protect you,' her mother protested and Olivia was surprised by the passion her words carried. 'The next time Yusuf came calling I admitted who I was but told him you had died in Athens. At first he didn't believe me,' a shadow crossed her face, 'he got a bit rough again but I showed him the list of the dead that the authorities in Athens had produced but he got angry and smashed the gallery up but I thought he was off your back.'

Olivia remembered when her mother's studio had been damaged and she had told her that someone had forced their way in and she remembered her mother's bruises and she knew that it had been Yusuf. Then she remembered the other two times she had said she had fallen down the stairs and she knew without a shadow of a doubt that the injuries had been down to Yusuf. Tears sprang to her eyes, 'I'm so sorry.'

They sat for a few moments before Olivia said, 'So many lies. He's thought I was dead since 1999. He wasn't looking for me at all.'

'Jimmy and I were concerned that Yusuf might not believe you were dead and we were worried for your safety so Jimmy got a death certificate for you,' Catherine said and saw the horror on her daughter's face, 'well it's a good job he did because that monster returned two years later but when I showed him the certificate he seemed satisfied but I could never be sure.'

'But what if he did believe you?' Olivia said, 'all those years wasted, It could have been so different. Perhaps it would have worked with Jack. Instead I've spent all these years alone and scared.'

'I could never be sure you were safe besides when you came here after Turkey you were broken,' Catherine said, 'it took so long for you to even partly recover. You weren't the same girl anymore. It had been years since you had left Jack and I was sure he would have moved on and I couldn't bear you getting hurt anymore.'

Olivia suddenly felt very angry, 'Oh my God mother,' she said accusation in her voice, 'how could you? You should have told me.'

'I was afraid for you,' Catherine answered but Olivia's anger didn't abate.

'It's not for you to decide how I should live my life,' she said between clenched teeth, 'I could have gone to the authorities,' she trailed off. It was Greece not England and she knew it would have been very difficult. She looked at her mother's face as she saw pure anguish there and her heart softened, 'Oh mum,' she choked, tears in her eyes as she realised that her mother truly loved her. She smiled at her, 'Where on earth did Jimmy get a false death certificate?' Her mother told her not to ask and they laughed lightly then Olivia said, 'That death certificate saved my life.'

'I think it saved both our lives,' Catherine said and then they sat for a few minutes in silence both lost in thought until she said, 'It doesn't matter anymore Olivia.'

No it didn't matter, she thought as any remaining anger melted away and she leant forward to hug her mother, 'Oh my God,' she said pulling back, 'if the authorities think I'm dead I can never get another passport.'

Catherine smiled, 'It was only meant to convince Yusuf. I never registered it.'

She brought herself back to the present as the plane touched down. She managed to get the last ferry of the day to Skopelos and arrived home, closing the door behind her she felt a great sadness. She was exhausted but hardly slept that night thinking about Jack and eventually cried herself to sleep. She was awoken by her door bell ringing and she looked at her clock. It was eight o'clock in the morning and she wondered who it could be.

She felt dreadful, her limbs were heavy and her spirits were low as she made her way to the door. She opened it and had to hang on to the handle to support herself as she saw Jack standing there. He must have caught the first ferry that morning over to the island.

'Bloody hell Liv, will you please stop running away,' he said.

'I thought you'd moved on,' she said.

He laughed and she stood back so he could come in. He opened the door out to the veranda and she couldn't help smiling as he made himself at home. She followed him out and he turned to her, 'I need to ask you one thing,' she looked up at him 'do you still love me Liv?'

She felt tears prick her eyes, 'Still?' she said in wonder, 'I never stopped.'

'That's good then,' he said, 'because I feel no different today than I did when I lost my heart to you in that bar in Barcelona.'

She was stunned then started to laugh and cry with joy but she didn't know what to say, 'I look such a mess,' was all she could manage.

He laughed out loud, 'I'll get used to it,' he said smiling at her and then turning back to the sea view he added, 'I've always wanted to live here.'

'

Printed in Great Britain
by Amazon